PLAYING THE GAME

JIMBOB STRYKER

To Donna and Kristen, and to all the kids who helped me learn how to play the game.

- 1 -

MEET SEAN PORTER

You wonder, sometimes, how you get yourself into situations like these. Looking back, I have to believe that, somewhere along the timeline of my life, I was led to this point—that I would be here no matter how I led my life. But I digress...

Flash back to 1980. At that time, I was a fifteen-year-old jock, having spent the past several years honing my skills on sandlot baseball fields. At some point during the previous year, I caught the soccer fever that was just beginning to grip the American landscape. By the end of that summer, I was playing on two teams and earning a little side money as a youth referee. Since they had some trouble getting enough qualified adults to be referees, I had the chance to work games played by kids older than I otherwise would have been allowed to referee.

Typically, I would be a referee for the real young ones, say six to eight years old. These kids would play what I liked to refer to as "swarm-ball." Every kid on the field, except the designated goalkeeper, would swarm to the ball like bees around a hive. No matter where it was on the field, they would kick at the thing as if it were a biting dog, all the time laughing, shouting, and having absolutely no idea where it was going to go next. The coaches and parents, meanwhile, would be screaming on the sidelines, as if the sheer weight of their voices would make little Kimmie or Matthew suddenly do a bicycle kick like Pele and score the game-winning goal.

A couple of times that year, I was given a game with older kids, usually in the under-fourteen girl's division. These kids were generally fairly new to the game also, but they were a lot more coordinated in their athletic abilities. The older players could see how a play might develop, so they tended to play positions a little better than the young ones. Their games were a lot more fun to officiate, and the girls were a lot more fun for a fifteen-year-old guy to watch running up and down the field.

Many of these kids were the little sisters of friends of mine, so I knew a lot of their names. On the soccer field, though, I began seeing them as individuals instead of as those annoying kids who were trying to hang around with us older guys. At the first of these games that I officiated, I could see groups of girls huddled together, glancing over at me before the game started, talking and giggling. But I thought of myself as an official, and acknowledging that I knew some of them was beneath my dignity. During the inspection and instruction prior to the game, as I checked cleats and shin guards, a couple of the girls who I knew softly said hi to me, almost embarrassed to know me.

As the game progressed, I forgot about who they were and concentrated on the play. Some of the girls had been playing for several years, and others were just learning the fundamentals. Nearly all of them, regardless of skills or experience, played enthusiastically and played hard. It was kind of a revelation to me to see these kids running up and down the field, heads down, shoulders and hips and feet fighting for possession of the ball, and sweating. Not glowing, not perspiring, but honest-to-God, hard work *sweating*. My estimation of their commitment to athletics climbed, and I decided then and there that I would never again think of them as annoying little kids.

I learned a lot about those kids that day, and I learned a little about myself, too. I didn't have any idea then, of course, but I would learn a lot more about them…and me.

- 2 -

FIRST AID

It was a couple of weeks before school was supposed to start, and my friends and I were not looking forward to the end of summer vacation. I rode my bike over to my buddy Jake Lehigh's house, hoping to scare up enough guys for a pickup baseball game. I dropped my bike to the ground, walked up to the front door, and knocked. There was no answer, but as I was walking back down the sidewalk to my bike, I heard some noise from the field behind his house. I walked around to the back and saw Jake's little sister, Kayla, and two of her friends playing around with a soccer ball. Kayla was thirteen, slim, and athletic for a kid her age, and was just learning how to play soccer. She had been on the field when I worked as a referee the previous Saturday, as had her two friends.

I was about to turn around and continue my search when Kayla looked over and saw me. She began waving and calling out to me.

"Sean! Can you help us?"

I sighed and began walking back to the field. Kayla had the soccer ball between her feet as she was readjusting her ponytail, pulling her long, pale blonde hair through a thick holder. Her hair was so light it was almost white, and even tied back, it reached nearly the middle of her back. She was dressed in a loose-fitting tank top and short shorts that looked like they were tight

5

enough to inhibit her circulation. I knew her fairly well since she was the sister of one of my best friends, but it was like I was seeing her for the first time. *Damn,* I thought to myself, *this isn't the little kid I used to see hanging around.*

With her was Jaimie Jacks, who was fourteen and Kayla's best friend. The third girl was Jaimie's twelve-year-old sister, Tara. Jaimie was shorter than Kayla, barely five feet tall, but she had a more grown-up shape to her. Her hips were not boy-slim like Kayla's, and her chest was much more pronounced. She had dark brown, slightly curly hair, cut just to her shoulders, with thick bangs brushing her eyebrows. Tara was even shorter but much thinner than her sister. She was just developing and hadn't blossomed to Jaimie's proportions as yet. She had always kept her dark hair cut very short but was in the process of letting it grow out. It gave her a bit of a wild look. Of the two of them, Tara was the more athletic, having played soccer and other sports since she was in kindergarten.

Kayla picked up the ball to try to juggle it, bouncing it on her knee, and not having much success that I could see. After it bounced away from her, she turned to me and said, "Can you please show me how to do this? Jaimie and I are really having a tough time learning how to keep the ball bouncing."

Tara puffed up a little and said, "Yeah, these klutzes can't do anything. We were trying to pass the ball to each other without letting it hit the ground, and Jaimie and Kayla kept on missing it."

"Well," I said to her, "you've been practicing for a lot longer than they have, Tara. Just because they can't pass the ball in the air doesn't mean they can't pass the ball on the ground, does it?"

"No, not really, I guess," she replied. "But juggling skills are still important, according to my coaches."

"Sure," I said. "Juggling is good for your hand-eye coordination. Or should I say foot-eye coordination?" All three girls giggled. "But," I added, "I know lots of really good players who have a tough time juggling. There are different skills required to juggle than to run and dribble and shoot the ball."

At that, I lashed out with my right foot and kicked the ball out of the air as Kayla was attempting to juggle. The ball bounced off my laces, up in the air. I trapped it and dribbled away a few yards. Tara yelped as I kicked out, and then ran after me to try to take the ball away. I called out to Kayla to get open, keeping my back between the ball and Tara, and whipped a pass across the field to Kayla as she sprinted past a startled Jaimie. Jaimie ran after her, and the game was on. It was two-on-two keep-away, a common soccer drill among many of the coaches in our area: Kayla and me versus Jaimie and her sister.

All of a sudden, just as I was about to pass the ball off, I heard Kayla cry out, followed by a thud. We all stopped and looked over to see her rolling over onto her back, holding her leg and grimacing in pain.

"What happened, Kay?" Tara asked anxiously as she ran over to her friend.

"I don't know," she said through gritted teeth. "I think I tripped over a rock and pulled a muscle in my leg."

"Let me see," I said as I ran up to her. Being the oldest and having taken first aid as part of my referee training, I was naturally going to take charge of the situation. I knelt down beside her and asked her what muscle she hurt.

She hesitated, then, almost embarrassed, said, "My…thigh muscle, I think."

I held her leg at her knee with both hands and tried to straighten out her leg. She grimaced with pain, still holding on to her upper thigh. She could bend her leg without any discomfort in her knee, for which we were all grateful, though we could see that she was in some pain from her pull.

"Can you stand?" I asked.

"I don't know, but I'll try," she replied. I held out my hands for her to grab, while Jaimie and Tara each grabbed an arm to help her to her feet.

"Oof!" She nearly collapsed against me when she tried to put some weight on her leg. I grabbed her around her waist and held her up.

"Here, Kayla, just hold onto me. I'll help you into the house," I said.

"You're going to have to help me walk," she said to me as she leaned against me. "I hope I'm not too heavy," she added.

"A little pipsqueak like you?" I teased her. "C'mon, squirt, I've got you."

I moved over to her bad side, grabbed her around her waist, and helped guide her as she hobbled toward her house. Because we had been running around, we were both a little sweaty. My grip on her waist kept on slipping, and she would slowly slide down a little at a time. The first time it happened, my hand just naturally found a convenient spot to grip, until it suddenly occurred to me that I was holding onto her in a very personal place. I stopped, flustered, and readjusted my hold on her. My mind was aswirl with conflicting feelings. *This is Kayla, after all, the kid sister of my pal Jake. What am I doing copping a feel? Uh oh, what if she notices? What will she say? Will she tell Jake what I did while she was helpless? Man, what a dilemma.* I wanted to help, but I didn't want to get into trouble with my best friend.

But then I felt her slip down again, and when she did, my hand ended up in the same place. I stopped again, pretending I was getting tired, and readjusted my hold on her once more. After I did, I thought I heard—or felt—her giggle softly. I could have been mistaken, though.

We made our way into their family room, and I set her down on the couch. I tucked some pillows behind her so she could sit up more comfortably. I went into the kitchen and got big glasses of water for both of us.

"Where is everybody?" I asked her.

"Dad's at work; Mom and Jake went to the store," she said. "Sean? Could you please massage this leg for me?"

She looked so hurt and vulnerable lying there. How could I refuse? I knelt down by her and started gently massaging her leg just above her knee. Her shorts were very tight, and they ended just an inch or so from the junction of her legs. Her skin was incredibly soft and smooth, and the big thigh muscles under the skin were pliant.

"Ooohh, that feels good," she sighed. "Go a little higher, please?"

Her head was back against the pillow, and her eyes were closed. I worked my way up her leg, from her knee up to mid-thigh.

"Where does it hurt the most, Kayla?" I asked.

"Up higher. I don't think it's a bad pull. I think I might just have cramped up. Do me a favor, Sean? In the upstairs bathroom, the one off the hall, there is a bottle of liniment. Could you go up and get it and rub it into my leg for me?"

"Sure thing," I said. I ran up the stairs to the bathroom and rummaged around in the closet until I found the liniment. I also grabbed a couple of towels and washcloths. I soaked one washcloth in cold water and carried everything downstairs.

As I came back into the room, Kayla was sitting up, taking off her shoes and socks. She looked up at me and smiled as I put my supplies down on the floor. She got both shoes and socks off her feet and then settled back, taking her hair out of her ponytail and giving her head a small shake. I couldn't help but notice how her boobs pushed out her top into small and enticing mounds. The sight of this very pretty, very young, blonde girl lying there began to have its effect on me. I quickly knelt back down and busied myself with getting ready to massage her leg for her. I handed her the damp washcloth, and she gratefully wiped off her face and the back of her neck.

"Okay," she said, "I'm ready for you." She smiled, pretending not to notice my discomfort.

I poured a small amount of liniment into my hand and started rubbing it into her skin. It seemed like her shorts were pulled up even higher than they were before. It was as if her entire leg was bare.

She had her left leg bent at the knee, and her injured right leg was straight on the couch so I could rub the liniment around on the top, the outside, and the inside of her thigh. As I started to massage her leg slowly, trying to push the heat from the liniment into her muscle tissues, she spread her legs apart slightly. I slowly worked my way up from her knee once again, moving up to about mid-thigh and then back down again. Each time I moved up, my hands crept higher on the top of her thigh. Then I worked them around to the sides and down again. Once again, her head rested on the pillows, and her eyes were closed. I glanced up at her and noticed her tongue was slightly sticking out of her mouth and there was a small sheen of perspiration on her upper lip. I thought she might have been breathing a little heavily, and every once in a while she let out a big sigh, never once opening her eyes.

My eyes, however, were wide open, and probably bugging out just a little bit. I had never been this close to a real live girl who was actually letting me touch her thigh before. Even though I was still thinking of this as a medical exercise, I was quite nervous—and intensely curious.

I massaged the oil into her skin with hard strokes, but then I couldn't resist lightly drawing my hand back down toward her knee, almost caressing her. I had never felt such smooth, supple skin before. I couldn't get enough of the feel of her against my fingertips. I could feel her leg quiver very slightly as I massaged her.

She apparently couldn't get enough of the feeling, either, for I heard her whisper to me, "Higher. Higher, Sean." I looked up at her, but her eyes were still closed. She may not have even realized that she had spoken to me.

I allowed my hands to travel all the way up her leg along the long quadriceps muscle, activating the heat of the liniment. As I got to the edge of her shorts, I rubbed down along the outside of her leg with my left hand and along her inner thigh with my right.

I was in turmoil. I was sweating, and my breathing was shallow. I didn't dare even blink for fear that I would break this spell and our session would end.

I needn't have worried. As I worked on her leg, she whispered a single word that held my attention: "More."

And so I followed her direction. I massaged her leg, and I took the liberties she was allowing. Kayla stayed as she was, leaning back on the couch and letting me minister to her. As softly and gently as I could, I slowly ran my hands back up her leg. I continued to work up onto the leg of her shorts before caressing down the sides of her legs, nervous I would be found out but unwilling to stop before Kala was ready for me to be done.

I glanced up at her face. Kayla was breathing heavily, her chest moving up and down in a rhythm as she took big breaths. *What the hell, nothing to lose by trying again.* I ran my hand back up again, teasingly slow, fingertips softly playing along her skin. When I neared the hem of her shorts, she reached down with both hands and pressed my fingers hard against the hot skin of her leg. She was trembling slightly, her eyes still closed.

She held my hands as her body tensed up. I could only kneel there, wondering in my male stupidity what was going on, when I felt her relax. Her back, slightly arched while she was pressing my hand to her leg, released its tension, and she nestled against the couch cushions once again. She softly grazed her fingers over my wrist as she came back into herself. Slowly, her eyes opened as she released my wrist and looked shyly at me. She looked down and then glanced up through her eyelashes at me. *Don't think badly of me,* she seemed to be saying.

For my part, I was in such a painful state I could not have stood if my life depended on it. I was also a bit shocked. Had I really been taking advantage of my best friend's sister? I was savvy enough to know that it wasn't strictly therapy on my part, and I didn't think Kayla thought of it as just a massage, either. What would she tell her brother? I was dreading seeing him next time, and I was dreading seeing Kayla next time, for fear of my reaction to either one of them. Even so, I desperately hoped that I would get another chance to be alone with Kayla once again, despite our age difference.

Kayla sat up and threw her arms around me in a fierce hug. She whispered in my ear, "Thank you, Sean. That's the nicest thing anybody has ever done for me. Thank you."

Well, that surprised me. I figured that I was the one who should be doing the thanking, but who was I to not accept a little heartfelt gratitude? Especially when it came from a thirteen-year-old fox, only recently putty in my hands.

I returned her hug, enjoying the feel of her against my chest. She looked up at me then, and quickly, softly kissed me. It was kind of a little girl kiss, puffy lips and closed mouth, but I didn't care. I wasn't even sure what a real kiss should feel like. And, at that moment, her show of gratitude was more than I could have wished for.

She lay back down on the couch, turned onto her side, and watched me as I busied myself cleaning up with the towels and washcloths. I fumbled around for a few minutes, desperately waiting for my body to recover before I ran out of things to do. I really didn't want to embarrass Kayla or myself by letting her see the effect she had on me.

Finally, I felt comfortable enough to stand. I gathered up the liniment and towels and stood up to take everything back upstairs. As I was climbing the stairs, I heard a car in the driveway. Jake and his mom were home.

They were surprised to see me, until Kayla explained about her accident. Her mom was effusive in her thanks to me for helping her out. Jake, meanwhile, had run upstairs to change into more comfortable clothes for baseball.

When I walked back into the family room, Kayla was watching TV while she was lying on the couch. I looked down at her and said, "Are you going to be all right, Kay?"

She sat up a little and said, "Yes, it feels pretty good now. Do you have to go?"

"Yes, I think I'd better. Jake will be down in a second."

She grabbed me around my leg as I was standing there, and pressed her cheek against my thigh. She looked shyly up at me. Very quietly, I heard her say, "I've never done anything like this before."

"I know," I said. "Neither have I."

"Can we do it again sometime, Sean?" I heard a touch of worry in her voice, as if I would jump up and start blabbing to the whole school about how easy she was or something. I gently removed her arms from around my leg and sat down beside her. She moved to rest against my shoulder, and I kissed the top of her head as I hugged her to me.

"Don't you worry, Kayla. You're my first, best girl, and we'll keep it a secret, okay?"

I felt her smile against me, and she wrapped her arm around me and squeezed. As I sat there, wondering at the odd turn that brought me there, I might have felt the saline warmth of her tears against my shirt.

She let go just as Jake ran into the room, and I scrambled to my feet. He grabbed my arm and began pulling me toward the back door. "C'mon," he said, "let's find the guys and get a game in before it gets dark."

With that, he pulled me out the door, grabbed his bicycle and baseball glove from his garage, and we were off.

✿ ✿ ✿

Late that night, I lay in bed thinking of Kayla. Visions of such a willing and lovely participant were fuel for a young boy's inspired fantasies, and it would be a long time before I was able to finally find the comfort of sleep.

- 3 -

THE TREE

The next morning, I was scheduled to referee an under-eight boy's game. All during the preparations for the game, I kept on thinking of my morning with Kayla. It wasn't until kickoff that I was able to even begin to get my mind on the game. During the game, I felt a little disconnected from things, and afterward, I almost went over to the two coaches and apologized. The game had ended in a 2–2 tie, so both coaches and all the players were happy. I opted to leave well enough alone and ended up not saying anything to them.

Right after the game, I had to hustle over to the high school for team tryouts. I had played on the junior varsity soccer team my freshman year, and I had dreams of moving up to play varsity. It was a long shot, because our head coach usually only chose one freshman and a couple of sophomores for the varsity team, but I was determined to give it my best.

It seemed like there were about a hundred guys milling about on the practice field when I got there. I walked over to join a group of my fellow JV players, who were congregated near one post of the goal on the field, waiting for tryouts to begin.

The coaches and the seniors on the varsity team divided everybody up into groups of five. There were circles of cones set up all around the field, and we had to work crossing passes in a star pattern among our circle of five. At the same time, we were to move counter-clockwise around the cones. The coaches were watching to see how we used our feet, both to move laterally and to trap and pass the ball. It was a fairly easy exercise for my buddies and me, but there were some kids who struggled. I could see, out of the corner of my eye, the coaches marking down comments on their clipboards. I concentrated on the ball, making sure it settled against my instep before I passed it off. I really wanted to make a good impression.

After that, the coaches put us through some conditioning tests, making us run the width of the field and back while dribbling a ball. Speed was a great advantage on the field, but speed without control was no good. We were being judged on our ball-handling skills as well as our speed and conditioning.

The last test they put us through was a shooting skill drill. Using both goals, they lined us up about twenty meters out from the nets. We were to make a crossing pass, leading the guy opposite us in line. That player, in turn, was to pass it back to us as we advanced toward the goal, using either a one-touch or a two-touch pass. Once we received the ball back, we were to take a shot on goal. We then rotated to the end of the other line and waited our turn to go again.

I had three more days of tryouts before the first cut. We wouldn't find out the coaches' decisions concerning team make-up for a couple of days after that. By the time I was walking back to my bike after that first day, I was very tired, but I was feeling confident I had done the best I could.

✿ ✿ ✿

As I was bicycling home from the tryouts, I decided to ride by Jake and Kayla's house to see if anybody was home. Jake was bouncing a tennis ball against his garage door, playing an imaginary baseball game.

THE TREE

"Hey," I said as I rode up his driveway.

"Hey," he replied as he whipped through a double play, shortstop to second to first, against the garage door. "Tryouts go okay?" Jake had football tryouts coming up, and he was a little nervous about how he would do.

"Yeah," I replied. "Today it was lots of stuff we've done a thousand times before. Running especially."

"It will probably be the same for me," he said as he fired a fastball into the inside corner of his imaginary home plate. "How was the soccer game this morning?"

"Two–two tie," I said. I caught his liner off the panel of the door and spun it back toward him off the same panel. "How's Kay feeling?"

"Leg's pretty good, I guess. Better now than when she got up this morning. I think she's downstairs now, anyway, watching TV with Jaimie."

He threw the ball back at the garage door for me to catch. "Want to do something?" he asked.

"I guess," I answered. "What did you have in mind?"

"Come on, I'll show you something," he said. He reached for the ball and put the ball and his baseball mitt into the basket on his bike, then climbed on. "Follow me. I found out something that I think you'll really like."

It sounded mysterious enough that he got my interest, so we pedaled off through the field behind his house, and into the woods on the other side. We dropped our bikes down onto the ground, and he led the way along one of the many paths that kids of a dozen generations had made through the small patch of woods. He branched off the path and headed toward the edge of the woods on the other side. Moving slowly through the woods, he came to a tree that had slats of wood nailed to it to make a crude ladder. Warning me to be quiet, he climbed easily up the tree trunk and then used branches to climb up a little farther. He motioned to me, so I clambered up until I was on a branch

opposite the trunk from the one he was perched upon. He pointed in the direction of a house about thirty yards away and leaned
toward me around the trunk of the tree.

"What do you see?" he whispered.

I looked, trying to figure out what it was he was showing me,
but I was stumped.

"Ummm…a house?" I asked.

"Yeah, idiot, a house. Whose house?"

"The O'Toole house," I said. *Why is he asking me whose house
this is? He knows as well as I do whose house it is.*

He looked at me as if I was the village dunce. "And who lives
in the O'Toole house?" he asked, speaking slowly as if to a very
dim child.

"Josh lives there," I said. Josh was another of our neighborhood gang, a good guy we both had been friends with since about
the second grade.

"And?" Now Jake was getting just plain annoying.

"And…" The light bulb went on, and I felt just as dumb
as Jake was thinking I was. "And Heather and Molly," we said
together.

Of course. Heather and Molly were Josh's sisters. Heather was
going to be a senior, seventeen years old and drop-dead gorgeous. She was a cheerleader and one of the most popular girls
at school. Molly, Josh's twin sister, was fifteen, just like us, and
was a younger version of Heather. I figured that Josh had to have
been walking around his house with a perpetual boner for about
the past three years, living with those two. He claimed, however,
that they were only sisters to him, just as annoying as typical
sisters were.

"So what are we looking at here?" I said to Jake.

"You see the window on the far left? That's Heather's room.
The window on the right is Molly's. That window in between, the
one you can see the mirror in, that's the bathroom they share."

"Yeah?" I said to him. "So what? The bedroom curtains are closed. How do you know?"

"Josh and I peeked into their rooms a couple of weeks ago," he said. "And just because the curtains are closed now doesn't mean they are always closed. Understand?"

I stared at him disbelievingly.

"It gets better," he whispered. "They hardly ever close the curtains in the bathroom. And the mirror you see just happens to be positioned advantageously in respect to the very branches in which we are perched," he finished with a smug little smile.

"Jake, old pal," I said, "you are my new best friend."

"I thought I was your best friend already," he said.

"Well, you were, but you've just confirmed my good taste in best friends," I replied.

We made plans to meet later that night to check out the windows and then headed back to Jake's house. As we were riding across the field from the woods, I couldn't help but notice (now that Jake had got me to thinking about windows and curtains) that Jaimie and Tara's bedrooms were at the back of their house, and they lived in a ranch house, so their windows were all on the ground floor.

The possibilities were staggering to a typical fifteen-year-old hormonally charged boy such as me.

Sometime after nine that night, Jake and I made our way back through the woods to the tree behind the O'Toole house. As quietly as we could, we climbed up the slats to the branches we had perched in that afternoon.

"Damn!" I heard Jake softly swear. "I meant to bring a pair of binoculars."

"That's okay. We're close enough for now," I said. I had to admit, though, binoculars would have been a great idea.

The mosquitoes were out in abundance, and Jake and I were getting bitten up sitting in the tree. There was no activity in the windows we were watching. After about an hour, we both had

had enough of branch sitting and mosquito swatting and dark house watching, so we gave it up and climbed back down. On the way back out of the woods, it occurred to us that maybe we should have called Josh to make sure they were home.

"Oh, well, so I'll call him tomorrow," said Jake.

We walked back across the field, and I glanced at Jaimie's house.

"Look!" I stopped Jake and pointed. Tara's curtain was drawn across the window, but there was a gap in Jaimie's. We quietly crept up closer to try to see into her room.

Jackpot! Jaimie was there, sitting on her bed, brushing her hair. We could hear the faint sound of a record playing, and she was nodding her head in time to the music as she was brushing her hair. She was wearing a robe, having apparently just gotten out of the shower.

"Oh, man, sweet!" Jake exclaimed. "Boy, would I like to get some of that."

"Why not ask her out, then?" I asked.

"I don't know," he whispered. "Maybe she's just too tight with my sister. I can't think that anything good could come of that."

"Aw, your sister's okay," I said.

"Easy for you to say; she's not your sister," he replied. I heard him sigh as he finally admitted, "I guess she's not so bad, but she's still a sister, you know?"

"Yeah, I guess," I said. Actually, I didn't know since I only had brothers, but it was easier to just agree with him.

We watched as Jaimie got up and left her room. She came back in a few minutes later and hung up her robe. She was wearing a thick nightgown, covering her from her neck to her knees. She pulled back the bedspread, got in her bed, and then turned out her light.

"Show's over," Jake said, and we started back toward his house.

"Hey, Jake, you want me to see if I can talk to Jaimie? Maybe I can see if she likes you, and then maybe you can get together with her."

"That's okay," he said. "I'll think about it. I don't know. Christ, why is this all so difficult?" He shook his head as we walked across the lawn toward his house. "Oh, well, see you tomorrow," he said desultorily. He slowly climbed the back steps, head hanging down.

Yeah, Jake, I thought to myself, *sometimes we really make it tough on ourselves.*

- 4 -

TRUTH-OR-DARE HEARTS

Two days later, Jake and I were over at his house playing his Pong game in the basement. It was raining buckets outside, and we were bored. We heard the back door open, and Kayla and Jaimie came pounding down the stairs, laughing and shouting. They burst into the playroom and stopped suddenly when they saw us there. They obviously weren't expecting us to be downstairs. They were soaked through, hair plastered to their heads, and their T-shirts were nearly transparent. They both crossed their arms in front of themselves and ran into the laundry room, squealing. Jake and I started laughing and hooting.

"Come on, ladies, come out. Nothing to be afraid of out here. Come on!" shouted Jake.

"Hey, sissy girls, come on out! We promise not to stare too hard," I added.

We heard Kayla's muffled voice. "What are you doing here?"

"Just playing games. Come on out, we've got sodas. It's okay. I'm your brother, after all. It's not like I've never seen you naked before."

"I'm not naked. I'm also not seven anymore, brother dear."

"So what? Neither am I. It's okay, really," he insisted.

We could hear them talking to each other through the door.

"Turn the light out," said Jaimie, "and we'll come out."

Jake scrambled to his feet and turned off all the lights but left the television on. He gave the girls the all clear.

The door opened just a crack so they could check to make sure we weren't fooling them, and then they came out and sat by us. They each had a towel to dry off with. Jaimie was using hers to fluff her hair, and Kayla had hers wrapped around her head. Jaimie kept on pulling at the front of her shirt, trying to pull the clinging material away from her, very self-conscious about how wet her shirt was. Kayla, on the other hand, was pretty much unconcerned about it as she sat down next to me, though I thought I could detect the slightest trace of a blush on her face. The low light coming from the television set across the room gave us just enough light to see each other.

"Your leg's better, I see," I said to Kayla.

"Yes, it feels pretty good," she replied. "What are you guys doing?"

"Nothing much," said Jake. "Just sitting down here wishing the rain would stop. What were you guys doing?"

"Getting wet, unfortunately," said Jaimie. "And this was just from coming from my house to here."

"So, what do you guys want to do?" asked Jake.

"I don't know. What do you want to do?"

I knew what Jake was thinking. He wanted to tell Jaimie that he wanted to rip her clothes off and jump her bones. He couldn't say it, though, so he just shrugged and tried to act nonchalant.

Kayla said, "How about playing Hearts? We could play Truth-or-Dare Hearts. Instead of keeping points, whoever ends up with the queen of spades has to do a Truth or Dare."

"Yeah, okay, why not?" We all agreed, so Jake opened the walk-in closet and found a deck of cards. We cut for the deal, and the first hand was dealt out. I had a great hand and was able to pass off the queen of spades to Jaimie on my left. At the end of the hand, she was forced to eat the queen.

"Okay, Jaimie. Truth or dare?"

"Ummm…truth, I guess," she said.

With a smile on her face, Kayla said, "Truth, Jaimie. Have you ever French kissed a boy?"

It was Jaimie's turn to blush. "No," she said.

"Next deal!" cried Kayla. She was really getting into this game. I hoped it didn't backfire on her and get us both in trouble.

On the next hand, we passed to the right. I passed the ace of spades, the king of hearts, and the five of hearts. Jaimie passed me three diamonds, trying to void her hand. I didn't think I would be hurt, and play began. This time, Jake ended up with the queen of spades. He chose *dare*.

"Okay, Jake," I said with a grin. "Your dare is to give Jaimie her first real kiss."

Jaimie looked as startled as Jake, but she was a good sport. Jake crawled over to her, put his arm around her shoulder, and kissed her on the mouth.

"No fair!" cried Kayla. "The dare was a French kiss!"

Both Jaimie and Jake shot her a look but turned back to each other. Jake reached out to her and kissed her again. We could see their mouths opening against each other, and Jaimie reached out to slide under Jake's arm to hold him for a longer kiss. When they stopped the kiss, they were both panting. Jake looked a little shell-shocked as he sat back down but quickly gathered his wits about him again and shot me a quick grin.

"Let's play!" he said.

Jaimie lost the next hand, but it was a little suspicious. She played the king of spades over my nine, and Kay gave her the queen.

"Truth or dare, Jaimie?" she asked as she played her card.

"Dare," she said defiantly.

"Okay, here it is. Without using your hands, you have to pass this empty soda can from under your chin over to Jake, who has to grab it under his chin without the use of any hands."

It seemed like a pretty innocent challenge, so Jaimie picked up an empty can and placed it under her chin. She leaned over toward Jake and tried to pass the can to him but discovered that it was nearly impossible to do without rubbing up against him. After several hilarious attempts at it, they got serious about finishing the task. They twisted and turned at each other, getting more and more frustrated at not being able to do it. Finally, Jake ended up lying on the floor on his back, and Jaimie lay down practically on top of him before they were able to successfully pass the can. By this time, Kay and I were laughing so hard, we were rolling on the floor. Tears were tracing down both our cheeks, and our sides ached.

On the next deal, there was no passing of any cards. We had to play the cards we were dealt, and I had a loser of a hand. I ended up with the queen, which put a smile on Jake's face.

"Okay, Seanster, what's it to be?" he asked.

"Truth," I said.

Jaimie jumped in with the question.

"Have you ever done anything with a girl?" she asked with a big grin. "And don't pretend you don't know what I mean," she warned before I could protest.

Here it is. I knew that if I lost any more hands, I would have to go with dares, because the next truth question I would be asked would be to reveal the girl's name, and I really did not want to do that.

"Yes, I have," I said, "but that's all I'll say about it."

"Awww, not fair," said Jaimie.

At the same time, Jake, looking startled at my answer, said, "Hey! How come I didn't know about this?"

"Too bad, so sad," I said. "Whose deal is it?" I asked, grabbing up the cards.

On the next hand, Jake was forced to take the queen, even though he was really trying to make sure I got it. I knew he wanted the name of the girl.

"Dare," he said.

Kayla had a smug look on her face. "Take the person of your choice back behind the couch for five minutes. Nobody will peek, I promise. We'll come get you as soon as the five minutes are up."

If she expected him to be upset, she was disappointed. I had a feeling that Kayla had already figured out that Jake really liked Jaimie, and I was beginning to think maybe Jaimie was also interested in Jake. At any rate, Jake stood up and, without hesitation, held out his hand to Jaimie. They walked over to the small space behind the couch and lay down on the floor. Almost immediately, we could hear murmurs and the liquid sound of kissing.

Kayla turned to me with an expectant look on her face and reached over and pressed her soft lips to mine. I put my arms around her and pulled her tightly to me, and we felt ourselves practically floating down to lie on the floor together.

Just as things were getting interesting, Kayla let go of me, looked at her watch, and called out, "Time!" She jumped up onto the couch and looked over the back, hoping to catch her brother in a compromising position. Jake and Jaimie sat up, looking a little flustered, and came back out to the game.

"Somebody deal the cards," said Jake as he sat back down. At this point, I think both he and Jaimie were going to try to lose. Unbeknownst to them, Kayla and I were just as willing to lose as they were.

I got the queen. Under other circumstances, I would have been railing about my bad luck, but this was an unusual card game, to say the least.

"Dare," I said quickly.

Jake looked a little disappointed he couldn't weasel the name of the girl from me, but then he realized what possibilities could lie ahead with my dare.

As he grinned at Jaimie, I could see the wheels turning in his mind. With no thought of the consequence of sending Kayla away with his best friend, but instead intent on providing the two of them with some time by themselves, Jake said, "Your dare is to take Kayla into the closet for five minutes."

"Make it ten minutes," suggested Jaimie with a grin, to which Jake readily agreed.

Feigning reluctance, I stood up, grabbed Kayla by the hand, and headed for the closet.

"Be sure to knock before you open the door," I said.

Jake looked dubious but said, "Sure, whatever you say. Have a nice time keeping my kid sister company. Hah!"

As soon as we closed the closet door, we could hear giggling and shuffling noises coming from the room. Kayla moved up very close to me and whispered, "We've got ten minutes."

We fell to the floor and immediately our lips found each other. It was a dangerous game, with her brother in the next room, but I was certain he was involved in his own pleasures. I knew this was a chance worth taking, as long as we didn't take it too far. We didn't want to be struggling to rearrange clothes at the end of our ten-minute limit, so we tempered our enthusiasm.

All too soon, there was a knock at the door. As Jake opened the door, the timid light from the television set seemed bright after the darkness of the closet. Jaimie's hair was tousled, and Jake's eyes were slightly glazed. I was in no position to smirk, however, as I could not stand up very straight. Kayla, of all of us, looked the most presentable.

"Whose turn is it to deal?" Jaimie asked. "Never mind, I'll just do it."

She grabbed the cards, and without waiting for us to sit down, began to deal out the deck.

"Oh, never mind the cards," she suddenly said. She looked up at us with shining eyes. "Kayla, truth or dare?"

Kayla looked at her a little fearfully before answering.

"Dare," she said quietly.

"Show us what you and Sean were doing in the closet," said Jaimie.

"Why?" asked Kayla, showing a little irritation with her friend. "Why do you want to know?"

"I just do," said Jaimie. "I want to know if you two were fooling around in there."

"Oh, yeah? Well, what about what went on out here? Are you going to tell us about that?" Kayla retorted. "I know how hot you think my brother is."

She immediately regretted her words. Jaimie looked like she had been hit in the stomach, and Jake was standing there a little shocked himself. After all, he never expected to hear that Jaimie might have the same thoughts about him that he had over her, in spite of the activities of the afternoon.

Before this line of conversation disintegrated any further, we heard a door slam upstairs. It got our attention, and we looked around at each other, each of us feeling a little chagrined.

We started making some noise until we heard Mrs. Lehigh at the top of the stairs.

"Are you kids down there?" she called out.

"Yes, Mom," shouted Kayla. "Jake and I are here with Jaimie and Sean. We're playing cards." She looked at us and grinned.

"That's nice, dear," said Mrs. Lehigh as she turned from the doorway. "Dinner will be ready soon."

"What time is it?" Jaimie suddenly said. She glanced at the star-shaped wall clock hanging over the television. "Oh my God, I was supposed to be home twenty minutes ago!"

She hustled around, helping us to straighten up the room, and then headed up the stairs.

"Wait up, Jaimie. I'll walk out with you," I said. I followed her up the stairs, then called back down, "Thanks, guys, for a fun afternoon!" All four of us chuckled, our little private joke.

Jaimie and I walked outside. It had stopped raining, and the sky was clearing. As we walked toward her house, I put my arm around her shoulder. She looked startled but then relaxed and accepted it.

"So, I take it you like Jake?"

"Yeah. I've been hoping he would notice me. I only live next door to him and have since I was six. You'd think he never saw me before today," she said quietly.

"Hey, it's nothing to worry about. He's a guy, and guys are pretty unsure about things like that. We really, truly don't have a clue about girls, you know."

"Not you," she said. "Kayla says you pick things up pretty quickly."

"Don't believe everything you're hearing," I said. "Really, I'm just as clueless as Jake most of the time. About girls, anyway."

By this time, we were in front of her house. I let her go and turned to continue on home.

"Sean?"

I turned around and walked back to her.

"Thanks."

"For what?" I asked.

"For not making fun of me, or of Jake…you know."

"It ain't nothing," I said to her. I'm not sure I followed her, but if she thought I deserved some thanks, I wasn't about to disregard it.

"See you tomorrow, Sean." With that, she reached up on her toes and gave me a sisterly kiss on the cheek. She smiled happily and then ran up the stairs to her door.

I stood there for a moment, trying to figure it out. Finally, I had to admit to myself that I couldn't.

Girls. Go figure.

- 5 -

LORI AND DAVEY AND KIP

The next day, I got a call from the lady who was in charge of assigning referees to the soccer games sponsored by our soccer association.

"Hello, Mrs. Dailey," I said. "Is there going to be a schedule change?"

"No, Sean," she answered. "I got a call from one of the parents at a game you officiated that I need to talk to you about."

"Oh?" I asked with some apprehension. "Did I do something wrong?" I was thinking about that game that my concentration was not on after my experience with Kayla.

"No, Sean, not at all. This was one of your under-eight games from a couple of weeks ago. It seems you impressed some of the parents. This particular mom wanted your name and phone number to ask if you would be interested in giving some private soccer lessons to her children. Since it's not our policy to just give out telephone numbers, I told her I would call you and give you her name and number, and if you were interested, you would call her instead. She agreed to that, so I have her information if you would like it."

"That's great, Mrs. Dailey. I really appreciate it."

"You know, Sean, usually when I get a call from a parent, it's to complain about one of our officials. It's a pleasure to be able to pass along one of the few compliments we receive. You should feel good about the job you've been doing out there, and I for one really appreciate the work you've done."

"Aw, jeez, Mrs. Dailey, you're embarrassing me, but thanks."

"You're very welcome, Sean," she said. "And thank *you*."

She gave me the information. The call was from a Mrs. Wilkinson, and she was interested in beginner lessons for her boys. I called her and introduced myself, and we chatted for a few minutes.

"So, Sean, you were the referee at my son's game. I was really impressed with how well you were able to communicate with the kids. Kip is seven, and his brother Davey is eight, and they both say they want to learn how to play better. Would you be interested in helping them? I'll be glad to pay you by the hour."

"Sure, Mrs. Wilkinson. I'll be happy to help them."

And so arrangements were made. The Wilkinsons lived about half a mile from my house, so I agreed to meet the boys that afternoon at their house to start their lessons.

After lunch, I loaded up my gear in a backpack and rode my bike over to their house. I rang the bell, and a lady answered the door.

"Yes? Oh, hi, Sean. I remember you from the game. I'm Lori Wilkinson. Come on in and meet the boys."

I was a little shocked that this person was really Mrs. Wilkinson. She looked to be barely into her twenties. She was average height, slender, with light brown hair cut just to her shoulders. She was very tan and lean. The halter top she wore accentuated her small waist and made her top look bigger than it probably was, and the white shorts made her tan legs look like they were about a mile long. If she hadn't introduced herself, I would have assumed she was a college-age baby-sitter or something.

I followed her back into the house. In the kitchen, she offered me some lemonade and then poked her head out the patio door.

"Kip!" she called. "Davey! Come in for a minute, boys!"

I heard them before I saw them. They were yelling and tumbling and practically doing somersaults over each other on their way into the house. They stopped for a second when they saw me by the kitchen table, and Mrs. Wilkinson introduced us.

"Are you going to teach us soccer?" asked Davey.

"You were the referee at my game," said Kip at the same time.

"Yes and yes," I answered. "Do you want to learn?"

"Yeah!" they both yelled. "I'm gonna play for the Chicago Sting!" shouted Davey.

"Oh yeah? Well, I'm gonna play for…for…the *Cubs*!" yelled Kip.

"You dope, the Cubs play baseball, not soccer," sneered Davey.

"Not by the time I'm playing for them, they won't be," insisted Kip.

"All right, boys, enough! Grab your soccer gear and don't forget your shin guards, and follow Sean, all right? And listen to what he says, and no smarting off to him. He's the boss. Got it?" Mrs. Wilkinson pinned them both with a stern eye. "No trouble from you two hoodlums, okay?" she added.

"Okay!" they shouted in unison. And off they went to collect their gear.

Mrs. Wilkinson watched them go and then turned to me.

"They're good boys," she said. "Just a little rambunctious. They'll listen to you. They really like to play soccer, and I think they really want to learn."

"Don't worry, Mrs. Wilkinson, we'll be fine. I like little kids, and your boys look like they know how to have fun. We'll have a good time, I know we will."

"Thank you, Sean. And please, call me Lori." She poured us both a little more lemonade while we waited for the boys to come back.

☆ ☆ ☆

I was right about Kip and Davey. They were very active little boys, and we had a lot of fun. They were also happy to listen to what I had to say, as long as I didn't talk too much. A lot of soccer is learned by kicking and dribbling, not from lectures, so the boys and I had a great time at our first lesson, working on basics. By the end of the lesson, they were actually passing the ball pretty much in the direction they wanted it to go and were running ahead of me as we made our way from the park back to their house. The kids were passing the ball back and forth and staying about five feet from each other, as I had taught them.

When we got to their house, they opened the door and burst in, shouting and yelling to their mother about their lesson. Lori came out from the back of the house and poured us all more lemonade as she listened to their excited chatter about everything they had learned. Every once in a while, she would glance up at me and give me a big smile.

Finally, she clapped her hands and said, "Okay, boys, way to go. Everybody upstairs now, and wash your hands and faces. You guys are filthy!"

Kip and Davey slammed down their glasses and ran up the stairs, in constant motion. Lori refilled my glass and reached for her purse.

"Thank you so much, Sean. I really appreciate the time you took with them. I know they can be a handful sometimes."

"They're great kids, Lori," I said. "They're enthusiastic, they're friendly, and they really are interested in learning how to play soccer. They may be a lot of work, but they seem to be a lot of fun, too."

"They are a lot of work, especially for a single mom. But you're right; they are fun. Anyway," she said, handing me the money, "here's for today. Can you come back tomorrow?"

"Sure, and thanks for letting me work with them," I said. We walked to her front door, and I yelled up the stairs to the boys. "See you tomorrow, guys! Good job!"

"Bye, Sean!"

"See you tomorrow, Sean!"

"Good-bye, Sean. And thank you for taking such good care of my little guys." She touched my arm lightly as she said good-bye. I hopped on my bike and rode home, turning back to wave as I rode down the street. Lori was there, in her doorway the whole time, watching me ride away.

- 6 -

THE MOVIE

When I got home, I took a shower and grabbed something to eat. I had another game to work, so I headed over to the soccer fields. I was working as a line judge for a girl's under-sixteen game. Working as a line judge was easy. Plus, since I was only working half the field, I could talk a little with some of the kids on the teams while they were on the sidelines. Since both teams, the Sting Rays and the Kickin' Chicks, were from our school, it was a friendly game, with the girls on both sides just as ready to joke with their opponents as try to steal the ball from them. Molly O'Toole was a midfielder on the Sting Rays team, and I saw Josh and his mom sitting in the bleachers, watching the game.

After the game, Josh came up to me and said, "Sean, a bunch of us are going to the Dairy Queen. Want to come along and hang out?"

"Sure," I said. "Who all is going?"

"Oh, me and Shayna and Molly and Tessa and Jen and Sam and Toby and maybe some others. The girls want to shower and clean up from the game, so they are going to meet us there in about an hour."

"Sounds good. Maybe I'll swing over to Jake's house to see if he wants to come, too," I said.

"Okay, great. I'll see you there, then," he said. He ran to catch up to his mom and his sister.

Shayna Gallagher was Josh's girlfriend, a rough-and-tumble girl who played soccer with abandon, heedless of injury. She had only been playing for about a year, but she had already earned a bit of a reputation as a player to be careful around. She would knock you down and run right over you without a glance. On the other hand, she would take a hard check from an opponent without a second thought, considering it all a part of the game. Most other girls around our age tended to take rough treatment on the soccer field almost personally instead of adopting Shayna's *laissez faire* attitude. She had bright red hair that she kept cut short, and was attractive in a tomboyish kind of way.

Molly, like her older sister Heather, was a real Irish beauty, with long, curly, red-gold hair. I'd heard people call her hair color strawberry blonde, and I guess that's an accurate description. She was on the junior varsity cheerleading squad during our freshman year and was looking forward to joining her sister on the varsity squad this year. She was tall and slender and looked really good in her letter sweaters and pleated skirts.

Tessa Navarrone was Molly's best friend and her physical opposite. Tessa was short and dark and looked slightly overweight (a mistake her opponents on the playing field often made, to their dismay), with coarse black hair. She was a bulldog on the soccer field, though, playing at the keeper position. She had two special attributes as a goalkeeper: she could punt the ball into the opponent's half of the field, and she was steadfast in her defense of a breakaway or a penalty kick. She tallied more shutouts than anyone else I had ever heard about around our area. She would often use her loud voice to move her defensive teammates around or to rally her team to greater efforts, taking a leadership role on the defensive side.

Jen Davies and her boyfriend, Sam Loggins, were both a year younger than the rest of us. Jen played forward for the Kickin'

Chicks and was their leading scorer. She was tall and gangly, excruciatingly thin, and could pump her long legs fast enough to leave everyone around her in her dust. I thought her ball-handling skills were only average, but her speed made her a formidable player. She and Sam had been going together just since the spring, but all summer long you never saw one without the other being nearby. Sam was also very tall, well over six feet, and as a freshman was considered to be the future star of our high school basketball team.

Toby Mueller was the runt of the group, a practical joker and Energizer bunny. I always told him he was a perfect Ritalin kid, and he never disagreed. I thought he was as manic as he was so people wouldn't care quite as much about how small he was, and it mostly worked. He was smaller than Jaimie's sister Tara, even though he was fifteen like most of the rest of us. He even had to show his school ID when he went to a PG-13 movie. And in a bit of a perverse twist, I knew he really had a serious thing about Jen. Just the thought of six-foot Jen walking around with tiny Toby was enough to make me bust a gut. However, I kept his secret to myself and didn't laugh even when he told me about his feelings for her.

I hopped on my bike and raced over to Jake's house. He was home, in the basement playing a game of Pong.

"Come on," I urged. "No time to waste. Let's go, now!"

I grabbed the controller out of his hand and threw it down. I grabbed him by his arm and practically pushed him up the stairs and out his back door.

"Get your bike and follow me," I yelled as I took off across the field behind his house.

"Sean! Wait up!" I could hear him struggling to catch up to me as I dropped my bike at the edge of the woods.

"Come on," I yelled. "You're going to owe me big time for this!"

He finally rode up, out of breath, and I headed into the woods with Jake at my heels. I turned and put my finger to my lips, silently indicating to him to be quiet, as we approached the ladder on the tree behind the O'Toole house. We climbed up to our perches, and I pointed toward the bathroom window.

We didn't have to wait long. After a few minutes, a lovely and apparently naked Molly stepped from the shower. We couldn't see anything but her head and shoulders, because of the position of our branch and the angle of the mirror, but it was enough to fuel our imaginations. We watched as she wrapped a towel around her wet hair and reached back to take another towel off a shelf. She wrapped that larger one around herself. She opened the bathroom door, disappearing from our view. Since the curtains to her room were still closed, Jake and I scrambled down and out of the woods to our bikes.

"Did you see that! So close!" Jake exclaimed. "Un-freaking-believable! How did you know she would be there?"

I told him about the soccer game and Josh's invitation as we climbed back on our bikes and started back across the field.

"All right, I'm there! Let me just let my mom know where we're going and I'll be right back out," he said as he dropped his bike and headed into his house.

We rode together over to the Dairy Queen. Toby, Sam, Jen, and Josh were already there, sitting around two picnic tables set up behind the building. Jen and Sam were holding cones and sitting together, and Toby and Josh were holding the other table for the group. Jake, Josh, and I went in and ordered, and by the time we got back out, the rest of the group had arrived. Jake looked at Molly and immediately turned red and looked away. In my mind's eye, I could see her as she was just a few minutes ago, damp and fresh as she stepped from her shower. I knew that Jake was thinking the same thing. Luckily, Molly and Tessa ran into the store, along with Toby and Shayna, to place their orders, without noticing Jake's discomfort. By the time they came out with their ice cream, we were all back to our usual rowdy selves again.

THE MOVIE

Sam, Jen, Josh, Shayna, and Toby were sitting at one table, and the rest of us were draped around the other one as we indulged in the delights that can only be had on a late summer day in the sunshine. Molly and I were on one side of the table, and Tessa and Jake were across from us.

"Hey, Sean," said Tessa, "I hear you're giving soccer lessons."

"Yeah," I said. "Where did you hear that?"

"I heard it," said Molly. "I baby-sit for Mrs. Wilkinson sometimes, and she asked me if I knew you."

"Wow," interrupted Toby as he hopped up onto our tabletop from his seat. He squatted down so that he was nearly eye level with us. "And she hired you anyway?"

We all laughed, and Tessa pushed him off our table. "Back where you belong, Monkey Boy," she said.

"Where I belong," he said, crouching on the ground, looking up at Tessa and batting his eyes, "is in your lap, sampling your considerable charms."

"Here, sample this," she shot back at him, flipping him the finger.

"See?" he said, standing and turning to his companions at the other table. "Completely and utterly charming." He shrugged and sat back down. Everybody at both tables threw wadded up napkins at him.

"What do you know about the Wilkinsons?" I turned to Molly.

"Well, you know Davey and Kip, right?" I nodded. "They're good boys," she continued, "but boy, are they ever active. I think Mrs. Wilkinson just has me come over so she can relax by herself for a while and not worry about her kids."

"She told me she was a single mom. What happened to Mr. Wilkinson?" I asked.

"I don't know for sure," she said. "All I know is that he died, but I don't know what happened. She really misses him, though. Sometimes while I'm giving the boys a bath, I can hear her crying in her bedroom. It's really sad."

"Boy, I didn't know any of that. I'll have to watch my mouth," I said.

"How often are you going over there?" asked Tessa.

"She wants me to come every day I can until school starts," I said. "So, unless it rains or something, I'll be there just about every afternoon for an hour or so."

"That's really great," Molly said. I felt her slide a little closer, until our legs were just barely touching. "Creating future soccer stars, I present to you, Sean Porter, instructor of the year!" She patted me on the back. Everybody applauded, with Toby and Jake adding whistles and cheers, while I bowed in mock humility.

The sun was starting to go down and it was cooling off. We all split up, and Jake and I rode back to his house. As we rolled up to his driveway, Jaimie and Kayla came out of Jaimie's house. They stopped when they saw us and put their heads together for a moment before coming down to us.

"Hey, Jake, you want to come over and watch TV?" asked Jaimie.

Jake looked over at me inquisitively. I gave him a small, quick nod.

"Sure," he said.

"Sean? You want to come, too?" asked Kayla.

It was my turn to glance at Jake. He shrugged, leaving it up to me. I looked over at Kayla and saw a little eagerness in her expression, enough for me to agree.

"Okay," I said.

We dropped our bikes on the front lawn and went with the girls into Jaimie's house.

Tara was in the kitchen, helping her mother with the dinner dishes. As Jaimie turned the television on, Mrs. Jacks came out.

"Are you hungry?" she asked with a smile. "We just finished dinner, but I could make you boys something..."

"No, thank you; we're fine," said Jake.

"We just came from the Dairy Queen," I added.

"Oh, I see," she said. "Well, if you need anything, Jaimie can get it for you."

"Thanks, Mrs. Jacks," Kayla said.

The four of us settled down on the floor, leaning back against the sofa. Jaimie found a cable offering of *The Sting* just beginning. Tara came in and flopped down on the sofa behind us just as the opening credits began.

I put my hand down on the floor, between Kayla and me, and sent up a silent and nerve-racking plea for her to notice it. Eventually she did, and she put her hand down next to mine. After several excruciating minutes, our little fingers were touching and then twining around each other. By the end of the second reel, we were holding each other's sweaty hands, trying to be surreptitious in the company of our friends. We leaned in toward each other until our shoulders were touching. We stayed that way until the end of the movie, alternately paying attention to the twists and turns of the plot and listening to the internal message of our own intricate dance.

- 7 -

AT THE DRUG STORE

For the next three days, I biked over to the Wilkinson house and took Davey and Kip to the park to work on their soccer skills. Every day, they came tumbling out of the house to meet me. The two of them then ran nonstop until I brought them back home an hour later. Lori Wilkinson always invited me in afterwards to have some lemonade, and we sat at her kitchen table while the boys ran upstairs to clean up after soccer.

Each time I took them out, I could see improvement in their skills. They still had the attention span of young boys, but they both loved to play soccer, and they loved kicking the ball to each other. By the third day, we were playing a game I called Heads Up. The three of us were in a moving, revolving triangle, each about twenty feet from each other. We were constantly passing two soccer balls, first clockwise and then counterclockwise. The exercise kept them moving (which they were prone to do anyway), and it helped to develop their passing and trapping skills using both feet. By the end of the day, they were both passing equally well with both the insides and outsides of their left and right feet, an accomplishment that not many kids their age could claim. It would give them a distinct advantage in their games.

The three of us dribbled our soccer balls back to the house from the park. One of my rules for the boys was that they couldn't pick up and carry a soccer ball. They had to dribble it wherever they went, except for crossing a street. When we came to a corner, they had to pick up their soccer balls and wait for me so we could cross the street together. They were very good about following this rule, and they learned very quickly not to let their dribbling lead them very much as we got closer to a street corner. While we were in the middle of the block, they were running ahead of me and then turning and dribbling back to circle behind me before racing ahead again, using both feet to keep the ball moving. They were both anxious to show their mom what they had been learning, and I was very pleased with the way they had taken to the game with such enthusiasm. When we got to their front lawn, they both left their soccer balls on the grass as they raced each other, both trying to be the first to tell Lori about their progress.

"Mom! Mom! Come out and see!"

"Come out, Mom, and we'll show you what Sean's been teaching us!"

They were shouting and jumping as they hit the front door. In just a few seconds, each had one of Lori's hands, and they were both pulling her out the door.

"Watch this, Mom!" shouted Davey. "Kip, go over there, and I'll pass it to you!"

Kip ran across the yard, and Davey kicked a pass to him with his right foot and took off running at a right angle. Kip neatly stopped the pass, turned, and led Davey with a pass off his left foot. As soon as the ball left his foot, Kip started running back to where Davey had been, ready to receive the ball back from his brother. They wove in and out of each other's passing lanes for a few minutes, all the time shouting out directions to each other, proud to show off for their mother. Lori stood on the front steps, watching her boys with a big smile.

She clapped her hands as she said, "That's great, guys. I am really impressed!"

She turned to me and said, "You've done a truly amazing job with these ruffians, Sean. I can't thank you enough."

"Aw, shucks, ma'am," I said in my best Southern drawl. "It twern't nothin'."

"Well, come on in, then, sheriff, and pull up a barstool while I serve you up some sarsaparilla," she countered as she opened the door and led us into the house.

The boys ran and jumped up the stairs to get cleaned up while Lori and I went into the kitchen for some lemonade. She set out a plate of cookies and filled four glasses with ice and poured freshly made lemonade into two of them. She handed me a glass and tipped hers toward mine in a silent toast before taking a sip. She sat down next to me at the table.

"Do you have a girlfriend, Sean?" she asked after a moment.

"Ummm…no, not really," I replied.

"I guess you know Molly O'Toole, don't you?" she said almost to herself.

"Yes, I know her and her twin brother. She was telling me that she baby-sits for you sometimes."

"The boys just love her," she said. "She doesn't seem to mind at all when they get rambunctious on her. She handles them beautifully."

"I know I've mentioned it before, Lori, but it's true. Davey and Kip are really good kids. There's no reason not to like them."

She sighed and said, "I know, but I worry anyway." She reached for her purse on the counter and opened it. "Oh no, I'm sorry, Sean. I forgot to stop at the bank to get some money. Can you stop by later tonight? Or do you have plans?"

My only plan was to see if Kayla was home. I figured I could stop by here first, so I said, "Sure, I can stop by. Or, if you want, you can just pay me tomorrow."

"Are you sure that's okay, Sean? I'd be just as happy if I could pay you tonight."

"No, tomorrow's fine," I said. I got up to go. "But thanks, I appreciate it. I'll see you tomorrow, Lori."

☆ ☆ ☆

"Sean! Hey, Sean, wait up!" Josh O'Toole was jogging across the park toward me as I rode by.

I stopped and waited for him to catch up. "Hey, Josh, what's up?"

"Not much," he said, trying to catch his breath. "I was thinking about going over to Lehigh Drugs. Come on along with me, won't you?"

I shrugged. "Sure, why not? What are you getting there?"

He leaned in closer and lowered his voice. "Condoms," he said. "Shayna wants to do it with me, but I've got to get condoms first."

"Wow," I said. "That's a big step, dude. When is this happening?"

"That I don't know yet," he said. "We were fooling around last night over at my house, and she says she thinks she's ready. I tell you, Sean, I nearly popped a nut right then and there when she said that."

"Yeah, I'll bet," I said. "Then what happened?"

"Well, we're making out on the floor, you know? And she's getting all squirmy and all, and then she goes, 'Yes, yes, I'm ready,' and starts calling my name, you know? Well, I thought she meant right then she was ready, so I try to get her clothes off, but she pushes me away. She's really in a huff now, thinks I'm just trying to get to her when she's, what did she call it? Oh, yeah, In a Weak Moment. I could almost hear the capital letters on the words, you know? Anyway, she says nothing doing until I get us some protection, and until I do, it's no-go for anything. She won't even give me a kiss until I can prove to her that I really love her or something, I guess."

"So, you're going down to the drug store to get some rubbers, and that's supposed to prove that you love her? That doesn't make any sense, Josh."

"Aw, hell, don't I know it. She's a chick, man, and that means she's confusing. All I know is that my first mission is to pick up some condoms for the next time she says she's ready. And who knows when that will be, you know what I mean? Anyway, the next time she says she's ready, I'll be ready."

"That's really messed up, Josh."

"Hey, it's not my logic, dude. You want to come along? I don't want to stand in that cashier line by myself holding a box of Trojans, you know? I could use the moral support. How about it?"

This was a perfect opportunity to supply myself. I had vague thoughts about how maybe, eventually, Kayla might be a willing partner instead of merely a figment of my overheated imagination. I hadn't ever considered acquiring protection, but now that Josh was on the cusp of becoming a man, I had to think about it. Like Josh, I too would not be looking forward to purchasing my first box of condoms by myself. Now, together, neither of us would have to.

"Yeah, okay, I'll come along. Why not?" I said.

We had to go past my house to get to the drug store, so we dropped off my bike on the way and walked over a couple of blocks to the shopping center. When we got there, we were confronted with a dizzying array of prophylactics in the back of the store.

"Shit, man, what do we get?" complained Josh. "I just thought we'd be able to come in here, grab a boxful, and take off again. Why are there so many choices?"

"I don't know. Lubricated, non-lubricated, ribbed, ultra-thin…what's this? *Flavored* condoms?!" I picked up a box.

A grown-up's voice from behind us startled us, and I dropped the box of condoms I had been holding.

"Hello, boys, can I help you with anything?"

I spun around in surprise, and my jaw nearly hit the floor. It was Mr. Lehigh, the owner of the drug store, and Jake and Kayla's father.

"Why, hello, Sean. I didn't expect it to be you here in the birth control aisle. Hello, Josh. Well, boys, I take it you are anticipating some adventures, right?" he said with a smile.

"Well...umm...just trying to be prepared, Mr. Lehigh," stammered Josh lamely. His face was bright red with embarrassment.

"It's nothing to be ashamed of, Josh, being here. It's a wise young man these days who thinks first about these things, instead of getting carried away in the moment, if you know what I mean," said Mr. Lehigh. "Now," he continued, "since this seems to be your first purchase, let me help you out. Try a box of these and see how you like them." He took a box of standard lubricated condoms off the shelf and handed them to Josh. "You can always experiment with other options the next time around, but these are good, basic items that will give you the protection you want while you learn how to use and enjoy them."

"Uh, that's great, Mr. Lehigh. Thanks a lot for your help," said Josh.

"You're welcome, Josh. Any other questions, boys? Sean, are you getting some of these, too?"

"Ummm...yeah, maybe I will. Thanks, Mr. Lehigh," I said.

He handed me a twelve-pack like Josh's and then casually waved and moved off to wander the aisles, looking for customers with questions. I watched him walk away and couldn't help wondering if he would have been so helpful if he had known that it was his own young daughter who was the object of my lustful fantasies. Somehow, I didn't think so.

Josh and I paid for our purchases and walked out the door, relieved to be hiding our stuff in plain brown paper bags, just in case we ran into any more parents we knew.

- 8 -

BEING PREPARED

It turned out that I was wrong about something that afternoon, since it wasn't Kayla who I was with when I opened up my first condom.

Josh and I went back over to his house after we left the drug store. We went upstairs to look for a good hiding place for his rubbers, someplace neither his parents nor his sisters would look. He finally decided to open up the box and hide the packets in some of his balled-up socks in the back of his underwear drawer. He also tucked two into his wallet. "For emergencies," he pronounced seriously.

"Emergencies!" I howled, and laughed until I cried. "At least I know who I can come to in case of emergency," I said, wiping tears from my eyes.

"Hey, you guys," came a voice from the doorway. "What's so funny in there?" Josh's twin sister, Molly, stuck her head in the room. "Hi, Sean. What are you guys laughing so hard about?"

"Nothing," grumbled Josh. "Just some guy stuff you wouldn't understand."

"Guy stuff? That sounds like a convenient excuse just to not even try to explain," said Molly with a grimace. "Come on, give it up. What are you guys doing?" She stepped into the room and stared us both down. She was dressed in a halter top and shorts that left her stomach bare. *Why is it that a bare midriff on a fit, young female is so appealing?* I couldn't stop looking at her.

I sat down on the bed, crossed my arms, and openly stared at her, enjoying the view.

"Christ, Molly, why is it that only girls can have secret stuff to talk about? Sean and I were just bullshitting. Really. We weren't talking about anything in particular."

"Yeah, right," she replied sarcastically. "Just bullshitting. Well, I know that's what you're doing now—to me, anyway."

I decided that I would let the two stubborn Irish kids butt heads for a while. *No sense sticking my nose in and getting it bent,* I thought as I sat back to enjoy the fireworks.

I had known both Josh and Molly since about forever, and they both had flashpoint tempers that could go off at any time. Both, however, were just as quick to get over it, and to the best of my knowledge, neither of them had ever carried a grudge away from any argument. Their fiercest fights were with each other, as was to be expected of brothers and sisters. But they also were the first to jump to each other's defense if someone else was involved. It was a little complicated for a dumb jock like me to figure out, so I usually let these things run their course with no interference. I figured that if I kept my mouth shut, I couldn't get into any trouble saying the wrong thing. It worked more often than not for me, and it worked this time, too.

Besides, just sitting and watching Molly while she was otherwise occupied was pleasure enough for me.

So there I sat, not paying any attention to what was being said, letting their voices wash over me while I contentedly watched Molly's skin flush with anger, when she suddenly reached out and grabbed from the floor the paper sack that held my purchase.

"Hey!" I shouted, reaching for the bag a fraction too slowly. Molly opened the bag and looked in, just out of my reach.

"And what do we have here?" she murmured as she pulled out the box of condoms. "Why, Sean, you little devil. Are these yours?" She looked at me coyly, with a big smile on her face.

"Sure," I said as bravely as I could. "They're mine. Of course they're mine. Who else's would they be?" I sat back down again, feigning indifference that she had found them.

She looked at the sales receipt and broke into a wide grin. "Well, well. It seems that you got these today." She put the receipt back in the bag and examined the box. "Hmmm…lubricated…medium…box of twelve." She looked up at me, a gleam in her eyes. "How long do you think it's going to take you to use a dozen of these things? Or is this your yearly supply?"

I stood and grabbed the box out of her hands and roughly shoved it back into the bag. "Very funny, Moll. A year's supply, huh."

"Wait a minute!" she cried suddenly. "Now I understand! Josh, you are a sneaky one. If Sean just bought these, that means that you got some, too, didn't you?" She walked over to his dresser and started opening drawers to search for them. "Where are they? Come on, Josh, show me."

Josh ran over and shoved his dresser drawers closed. "Cut it out, Molly," he said.

"I know you've got them here, Josh. Just show me where. I promise I won't tell anybody." She looked over at me and moved toward me and leaned down to grab my hand to pull me up. "Come on, Sean, show me where he's keeping them."

I resisted, making her pull a little harder. She couldn't pull me up, so she dropped to her knees and clasped my hand to her bosom and batted her eyes at me. "Please, Sean? Show me? As a favor to me?"

A lot of evil thoughts played themselves out in my mind at her words as she clutched my hand to the swells of her chest. She was making it hard to think straight. I distractedly noticed that the tops of her tanned thighs were very lightly freckled.

"Molly, let him go. All right, I'll show you. Christ, but you're a pain sometimes," grumbled Josh.

Molly jumped up with a squeal and hopped over to Josh as he opened his socks drawer. "They're right here," he said as he unrolled a pair of his socks. Four packets tumbled out, and Molly picked them up.

"Neat!" she cried as she turned the packet over. "How do these things go on?" she asked, almost to herself.

"Well, I'm certainly not going to show you!" huffed Josh, a shocked look on his face.

"I wasn't talking to you, brother mine," said Molly, punching him in the arm. "I was speaking hypothetically. I don't want you to *show* me, for God's sake."

"Oh," mumbled Josh. "Sorry. Well, you just roll it on, I guess."

"I guess," said Molly quietly as she examined the packet. "So," she said as she tucked the packets back into Josh's sock, "you think Shayna's ready for this?"

Josh shut his dresser drawer and sat down on the bed next to me. Molly sat down on my other side and leaned back on her arms so she could to talk to Josh.

"She says she is," Josh said. "I just want to have everything set, anyway."

"Just like a Boy Scout, right? 'Be prepared.' Who are you prepared for, Sean? I didn't know you were going out with anyone."

"I'm not going out with anyone," I said. "But it never hurts to be at the ready, does it?"

"Well," she said almost to herself, "I guess not. It's just that I don't know if I will ever find anybody to be ready for."

"What's the matter, Molly? Your love life got you down?" Josh didn't sound very sympathetic.

"What love life? I don't have one. I've never had one. I probably never will have one." With that, she shoved herself up and walked dejectedly out of the room.

"What's up with her?" I asked. "What did she mean by that?"

"Aw, she's just upset because she's never been out on a date. She sees me with Shayna, and she thinks something's wrong with her because no boy's ever asked her out or anything."

"You're kidding. She's drop-dead gorgeous, and she's never gone out? That's pretty strange."

"It's true, though. I get guys asking me all the time about her, but I guess they're just too shy or something to call her. She gets depressed about it sometimes, that's all."

"Wow, I never would have thought it. You just sort of assume that the really pretty ones are always out on dates and chasing them away with a stick. Hey, but what about Heather?"

"Oh, Heather's a different story. She's been going out with Evan ever since sophomore year. I think that bothers Molly, too, that Heather found a boyfriend she's kept all this time while Molly has never had the opportunity."

"Man, I'm blown away. I never would have guessed."

"Hey, Sean, why don't you ask her out? I know she likes you."

"Oh, man, I don't know..."

"Yeah, go ahead. You two would get along fine," Josh said. "Just don't let me hear that you're planning on using these things on her, okay?" he added, kicking at my sack of condoms. "She is my sister, after all."

"Okay, Josh, I'll think about it. Calling her, I mean."

"No, man, don't call her. Do it now. Go down and knock on her door and talk to her."

"Now? I don't think so. What if she says no? I'd rather do it on the phone."

Josh looked disgusted. "What a chickenshit. Go, Sean. Knock on her door and just talk to her for a little bit. I've got to call Shayna anyway, so while I'm on the phone, just go say hi to her."

He left the room to call his girlfriend, leaving me alone and nervous about talking to Molly. Finally, I decided that I really had nothing to lose by going down and just saying hello. I left Josh's room, went down the hall to Molly's room, and knocked on the door.

I heard her muffled voice call out, "What do you want, Josh?"

"Um...it's me, Sean. Josh went downstairs to call Shayna."

The door opened just a crack. "Oh, hi. What's up?" Molly asked.

"Uh, nothing...I just thought I'd come down and see what was up with you while Josh was on the phone."

"Sure, okay," she said, opening the door. "Come on in."

I walked into her room and automatically looked at her window. The blinds were up, and I thought I could figure out which tree I had been in at the back of their yard. "Look, Molly, I'm sorry if Josh or I said anything to get you upset," I started.

"No, no," she interrupted, "it's not anything you guys said. Well, not anything you said, anyway, Sean. Josh just knows which buttons to push, though, and he loves pushing them. But don't worry about me. He's got buttons I know how to push, too."

I laughed, and she smiled at me.

"Hey, Sean, I'm baby-sitting over at the Wilkinsons tonight. You want to come over and watch TV with the boys and me?" she asked.

"Okay, sure. What time?"

"Come over about seven thirty or so. The boys will still be up, and we can goof around with them for a little before they have to go to sleep. Mrs. Wilkinson will be out until about ten o'clock."

"Okay," I said. I got up to go find Josh again, mentally shaking my head. *Now why were you getting all worked up and nervous for nothing?* I thought to myself.

Sometimes life takes a right turn on you, just when you thought you were looking at a nice, straight road to travel.

- 9 -

THE BABY-SITTER

So there I was, ringing the doorbell at the Wilkinson house at seven thirty sharp. I was freshly showered, and I had shaved off the peach fuzz from my chin. I looked presentable enough in my Chicago Sting jersey. When I rang the bell, I heard the pounding of small, active feet running inside, and the door was thrown open. Davey and Kip flew out and tried to gang-tackle me on the front steps, very nearly succeeding before Molly came out to rescue me.

"Davey! Kip! You're going to tear him in two! If you will just let him go for a second, he'll come in and play," she said laughingly.

"Sean! I didn't know you were coming over!"

"Sean! We're making popcorn! Come in, come in!"

I let them pull me into the house, and we stumbled into the family room. They were getting ready to watch a movie called *The Bad News Bears*. I could smell popcorn popping in the microwave. The boys jumped onto the couch while Molly went into the kitchen to get drinks for everybody, and I slipped the tape into the VCR. Kip and Davey were fighting for supremacy over one of the pillows on the couch, until I finally took it away from them both and plopped down on the floor with it. Molly came in with platter loaded with a big bowl of steaming hot popcorn and four glasses of ice with matching cans of soda. The boys each settled into a corner of the couch. Molly and I sat next to each other on the floor, leaning back against the sofa. I pushed the button on the remote, and the movie started as we dug in and devoured the entire bowl of popcorn.

After about forty-five minutes, I stopped the movie so the boys could get ready for bed. We promised them that they could watch the rest of it with us, as long as they brushed their teeth and put on their pajamas. They raced each other to see who could be the fastest. Davey, being a year older, ran down the stairs first, reclaiming his corner of the couch. Kip was right behind him, and when they both were settled, I started the movie back up. While the boys were getting ready for bed, Molly and I had cleaned up the spilled popcorn and carried the dirty dishes and glasses into the kitchen. Molly rinsed everything off, and I took a dishcloth and wiped down the coffee table in the family room. When the boys came back down, Molly and I sat back down on the floor, our knees and shoulders just touching. By the time the movie ended, Molly had her head resting on my shoulder, my arm was draped around her, and the boys were fast asleep on the couch. We shook them gently awake. Molly and I each accompanied one boy up the stairs and into their beds, tucking them in and turning out the light. We shut their doors and went back downstairs to the family room.

We found a dark, black and white movie from the thirties on some channel and let that play as we sat back down on the floor. I was suddenly very nervous again, unsure of what to do with my arms or hands. Molly turned toward me, looking into my eyes, and I could see that she was just as nervous as I. Oddly, this had a calming effect on me, and I put my arm around her shoulder. She naturally, almost unconsciously, moved closer to me, and she snuggled into my arm. We stayed just like that, watching the scratchy images float across the glass of the television screen, until we heard a car pull into the driveway. Startled like two deer stranded on the side of a highway, we stared out the window, still clutched together, until the slamming of a car door shook us from our frozen state. We scrambled up, both secretly grateful that we hadn't done anything we shouldn't have done. We fluffed the pillows on the couch and checked once more to make sure the room was clean and presentable.

The back door opened, and Lori called out, "Molly? I'm home."

"Hi, Mrs. Wilkinson," Molly said as she got up and walked toward the kitchen.

Lori stepped into the doorway and saw me just as I was getting up from a chair. "Sean! I didn't know you were here."

"I'm sorry, Mrs. Wilkinson," said Molly. "I should have told you, but I invited Sean over to watch TV with us. I hope it's all right. I know how much the boys like him, so I thought..."

Lori gave us both an appraising look. Molly seemed to be a little flustered. I was very self-conscious as Lori examined us.

Finally, Lori relaxed a little, apparently satisfied with what she saw. "No, Molly, it's fine. I don't mind. I just wasn't expecting to find him here, that's all. Sean, of course you are welcome anytime," she said, looking at me. "Did you have a good evening?"

"Yes, we did," I said. "We watched *The Bad News Bears* until Davey and Kip fell asleep. They'll probably be dreaming of baseball and popcorn all night."

"Just as long as they stay dreaming all night," said Lori with a small smile. "I hope they decide to sleep in tomorrow morning, so I can get some rest." She looked around the room absentmindedly. "Grab your things, and I'll give you both a lift home."

"Oh, no, that's okay, Lori. I've got my bike here, so I'll just ride home," I said.

"And I live on the way, so I'll just walk with Sean, if that's all right," Molly added.

"Are you sure? I really don't mind driving you."

"No," we both echoed. "We'll be just fine," I added as we headed for the door. "Good night, Lori. Hope you're able to sleep in tomorrow."

Molly and I stepped outside. I picked up my bicycle, and we walked down the sidewalk, aware that Lori Wilkinson was watching us until we rounded a corner and moved out of her sight.

We walked slowly toward Molly's house, reluctant to part company. We talked quietly about the upcoming school year, about soccer, about nothing. When we stopped in her driveway, her house was dark.

"It doesn't look like anybody's home," I said.

"I guess not. Heather had a date, and Mom and Dad were going out with some friends, but I thought Josh would be home."

"Maybe he's over at Shayna's," I said.

"Maybe," she said. She looked over at me. "Do you have to go home right away? Or can you come in for a little while?"

"No, I can stay for a little," I said. We walked together around the side of the house. I set my bike down on the ground beside the garage, out of the way. Molly held my hand as we walked around to the back door and went into her house. Her palms were sweaty, and I could feel just the faintest tremor in her hand.

"We can go upstairs and listen to some music," she said quietly as she led me through the darkened house. We walked down the hall to her room. She opened the door but didn't turn on the light. Instead, she turned on the light in the closet and closed the door until just a sliver of light came through, keeping the room dim. She walked back to me and unhesitatingly stepped close to me. She was only a couple of inches shorter than me, so she didn't have to raise herself up very far to put her arms around my neck and press herself close to me. I accepted her invitation, and I put my arms around her waist and pulled her close. She lifted her face to me, her expression serious.

Our lips came together, but this was no chaste kiss. I heard a moan, but I couldn't tell if it came from me or from Molly. It didn't really matter. We were both too wrapped up in our sudden incendiary feelings to care about much beyond the immediate.

Her hips started moving of their own volition, side to side, creating exquisite contact at our most sensitive places. I could feel her soft hair brushing against my arms and hands as her head moved during our kisses. The combination of sensory signals racing through me created a nearly unbearable pressure in my chest and solar plexus, and I was sure Molly was feeling a similar barrage.

Nearly simultaneously, she grabbed at the hem of my jersey while I found the buttons on the back of her halter top. She pulled my jersey up and off as I raised my arms, and then she reached behind her and practically ripped her own top off, bra and all. Even in the dim light, just before she clutched me to her again, I could see a light pattern of freckles across her chest. She pushed me back, forcing me to step backwards until I felt the edge of her bed against my knees. I sat down when she pushed, and she kept on coming, forcing me onto my back with her on top of me, her lips once more searching for mine.

She was an animal, out of control and not to be denied in her quest toward satisfaction. I didn't know if it was because she liked me or if it was just a case of being in the right place at the right time, but at the moment my mind quit functioning rationally, so the pondering of such a question was no longer possible.

She lifted up from me. She sat up, grabbed at my shorts, and pulled them from my body. Only after I was naked did she stand up and yank her own shorts off, pulling down her panties with them. She held up her shorts, reached into a pocket, and withdrew a small, familiar-looking packet. She concentrated as she tore it open.

"I stole this from Josh this afternoon," she said seriously. "I wanted to see how it worked. Now's a good time to find out."

With that, she took out the condom, placed it carefully, and rolled it down. I involuntarily spread my legs a little as she was fitting it on me, and she bent over me, examining me as she concentrated on her task.

With virtually no preliminaries, she straddled me. I was watching her face, and I could see she was biting her lower lip, her eyes glazed, as she concentrated on her mission. She sat up slightly and flexed her legs. Her torso dropped, and the deed was done.

The only thing my mind would sensibly process for the next several minutes was *Oh my God.*

At the end, she rested her head against me. Her back was sweaty with her exertions, as was her forehead, and her strawberry blonde hair was sticking to her. All in all, I had never seen her more beautiful.

She lifted up and lay back on her side next to me, her arm around my chest. "Mmmmm," she hummed, "if I had known this is what it all was about, I'd have found you a lot sooner."

I kissed her forehead. "It was pretty spectacular, wasn't it? I really didn't know what to expect, either."

She looked at me, a little startled. "You've never done this before?" she asked.

"No," I admitted. She nestled back down against my side, purring in her contentment.

"I'm glad it was with you," she said quietly. "And I'm glad your first was with me. It makes things even better."

My eyelids were getting very heavy. Just as I slipped off to sleep, I briefly wondered if Jake was up in the tree outside, watching.

It seemed like just moments later when I was awakened by a sudden noise. I looked up, muddled and confused about where I was, until I felt Molly's naked body next to mine.

"Oh, shit," I mumbled, looking desperately for a clock. It was close to midnight. I could hear muffled voices downstairs. I shook Molly, waking her, and motioned for her to be quiet. Her eyes were big and round, and she looked scared as she realized where we were. Her bedspread was rumpled, and the room reeked of sex. She slipped out of bed and locked her door. She tiptoed over to her window and opened it quietly to let in some fresh air and then came back over to lie next to me.

"Stay quiet," she whispered in my ear. "When they've gone to bed, I'll help you sneak out of the house."

We huddled together for what seemed like hours, knowing we were going to be caught. Somehow, we weren't. We heard footsteps tromping up the stairs and down the hall, and then the house was quiet. We waited another thirty minutes before getting dressed, sneaking out her room, down the stairs, and out the back door. As I stepped outside into the cool night air, Molly grabbed my arm and pulled me back. She gave me a hard kiss and whispered into my ear, "I love you, Sean." She whirled and closed the door before I could react.

I walked my bike through her neighbor's backyard before venturing out onto the street. I hoped I could sneak into my own house as easily as I snuck out of Molly's. Meanwhile, my mind whirled with distractions, images of a blonde thirteen-year-old intertwining with images of Molly, sweat-slicked at my side in post-coital languor.

- 10 -

THE MOTORCYCLE PROMISE

By the time I dragged myself out of bed the next day, it was almost noon. I had a soccer game to play. After that, I was supposed to go over to work with Davey and Kip again. I called Molly while I was eating a bowl of cereal for breakfast.

"Hi," I said when she answered the phone. "How are you feeling?"

"I feel great," she said. I could almost hear her smile in her voice. "A little sore, but even that's going away. How are you?"

"I'm a little tired, but I'll be okay. I've got a soccer game this afternoon, and then I have to go over to the Wilkinsons. Are you doing anything tonight?"

"I was going to go over to Tessa's. Want to come along?"

"Sure," I said. "What time were you going?"

"We're going shopping this afternoon, but we should be back around five. Ummm...Sean?"

"Uh-huh?"

"Bring along a couple of those...things you got yesterday, okay?"

It was a good thing I was sitting down, because my knees turned to water as soon as she said that. "Yeah, of course," I said. "Anything you say."

"Good. Just remember that, and you'll get along with this Irish lass just fine," she said with a laugh.

☆ ☆ ☆

The soccer game was a laugher. I was playing with a club team that consisted of guys from all over our area, not just from our community. The team we were playing was just a pickup team thrown together for the summer league, and they were not very good. All summer long, I had played just about every position on the field, including keeper, but I was learning that I really liked playing defense, especially right-side defense. My coaches discovered that I had a knack for stealing the ball more often on the right side, and I would streak up the sidelines until I was past the centerline. Depending on how my opposition reacted to this intrusion, I would either continue down the field, switching positions with my right midfielder, or I would loft the ball across to our offensive players in the middle and let them take over. Against teams with weak midfielders or defenders, I could make it almost all the way down to the penalty line before crossing the ball, and a couple of times I was able to waltz the ball in and score from the side when the defense was still scrambling around trying to cover all our players down the field. At any rate, the coach pulled most of his starters, me included, for the entire second half, because we were already up 6–1 by halftime. Even so, we ended up winning 9–3, and I was feeling pretty good.

I went right from the game over to meet Davey and Kip. We warmed up and stretched, and played Heads Up for about fifteen minutes. After taking a drink break, we started on a game of Keep Away with me in the middle. The boys were still prone to standing still and waiting for the ball instead of moving to it on a pass, and I hoped that Keep Away would make them see why they had to move on the ball. Passing into open space, give-and-goes, and leading the receiver were still too advanced for these little guys, but they were working hard toward being better soccer players. I knew that when the fall season began, they would be more skilled than most of the other kids in their age group.

We ended our session by playing Heads Up on the way back to their house again. As we got there, Lori opened the front door to let an older man out. He was dressed in a dark suit and was wearing a loud pink and yellow tie. He shook her hand, walked down to his car parked at the curb, and drove away without a second glance at the boys or the house. Lori, as usual, invited me in for lemonade while Kip and Davey ran upstairs.

"I hate having to do some of these grown-up things sometimes," she said, almost to herself, as she poured four glasses of lemonade over ice.

"What do you mean? Is it something to do with that guy who just left?" I asked.

"That was my insurance man. He was dropping off more papers for me to look over. Just when I think I'm healing, something comes up to open up old wounds," she muttered. Tears were starting to form in her eyes, and her lower lip was trembling.

I stood up, alarmed, and put my arm over her shoulder. "What's the matter, Lori?" I asked, concerned.

She dropped her head to my shoulder and sobbed. Her shoulders were shaking, and I could feel, underneath the weight of her hair, that the skin on the back of her neck was hot to the touch. After a few moments, she collected herself, straightened her shoulders, and gave me a quick peck on the cheek.

"Thanks, Sean, for your support." She moved over to the counter and pulled some tissues from a box and wiped her eyes. She stepped back to the table and sat down heavily.

"My husband died last year," she said quietly. She was looking down at her hands as they methodically tore apart the tissues. "He was in a motorcycle accident just about a year ago, over

Labor Day weekend. Massive head injuries, internal bleeding, broken leg, two broken arms, punctured lung. They had him on a...m-machine for five days, until they finally said that he was brain-dead and would never recover. I...I told them to pull the plug, and he died an hour later. He was twenty-nine years old."

She looked up at me then, and the tears started running down her face. "Don't ever get on a motorcycle, Sean. Promise me. My boys think the world of you, and I won't have them go through something like that ever again, if I can help it. Promise me, Sean."

Her eyes were pleading as she looked at me miserably. It wasn't a real big stretch for me to make such a promise, since my mom and dad had already forbid my older brother Michael from ever riding one. I knew my turn for the "Motorcycle Danger" lecture at home was next.

"I promise, Lori. No motorcycles."

She looked at me for a moment more, perhaps gauging my sincerity, before finally nodding, accepting my promise. She picked up the scraps of tissue to wipe her eyes, until she realized that she had torn them into useless bits. She got up and took a handful more from the box on the counter, crossed over behind me, and wrapped her arms around my neck, hugging me fiercely from behind.

"Thank you, Sean. I don't know what I'd do without you. I can't tell you what a huge difference you've made for me. And for my guys," she added. She let go and came back around to sit at the table again. Her eyes were still red, but she was much more composed now. "Anyway," she continued, "since then, I've had to do more of the grown-up things that Tom used to take care of for us, and I don't like it. But I do it, because the boys need me to do it. But really, Sean, I'm still just a kid at heart. I'm really not that far from being a teenager myself, at least in my own mind," she said with a rueful smile. "I know you probably think of me as being older, but I'm not."

"Actually, I don't. When I first met you, I thought you were the baby-sitter or something, maybe a college kid working for the summer," I said.

She blushed just a little. "Thanks, Sean. Even if it's a little white lie, I appreciate it. Are you sure you don't have a girl-friend?" she asked teasingly. "I may just claim you for my own, then."

Now it was my turn to blush.

- 11 -

INTO THE WOODS

By the time I got over to Tessa's house, it was nearly six in the evening. Molly and Tessa were sitting on the front step with Kristina Mendoza, a slender Hispanic girl who was fairly new to the neighborhood. She lived just down the street from Tessa, and they had become friends right away. Kristina played soccer for the Sting Rays and brought considerable skill to the team. Her family had moved here from Texas, where she had played soccer year-round, practically since she could walk. I didn't really know her very well, but Tessa and Molly both liked her, and the three of them had hung out together for quite a bit of the summer.

"Hi, ladies," I said as I walked up the sidewalk.

"Hi, Sean," they echoed in answer. *Is it my imagination, or are Tessa and Kristina looking at me funny?* I couldn't really tell. Molly stood up and came over to me. She grabbed my arm and pulled me over to sit by her on the bottom step.

"Have you eaten dinner yet, Sean?" asked Tessa. "My dad's going to barbeque some burgers and hot dogs pretty soon."

"Hey, that's great," I said. "You're sure it's okay with your parents if I stay for dinner?"

"Sure," she said. "Kristina and Molly were already staying, so one more won't matter."

"Even if it's a boy with an appetite?" I asked. "Between my brothers and me, we eat everything we find in the house. My mom is always complaining about how often she has to go food shopping for us."

"I don't think even you could out-eat my dad," said Tessa. "He eats more than anyone I've ever seen or heard of."

"It's true," confirmed Molly. "I've never seen anybody eat like Mr. Navarrone. My brother Josh eats a lot, but nothing like your dad, Tessa."

"That's right," added Kristina. "When we first moved here, Tessa's parents invited my family over for a cookout, and Mr. Navarrone cooked a whole huge turkey on the grill. Do you know that there was no turkey left by the end of the meal? And then, after dinner, your mom brought out all these pies and cookies and stuff, and we practically finished them off, too!" She started laughing at the memory of that meal.

"So," I said, "I don't have to be polite and not eat very much, then, is that what you're telling me? Yum, I can't wait!" I rubbed my growling stomach in anticipation.

Tessa instructed me on where I could find a telephone in their house. I went in and called my mom to let her know I was staying for dinner.

"You're sure it's okay with Tessa's parents, Sean?"

I favored her with a big, theatrical sigh that I was sure she would be able to hear over the telephone. "Yes, Mom, I'm sure."

"Make sure you thank them when you're done," she reminded me.

"Yes, Mom," I answered dutifully. "I will. I promise."

"Okay, then, have a nice time," she said. I hung up the phone and ran back out to the front to be with my friends.

In a little while, Tessa's parents called us into the backyard for dinner. It was quite a party, with the four of us, Tessa's parents, her two sisters and two brothers, plus an assortment of their friends, totaling about twenty people. We were spread out throughout the backyard, finding space on the deck or at one of several tables or on a retaining wall across the back of their yard. There was plenty of food and lots of sodas and iced tea, and Mr. Navarrone ruled it all from in front of his gas grill, cooking up a storm of hamburgers, hot dogs, bratwursts, and barbequed chicken. There was also corn on the cob, baked beans, salads, Jell-O, cold pasta salad, and chips, followed by homemade cookies and a chocolate cake with ice cream for dessert. By the end, I had downed two hamburgers, a bratwurst, and a huge mound of beans and pasta salad, and still managed to squeeze down a piece of cake and a couple of cookies. Molly, sticking by me throughout the meal, kept up a running commentary for her friends on my progress, until both Tessa and Kristina finally begged her to stop.

"Enough!" cried Kristina. "I'm going to be sick just hearing what he's eating, Molly!"

"Between you and my dad, Sean, you could clean out this house of food," complained Tessa good-naturedly.

"Someone is challenging me to an eating contest?" rumbled a gravelly voice from the other side of the yard. "Who's eating so much over there?" said Mr. Navarrone.

"It's Sean," cried Lisbeth, Tessa's youngest sister.

"What? That skinny little kid?" said Mr. Navarrone. "Where are you putting all that chow, Sean? In a hollow leg?"

"I'm a growing kid, Mr. Navarrone," I called out. "Besides, I'm just trying to be a good guest by cleaning my plate. It's not really my fault."

"A good guest? Hah! How about a bottomless pit?" said Molly with a laugh. "Aren't you afraid of getting too fat?"

"Nah," I said. "Not with all these beautiful women around here to chase. I'll work it off somehow."

Everyone laughed, and Molly slugged me in the arm in mock anger.

"If you're planning on chasing all these beautiful women," said Mr. Navarrone, "then you probably need one more cookie for sustenance. Some of them can run pretty fast, as I'm sure you know. Tessa, come get the plate of cookies for Sean, would you please?"

The last laugh was on me after all, when Tessa loaded up a plate with cookies and pieces of cake and brought it over to me. She handed it over with a flourish.

By the time we were done eating, it was dusk. The streetlights were buzzing and flickering to life, and porch lights throughout the neighborhood were switching on. Lightning bugs were making an appearance, and we all chased them around, catching them and putting them in each other's hair and on our clothes. As the darkness closed in, Kristina, Molly, and I said our good-byes to everybody. We thanked Tessa's parents for dinner, and then the three of us wandered down the street toward Kristina's house.

"Do you guys want to come in for a little while? Maybe there's a good movie on or something," said Kristina as we got to her house.

Molly and I looked at each other and nearly simultaneously said, "No, thanks. I've got to be getting home." We waved and continued walking toward Molly's house. Nervously, we reached for each other's hand, as if we were near-strangers on a clandestine mission.

When we got to her house, she led the way down her driveway and into the garage. "I've got some blankets stashed in here," she whispered. She went in through a side door and came back out again, carrying some folded blankets in her arms.

"Let's go back here," she said softly. "I'm not sure who's home, so we need to keep quiet until we get to the clearing."

She led the way to the back of the yard and into the trees. About twenty yards in, there was a small clearing, with a picnic table, an old fire ring, and a couple of bent and broken lawn chairs. It was obviously a long-time neighborhood hangout, but I hadn't realized it was there.

Molly knelt down. She spread out the blankets on the ground and sat down facing me. Silently, she patted the ground next to her, beckoning me. She was wearing a sleeveless shirt that buttoned down the front, and a pair of tight shorts. She reached up and took her reddish-blonde hair out of the ponytail, letting it fall down her cheeks and spread across her shoulders. I moved over to sit beside her. I reached around to put my arm around her shoulder and felt the weight of her hair against my arm as she moved into my embrace. We kissed, fumbling to find each other's lips in the dark. As we connected, we lowered each other down onto the blanket until we were lying on our sides, facing each other, lips locked together and arms entwined. I felt her hand running up and down my back, and I did the same, my fingertips sensing the soft cotton of her shirt, the bumps and ridges of her spine, and the extra thickness of her bra beneath her shirt.

I dragged my hand down, blindly searching for the hem of her shirt. The pressure of my hand on the small of her back and on her butt caused her to move her hips closer to me, until she was rubbing against me. I slipped my hand under her shirttail and brushed along the soft skin of her back, feeling the muscles underneath the skin flexing and relaxing with the unconscious movement of her hips against me. As I moved up her back, my arm pushed her shirt up until it started to bunch up under her arm. It must have irritated her a little, because she let go of me and started to unbutton it. I tried to help, but it's easier working buttons when they're on you, so I ended up fumbling around until she finished the job. She shrugged out of her shirt and settled back against me, reaching once more for another kiss. I put my arms around her again and enjoyed feeling her back tense and relax as I tickled up and down along her spine. Molly, in the meantime, found the hem of my shirt and started rucking it up my body, duplicating my movements.

I didn't have a lot of experience with the hooks and eyes of bra straps, but I managed to unhook Molly's with one hand after wrestling with it for a few moments. As soon as it was loose, I ran my hand around her so I could take momentary possession of her tender flesh.

Eventually, we crossed that invisible line. Molly sat up and looked down at me.

"Did you bring them?" she said quietly, her eyes shining in the dark.

I nodded and scrambled over to where my shorts lay crumpled in a pile. I dug into my pocket and pulled out one of the little foil packets, and I tore it open. My fingers weren't working properly, and I felt a little frantic as I took the condom out of the package and tried to put it on.

"Come here; I'll do that," she whispered with a giggle. She sat up, her small breasts jiggling provocatively, and knelt down in front of me. I handed her the condom and had to hold my breath when the sensations of what she was doing to me suddenly hit me like a giant wave.

She fitted the condom and then pulled me over on top of her. She spread her legs to accommodate me, and she guided me to where she wanted me to be.

Too soon, it was over. I was too quick, too overwhelmed, too young to know how to pace myself, though Molly didn't seem to mind. She started giving me small, quick kisses on my cheek, my neck, my ear. It got me out of my reverie. I lifted my head up off her and looked into her smiling eyes.

"How're you doing, Molly?" I asked uselessly.

"Pretty darn good, Sean Porter," she replied. "But you're kind of heavy. Do you mind sliding off for a minute?"

"Okay," I said. It felt like my brain still was not functioning at much more than half capacity, so I was tracking her a little slowly.

I lifted up and rolled off to lie next to her. I reached down to remove the spent condom and threw it off into the woods.

I thought I heard a noise from that direction, but I decided it must have been a squirrel angry at our intrusion. "Did you...?" I asked Molly, turning back to her and putting my arm around her.

She hesitated. "Um...no, not really," she admitted. "But I really enjoyed it, anyway," she added quickly.

"Hmmm..." I said, looking at her and smiling. "What can we do about this? I wonder..."

She reached over and gave me a playful slap and then rolled over into my arms and gave me a scorching kiss. Distractedly, I wondered where she learned to kiss like that, since she never had a real boyfriend. Very soon, though, I could not concentrate on anything beyond what was being inflicted on me by my companion on the blanket.

Before long, the girl took charge. She loomed over me, turned her hooded eyes toward me, and whispered, "Did you bring another one?"

I nodded mutely. She reached over me to my shorts, searching pockets until she found her prize. She tore open the package and took out the condom. She bent back over me, concentrating once more on rolling it on me. She swung her leg around me, put her hands on my shoulders, and watched my eyes as she had her way with me.

I learned from her, and was able to hold off my own climax until Molly reached her completion. At the end, as I had done before, she collapsed down on top of me in exhaustion. She was sweaty and tired, with her hair sticking to her back and neck. I softly caressed her back with both hands, trying to will away her weariness as she lay comfortably on me.

As her breathing eased, she lifted up her head and stared at me for a moment. She softly kissed me on the lips and said, "I really, really liked it like that."

I burst out laughing. "I could tell," I told her between gasps. She looked at me as if I had lost my mind and then started laughing with me.

Molly snuggled up next to me, my arm around her shoulder, both of us naked and unashamed in the darkness of the clearing. I could feel the softness of her breast as it pressed against my ribcage, a feeling I wouldn't mind getting used to.

"Sean?" she asked quietly after a few minutes.

"Molly?" I answered groggily. My eyelids were getting heavy.

"Will you be my boyfriend?"

That snapped my eyes open. I should have known that the things we had done the past two days would lead to this, but I hadn't been expecting it to come up right then. I thought about Kayla, and Jake, and Josh, and Kayla again.

"I'll try, Molly. But I'm not sure I know how," I told her.

She was silent for a moment more. "That's okay," she said. "I'm not real sure about how to be a girlfriend, either. But we can try, can't we?"

"We can try," I agreed.

- 12 -

FAMOUS LAST WORDS

Two days later, I was riding my bike down the sidewalk when I heard someone call out my name. I looked over, and Jake Lehigh came running up to me, just as I was stopping. He looked really mad as he reached me. I was off-balance, in the process of stopping my bike, when he shoved me down and off my bike.

"You *asshole!*" he shouted. "What the fuck do you think you're doing?"

I jumped up and got right back into his face. "What are you talking about, Jake?"

"I saw you and Molly."

Uh-oh, I thought to myself. I had a sick feeling I knew where this was headed. I couldn't back down, though, not to Jake.

"Yeah? What did you see, Jake?"

"I was in the woods the other night. I saw you and Molly walk back into the woods, so I followed you. I saw the whole thing."

"The whole thing?" I asked. "So you were peeping at us like a perv?"

"A perv? Me? Damn it, Sean, you almost hit me with that first condom you threw into the woods!"

I looked at him, not sure I heard him correctly. Just the image that conjured up in my mind was enough to make me bust out laughing. Jake looked at me as if I was crazy. Then he must have realized how funny it all was, because he just started laughing with me, until finally we were both sitting on the ground, our arms around each other's shoulders like the best pals we really were, laughing until the tears were racing down our faces.

I looked at him out of the corner of my eye. "Splat," I said. That started us going all over again.

By the time we were finally calmed down, we were lying on our backs on the ground, my bicycle still blocking the sidewalk as it lay on its side.

"Okay," wheezed Jake, "enough of this. What's going on? And, by the way, where did you get the protection?"

Well, that nearly got me going again as I described my trip into his father's drug store with Josh to buy the condoms.

"No shit, my dad helped you guys out? Man, I wonder what he was thinking," marveled Jake.

"It took us by surprise, believe me," I said. "I really didn't know what to say to him."

"Yeah, I'll bet," said Jake. "So, Sean, what are you going to do? After all, I've seen how you and Kayla act around each other. And Jaimie, well, even though they are best friends, she's kind of told me some things about you two."

I sighed. "I don't know, man. I mean, I really like Molly, and I don't want to hurt Kayla's feelings, because I really like her, too. But she's still in middle school, you know? We really can't be, like, going out or anything, can we?"

"Well, she's my sister and all, but you're right. Besides, Molly is a supreme-o hot babe. And I got to see her naked, which is even better."

"Yeah," I said, sitting up. "It's much better. But you've got to stop spying on us, Jake. I'm going to get the willies thinking about you being out there somewhere. Promise me."

"You really know how to spoil my fun," muttered Jake as he stood up and brushed himself off. "Okay, no more spying. But you've got to share some of your rubbers in exchange."

"What do you mean, share?"

"Hey, I can't walk into my own dad's store and just buy the things, can I? Besides, you still have a bunch. If you keep me supplied, I'll pay for the next boxful, okay?"

"Wait a minute, I smell a story here. What's going on, Jake?" I asked. I had a feeling things had progressed with Jaimie.

"Well...yeah, I need 'em," he admitted. "Jaimie and I... well...we kind of...um...did it the other day."

"You *did?* Man, tell me!"

"Well...it was uh, let's see...the day after we ran into Jaimie and Kayla coming back from the Dairy Queen. You remember that day? We watched TV at Jaimie's house? Anyway, Jaimie and I met at her house again the next day, and one thing led to another, and...uh..."

"And?" I prompted.

"And...we did it. Twice. On the couch in the family room."

"Twice? You dog, you!" I slapped his arm companionably.

He looked a little uncomfortable about his confession, but then he looked up at me and smiled.

"Oh, yeah," he said, grinning. "But you know how it is. I saw you do it with Molly twice that night."

"Oh, yeah, indeed," I said, grinning back at him like an idiot.

"Anyway, Jaimie got a severe case of the guilts afterward and will hardly talk to me right now. Maybe if I can show her I've got some condoms, she'll at least talk to me. So that's why I need them."

"Okay, pal, come with me. I've got them stashed at home. You can have a few, but if you get caught with them, you didn't get them from me, all right?"

"I won't get caught," he said. "You know me better than that."

Yeah, right. Famous last words.

So we went over to my house and up to my room. I thought that hiding them in rolled up socks, like Josh had done, was a pretty good idea, so I had done the same. I unrolled a pair of soccer socks and handed Jake four packets.

"Here you go, Jake. Two nights' worth, at your rate." I snickered just a little, until I looked at my meager stash. Already I was down to six condoms. And I had the feeling Molly was going to find a way to use them up quickly. Not that I was complaining, of course, but I hoped I wouldn't encounter Jake's dad if I had to go back for more too soon. He would really wonder what was going on then.

"Thanks, Seanster, you're the best. Oh, by the way, my parents are having a bunch of neighbors over tomorrow for a cookout and stuff. They're setting up softball and volleyball in the field behind our house, and I think there's a scavenger hunt after dark. Why don't you come over after you're done at the Wilkinsons?"

"Sure," I replied. "Sounds like fun. I can do that."

- 13 -

LIGHT AND SHADOW

I got over to Jake's house about three in the afternoon, just as the big softball game was being organized. Most of Jake's neighborhood was there, totaling about ten families, so there were lots of adults and kids running around. There were big galvanized garbage cans filled with ice and sodas, and a couple of coolers with beer and wine for the adults. Most of the moms were not going to participate in the game, but all the kids and a lot of the dads were already out there, setting bases and marking the field. Jake was standing out in right field with Jaimie, Kayla, Tara, and a couple of the younger kids from the neighborhood. Everyone was drinking sodas and waiting for teams to be chosen. Jake saw me first and waved me over. When Kayla saw me, she smiled and leaned over to whisper something to Jaimie, who laughed out loud, glancing up in my direction.

I grabbed a can of soda and ran out to where they were standing. Jaimie was wearing a tight T-shirt that accentuated her high, firm breasts. She kept on standing up straight, shoulders back, to make them stick out even more, and kept on glancing over at Jake to gauge his reaction. His reaction was to be a little nervous about having those things thrust at him when his parents and his sister were around.

Tara, Jaimie's sister, was apparently in some sort of competition with her, since she had on what looked like a man's shirt, the top three buttons left open and the shirttails tied around her to leave her flat tummy bared. Combined with a pair of shorts that were too short and tight, she exuded a sultriness that was far beyond her years

Kayla, on the other hand, looked fresh, young, and delicious in a tank top and soccer shorts. Her long hair was tied back in a ponytail that cascaded down her back, and the almost white color set off her tan beautifully.

The group of us walked back toward the sidelines, where the teams were being chosen. Mr. Lehigh and Mr. Jacks, Tara and Jaimie's father, were the team captains. They made sure each child was chosen for a team, starting with the youngest, before any adults or teenagers were picked. Jake and I were on opposing teams; Jaimie was on Jake's, and Tara and Kayla were on mine. We had some really small kids, four and five years old, playing on both teams, and Jake and I both helped our players when their turn at bat came up. We ended up playing two innings before the younger ones got bored and wandered away. The older kids and the adults kept on playing, and the game got more and more competitive. Finally, in the seventh inning, the whole game deconstructed on a double-play, a fly ball caught in left field and a runner picked off at first. The batting team called the runner safe; the fielding team called the runner out. After about ten minutes of arguing and discussing the play, the only conclusion that could be drawn was that everyone was hot, tired, thirsty, and hungry. We all decided to call it quits, and everyone headed in to the sidelines, where all these problems could be solved.

Jake and I each grabbed a couple of sodas and plopped down on the ground, sweaty and pleasantly tired. The three girls came over to sit by us, each with a soda of their own. For some reason, Tara bent over right in front of us to brush off the grass, giving Jake and me a peek down her shirt as it gapped open.

I leaned over to Jake and whispered, "What's up with Tara and her getup?"

He looked at me quizzically and shrugged. *You know as much as I do,* his expression said.

"Tara," Jaimie warned quietly.

Tara looked at her sister, who was scowling at her. Her face turned an angry red, and you could tell she was closing in on herself as she stood up. She looked down on Jaimie silently and turned and walked away. She tried to sway her boyish hips as provocatively as she could as she headed back over by some of the younger kids.

"Who is she trying to be grown-up for?" Jake asked.

"I really don't know," said Jaimie. "The past few days she's been in a strange mood. I hope she snaps out of it soon; it's getting on my nerves."

"Oh, forget her," said Kayla. "She's probably just PMSing and taking advantage of it."

"Maybe," admitted Jaimie. "I just hope she gets over it soon or I'm going to have to give her the 'big sister' cure."

"And what's the 'big sister' cure?" asked Kayla.

"That's the cure where I sit on her until she promises to lighten up," said Jaimie. "It's kind of like that fax joke that my dad has hanging in his office that says, 'The Beatings Will Continue Until Morale Improves.'"

We all laughed at the thought of Jaimie sitting on top of Tara until her mood improved. I thought she'd have to sit there for a long, long time.

✫ ✫ ✫

After dark, when some of the parents had taken the little kids off to bed, Mrs. Lehigh gathered the older kids around to announce the Grand Scavenger Hunt.

"Okay, kids," she said as she handed out the sheets of paper with the items to be collected. "Here are the rules. All these items must be collected within this neighborhood. All the parents know about the scavenger hunt, so you won't be surprising anybody by ringing their doorbell. No going to any stores or outside this area. You have ninety minutes to collect as much of the list as you can, and then you have to meet back here. There will be prizes awarded for the most items found, the quickest back to headquarters here, and maybe a couple of other prizes to be named later. You must buddy up. I don't want any kids going off by themselves, so pick a partner before you go. All set, everybody? Ready, set, *go!*"

All the kids started picking buddies to go out with and running off with their lists. Kayla grabbed my hand and said, "Wait a second, Sean." We slowly walked toward the street as she looked around. She made sure everybody else took off and then led me in a different direction, bags and lists in hand.

"Where are we off to?" I asked.

"Shhh…just follow me," she said secretively.

She kept us in the shadows, sneaking around the outside of the house while holding my hand and tiptoeing through the grass. She peeked around the corner to the front of the house to make sure the coast was clear, and pulled me behind her as she crossed the front yard to the front door of her house.

She opened the door into the dark house. We went in, back to the kitchen and downstairs into the basement. She closed the basement door and led me down the stairs in the inky blackness. I was blind in the darkness, but she moved through the basement without hesitation, to the couch.

"Sit here, Sean. I'll be right back."

I sat on the couch, wishing there was even just a pinprick of light to see something by. I heard Kayla on the other side of the room, rustlings and the soft whisper of cloth heard only due to the increased concentration on sound I was experiencing, thanks to the loss of use of my eyes.

"Kayla?" I whispered.

"Shhh..." I heard from across the room. I thought I heard a door quietly creak, but I couldn't be sure.

There was a small line of light coming from the frame of the closet door. As my eyes adjusted to this minimal amount of light, I slowly became aware of what was around me. It was a familiar room, so the furniture and walls quickly gained their proper place as I got used to the dark. I could just make out the shape of Kayla standing over by the closet door.

"Can you see anything yet?" she whispered.

"Not much," I said. "What are we doing down here? We're supposed to be on a scavenger hunt."

She reached for the doorknob and opened the closet door just a crack. Light from inside the closet seemed to flood out of the opening, and suddenly I could see Kayla standing there, the light seeming to focus on her features.

She had taken off her tank top and shorts, and she presented herself to my gaze in her underwear, her pale hair loose and falling down, spreading across her shoulders. Her small breasts, white landmarks on her tanned chest and stomach, were poking out of their hiding place behind her blonde hair. The light cascaded across her waist and narrow hips, highlighting her hipbone, swathing her navel in highlights and shadow. She reached up and, with just one finger, brushed her hair off her forehead above her eyebrow, the gesture less one of unconscious habit as one of sensuous anticipation.

I was speechless. I was riveted to the couch and could not move so much as an inch, so enthralled with the vision she presented was I. She stared at me for a moment, motionless. The image of Kayla standing there, innocent and beautiful, seared itself into my mind for all time.

She walked over to me, the light haloing around her body, and sank down onto the couch and into my arms. We kissed, a wet and soft joining that spoke of promise and fulfillment.

"I found my mom's list of the scavenger hunt items in her desk, so I've already collected most of the items," she said softly. "We have about an hour to ourselves."

"You are a sneaky little devil," I murmured into her ear.

She chuckled throatily. "Oh, yes, I am," she agreed.

Her head stretched back as I nuzzled her soft neck, my arms around her and my hands reveling in the feel of her soft skin. She twisted in my arms, crossing her leg on my knee. My hand fell quite naturally down onto her hip. Without consciously thinking about it, I let my hand stray from there to her butt, and as I caressed her, she squirmed against me in anticipation.

We played little kissing games, caressing games, learning about each other in a ritual as old as humanity.

At one point, I rolled over on top of her, but she pressed up on my hips with her hands and stopped me.

"No, Sean," she gasped.

"I've got some protection, Kay, if you want..."

"No. I can't do that, Sean. I'm too scared. Let's just do it like we were doing, okay?" She was whispering, a little quaver in her voice that nearly broke my heart.

"Whatever you want," I assured her. I rolled back off her and onto my side.

Finally, in the end, we collapsed together on the couch. *This effort at pleasing each other is tiring,* I thought as I pulled her over toward me. She rested her head below my chin, relaxing in my arms.

"Oh. My. God," she whispered tiredly.

"Times two," I added.

"Any more and I don't think I could survive it," she said.

"I'm not sure I survived this one," I answered. I was so tired, my eyelids were threatening to droop.

"You survived," she said. "I definitely felt a glimmer of life in you." I could feel her smile against my chest. She ran her hand down my arm. Our fingers found each other's and gently intertwined.

"That wasn't me. That was my evil twin brother. He killed me and took my place. Sean's too fragile to survive something like that."

"Oh, yeah? Well, evil twin, get up. It's late, and we have a scavenger hunt to complete." Kayla sat up and swung her legs down. She walked toward the laundry room, her narrow hips swaying just slightly. The contrast of light and shadow played on her backside, first revealing and then hiding her slender form. This created an image for me of just how lovely and sensuous a young girl can be without even thinking about it. At fifteen, I was thinking of myself more and more as a man of the world, and I couldn't think, at that point, of anything that could be more precious than the sight of Kayla walking away, blissfully innocent and unashamed in my presence.

But I had a real problem, and I knew I had to face it soon. Kayla and Molly, unbeknownst to either of them, were battling for my attentions in my own mind. As much as I enjoyed the affections of both, I was not happy about the deceits that I had inadvertently created. It was a conflict that I knew I had to resolve before too long.

I stood up and stretched. I heard water running in the laundry room, and a few minutes later, Kayla returned, dressed once again and carrying wet washcloths. She threw one at me.

"Here, Sean." Kayla walked around the room with an air freshener, spraying the room to rid it of the odors of our passion.

I wiped my hands and face and thought about my dilemma. How to break the subject?

"Kay?"

"Hmmm?"

"Ummm...I need to talk to you..."

"Okay, Sean," she said. She walked over and flipped on a light by the television.

"You know...uh...Molly O'Toole..."

"Sure," she said. "I know Molly and Josh, but I don't know Heather very well."

"Yeah, well...ummm...Molly and I..."

"Are going out? Yes, I know."

I sat down on the couch, a little stunned. "You know?"

"Sure. I heard Jake talking to Jaimie. I think it's great, Sean. You and Molly would make a really cute couple."

"What?" I couldn't believe what I was hearing. "Are you serious?"

Kayla came over and sat down beside me, taking my hand in both of hers. Her eyes were glistening in the pale light of the table lamp. "Sean, if I could, I would claim you for my boyfriend. But I know I can't. You're in high school, and I'm still in middle school. I love you, and I love what we've been able to do together. But I can't compete with Molly O'Toole, not with her being able to see you every day at school and all. I'm glad for you, Sean. I really am. Molly's a nice girl, and I like her a lot. Go out with her, have a great time. Just don't forget about me, okay?"

At that, tears started to spill down her cheeks. I really felt like shit as I watched her give me her blessing. She wiped her face with one of the damp cloths and sniffled a little. She stood up, looking down on me.

"But next year, when I get to that high school..." She left the rest of her comment unsaid, but I understood perfectly. All bets were off next year.

I stood up and gathered her into my arms and gave her a tight hug. She pressed her face into my shoulder and put her arms around me, clinging to me tightly.

"Come on, let's go upstairs before they send out a search party for us," she said. Her words were muffled as she pressed against me. "I've got the bag of scavenger items in the garage." She let go and took my hand, leading me toward the stairs. I followed along, numbly accepting direction from her as I tried to digest all that she had said.

I will never, ever understand girls, I thought to myself as we left the house by the front door and snuck around to the garage.

- 14 -

VARSITY SOCCER

School was starting in a few days, and the fall sports teams were busy. Football was practicing in the mornings, soccer and tennis in the afternoons. Josh and Jake had both tried out for the football team and had made the junior varsity team. I was on the varsity soccer team, playing my right defensive position behind Skip Horvath, a senior and one of the stars of our team. Skip was chosen for All-Conference honors as both a sophomore and a junior, and was second-team All-State last year. Given his reputation and skills, I wasn't planning on a lot of playing time this season, but I knew he could teach me a lot about the game. Even though I wasn't a starter, I was happy to be playing on the varsity team with Skip as my mentor. I knew that the position was mine for my junior and senior years, as long as I didn't screw up somehow.

When I got to the first practice, I was surprised to discover that I was one of only two sophomores on the varsity team. In addition, one of the backup keepers was a freshman I knew only slightly. He was Kristina Mendoza's brother, Jorge. Like Kristina, he had been playing year-round soccer for years in Texas. The other sophomore was Eric Johnson, a teammate from my club soccer team. Eric won nearly every foot race he ever ran in, from grade school through middle school. He ran on the track team in the spring, but he preferred soccer to cross-country in the fall. Because of his speed and stamina, he usually played midfield. He wasn't especially skilled with the ball, but he was so lightning fast that, like Jen Davies, he left his opponents in the dust, making him very tough to defend.

Part of the first day of practice was spent introducing everybody, from players to coaches to equipment managers, as well as getting the schedules handed out and assigning lockers and uniforms. The rest of the time was spent running on the track. We did a one-mile run, rested, did a half-mile run, rested, and finished with wind sprints. Eric and I were in pretty good shape from playing so much during the summer, but some of the kids were wiped out by the end of the afternoon. After the last sprint, we all pretty much collapsed on the grass of the soccer field, gasping and sweating. A couple of guys crawled over to the sidelines and threw up, something the coaches duly noted.

The coaches ordered us in to shower up. We all stood up to walk into the school, to the locker room. Three or four teammates were a little wobbly and needed support, and a bunch of others were still breathing very hard long after Eric and I and a few others had managed to catch our breath. We straggled along, glad the day's practice was finally over.

As I was sitting on the bench in front of my locker, removing my soccer shoes, socks, and shin guards, Skip came over and sat down beside me. He had already removed his gear and thrown everything, including his sodden T-shirt, into a pile.

"You came out of that torture in pretty decent shape," he said. "I take it you played a lot this summer."

"Yeah," I said. "I played on a recreational team this summer, and I also played on a club team. As a matter of fact, we have our last game on Wednesday morning. I was wondering if I can get out of team practice that afternoon."

He chuckled. "This is varsity soccer, Porter. No excuses for missing practice. You're gonna get your fill of running by the time you're done on Wednesday. Anyway," he continued, "we're having a little soccer team party on Saturday over at my house. Kind of a get-to-know-your-teammate party. You going out with anybody?" I nodded. "Bring her along. I've got a pool, so bring a suit and a towel. I'm telling people to get there anytime after one o'clock in the afternoon. We'll throw something on the grill for dinner, but you'll need to provide your own drinks. No booze. Okay?" He got up and walked away without waiting for an answer.

A senior talked to me like I was an equal! And not just any senior; it was Skip Horvath, one of the best-known and most popular kids in school. Now I felt like I had really made the team. I went home to mow our lawn, dog-tired but happy.

✿ ✿ ✿

The next morning, I rode over to the Wilkinson house to work with Davey and Kip. I had called Lori and let her know about my schedule. She was kind enough to let me switch to mornings with the boys.

We went over to the park and began stretching. I told them that I could only work with them on the weekends now that school was starting.

"But will you come watch our games?" asked Davey.

"Sure I will," I said. "Remind me to get a copy of your game schedule from your mom when we get back to your house, okay?"

"Are you gonna be our coach during the games, too?" asked Kip.

"No, sport. Your team already has a good coach. I'll just be there to cheer for you."

"Oh. Will Molly be there, too?"

"Maybe. I can ask her, if you'd like," I said.

"Molly's a good soccer player, isn't she?" asked Kip.

"Yes, she is."

"Well, why don't the two of you be our coaches, then?"

"I think it's because you're supposed to have grown-ups for coaches, Kip. Molly and I are still kids, too, you know."

"Really?" He had to think about this one. "I guess you are, if you are still going to school like Davey and me. But you look pretty grown-up to me, Sean."

I laughed out loud. "Hey, thanks, pal. But I really don't feel grown-up. I like being a kid, you know."

Davey looked at me as shrewdly as an eight-year-old could. "Yeah," he said, "being a kid is really all right, isn't it?"

"Come on, you guys, get up and get running. I think you're just saying this stuff to keep from working too hard," I said with a laugh as I climbed to my feet. "Ready? Last one to that willow tree over there has to be the monkey in the middle!" And off we dashed, running and laughing as we dribbled our soccer balls over to the tree.

I wanted to try to teach them about timing and space. I had Davey play defender while I had the ball. Kip was about twenty feet to the side, counting in seconds as the drill progressed. Davey started about forty feet up from me and, on my signal, started running toward me to take the ball away. At the same time, I dribbled up toward him and passed the ball to Kip when Davey got near.

"How many seconds did you count, Kip?" I asked.

His eyes were big and round, hardly believing his own counting. "Only two!" he said.

"How many seconds did you think it would take before Davey got to me?"

"About twenty," he said.

"That's how fast you have to look around for a teammate, watch your defender, and make a decision on what to do with the ball. Two seconds to do all that. Can you do it?"

"Yes!" cried Davey.

"No!" cried Kip.

We did the exercise again, and Kip was closer to being right than Davey was, but I wasn't disappointed. It's an extremely hard physics concept for little kids to grasp, time and two bodies in motion. I'd had teammates taking advanced classes in school who couldn't figure it out. Nevertheless, I thought that if I could get them to at least acknowledge the difficulty, then they would be another step up on nearly every other kid their age on the soccer field. After several frustrating tries at it, I finally had to make the defender start out nearly a hundred feet away from the player with the ball. This gave them four or five seconds to make their decision, and that was more achievable for both of them. We worked on this problem off and on during the whole lesson, even going so far as to chant during our water breaks, "One-potato look; two-potato pass. One-potato look; two-potato pass."

Two hours later, we were headed back to their house. We played our Heads Up game with three soccer balls but kept up the chant all the way home, passing the ball as we said the word *pass*.

Lori was on the front steps waiting for us when we got to the house, standing by the front door. She watched us completing our last passes as we came past the driveway and onto the front lawn.

"Who are these boys, Sean?" she asked. "They are too organized to be my Davey and my Kip." She looked down at the boys with a smile on her face. "Who are you, and what did you do with my sons?"

"It's us, Mom. Really, it's us," yelled Kip. He ran up the steps and hugged his mother around her waist.

"I know it is, Kip; I was just teasing. I hardly recognized you is all, you guys were so good at passing the ball!" She looked at me, eyes twinkling. "Come in and get something to drink, boys." She held the door open for us, and we filed in to enjoy our customary glasses of fresh lemonade.

"So this is the last summer lesson, I guess," Lori said as she refilled our glasses. The boys had run upstairs to get cleaned up, and I was hanging around for a few minutes before going home for lunch.

"Yes, it is," I said. "I've got a game tomorrow morning, and school starts on Thursday."

"Kip and Davey don't start until Friday. This summer really flew past. It seems like it was only yesterday that it was Memorial Day weekend."

"I know. I've been so busy this summer with soccer and stuff that I almost feel like I didn't get a vacation, and now school's starting again. Ugh!"

"Ah, but you did have a vacation," she reminded me. "You got to sleep in almost every morning, didn't you?"

"Well, yeah," I said sheepishly. "But those days are gone now."

"I'm not going to feel that badly for you, Sean," she said with a smile. "I haven't gotten to sleep in since the boys were born."

It was time for me to go. I stood up and carried both our glasses over to the sink and rinsed them out while Lori rummaged in her purse for my money for the lessons. When she handed me the bills, there was an extra ten dollars folded into the middle.

"What's this for?" I asked.

"It's for being so good with the boys," she said.

"No, Lori. I can't take it. They've been really good, and I've enjoyed—"

"Forget it, Sean," she said, "you're taking it." She wrapped my fingers around the money and then stepped into me, pressing herself up against my chest. She kept her eyes open as she kissed me softly on the cheek, her face slightly flushed. *She's a couple of inches shorter than me,* I thought to myself. *Why hadn't I noticed before?*

She stayed next to me for a moment more. Her dark eyes were serious, depthless pools of brown and black. She reached up with her left hand and squeezed my arm before stepping away. She seemed a little flustered, and I knew I was feeling the same way.

"Thanks, Sean," she said quietly. "Thank you for everything."

- 15 -

YELLOW CARD

That afternoon, the combined varsity and junior varsity soccer teams drilled together. It had turned into a cool, cloudy day, and I felt like I could run forever. We did really boring passing drills; we did three-man weaves; we did three-on-two defensive drills; we did four-on-two offensive drills. We ran laps around the field three times: once during warm-ups, once just before our water break, and as a final exercise. The coaches called it a "warm-down," but we got sweaty all the same. Having played on two teams most of the summer, I quickly got tired of drills and skill tests and was anxious to scrimmage and play games. About half the varsity team, and a few of the guys on the JV team, were of the same opinion, having played most of the summer also, but the coaches were going to do what the coaches were going to do, and no amount of interference from the players, especially underclassmen, was going to change their minds.

From our point of view, certain players on the teams had played together for such a long time, they knew what to expect in a game situation. But the coaches, not having watched us all over the past couple of years, were starting near ground zero. They had to evaluate each player according to his position, his skills and weaknesses, and his teammates. The learning curve was much larger for them than it was for us. Even so, there were a substantial number of guys I was not familiar with, as far as their soccer playing was concerned. By the time we played our first game, still more than a week away, I knew that I would have a good idea of the strengths and weaknesses of most of the players on both teams.

During our lap runs, we tended to run with our classmates or former teammates. The juniors and the seniors usually ignored us underclassmen, clumping together as if for protection. During the drills, however, Skip made sure I was partnered with him most of the time. He kept up a running commentary on defensive maneuvers as we drilled. It was his final year as a high school player, and he was being very generous in sharing his time and his experience with me. I knew most of the other guys at least by name, but after practice ended, Skip took me around to nearly all the upperclassmen and introduced me to them. Eric's eyes nearly bugged out when he saw that, and he began laughing almost uncontrollably. I shot him a look, but he kept on laughing and making quiet comments to Jorge and some of the other younger kids.

That evening, I called Molly and talked to her for about an hour. I told her about the team party at Skip's house, and she put the phone down to ask her parents if she could go. She came back on the phone, slightly breathless.

"They said I could go, but I have to leave the phone number with them, just in case," she said.

"Great. I'll get his number and give it to you tomorrow, okay?"

"Okay. I can't believe that tomorrow's the last day of summer vacation, Sean. I'm not ready to go back to school."

"I'm not either. I could live on summer vacation all year long."

"So, if tomorrow's our last day of freedom, can you come over?"

"I don't know, Molly. I've got an away game in the morning and then team practice in the afternoon. I'm going to be pretty wiped out by the end."

"Too wiped out to see me?" She sounded disappointed, and maybe a little angry.

"No, no, not too wiped out to see you, but I'll probably have to be home pretty early. What did you want to do?"

"I don't know, maybe go to a movie or something? Or we could just watch TV with some friends. I just don't want my last night before school to be wasted."

"I know; I agree. Tell you what. I'll call you when I get home from practice, and we'll figure something out, okay?"

"Okay, Sean. Good night. Dream good dreams of me to-night."

The huskiness in her voice sent sudden signals through my bloodstream. Her wish was going to make it difficult for me to get to sleep that night.

☆ ☆ ☆

The next morning was cool and rainy, one of those gentle summer rains that gets you wet but doesn't make you wish for shelter from the storm. Our team piled into cars and vans driven by our three coaches, and we drove the thirty miles to our last game of the season. Eric Johnson and I rode in the car with Mr. Reyes, our head coach.

On the way, Eric kept on pumping me for details about why Skip was having me tag along with him.

"Come on, Eric. I've told you all I know. If you want to know more, ask Skip yourself."

"Fat chance he'd even talk to a lowly scrub like me," he complained. "Why you, Porter? Are you the anointed successor?"

"Oh, give it a rest, would ya? I don't know, and I don't care. I just want to play the game, you know?"

"Maybe he don't like black soccer players. Maybe he's got a thing for your skinny ass. Maybe he's just setting you up for some elaborate joke. Maybe—"

"Maybe you could just shut up about it, okay?"

He gave me a big, theatrical sigh and rolled his eyes, as if I were the mosquito buzzing around his head instead of the other way around. I mentally shrugged my shoulders and stared out the window, ignoring everybody else in the car.

We got to the field about a half hour early. We all scrambled out of the cars and unloaded our gear. The coaches passed out the practice balls, and we all set up for warm-up drills without the coaches needing to tell us what to do. Another game was being played on the field, and there was a good local crowd filling about half the bleachers lining one side of the field. There was some enthusiastic cheering going on, despite the rain.

Just as the other game ended, we took off at a slow run to lap the perimeter of the field once and then picked up the pace for a faster run for one more lap. We then took the field and rotated around to pass out to a player, who then took a shot on goal, warming up our keeper.

The referee blew the whistle, and the starting lineups took the field. We had lost the coin toss, but with no sun, no wind, a light rain, and virtually no lengthwise slope to the field, there was no real advantage, other than psychological, to winning it. Our opponents, named the Stingers, elected to take the ball on the kickoff. The timers started, the whistle blew, and the game was on.

The Stingers tapped the ball forward and then immediately passed the ball back to their center midfielder. It's a basic maneuver for a kickoff, designed to keep possession of the ball (a key part of the game). If our opposing coaches and players understood the wisdom behind the play, they would continue to pass the ball back or across, keeping the ball and waiting for an opportunity to advance it up the field. If, however, they were performing it as a drill simply because they knew they were supposed to pass it back, we knew how to counterattack.

It became immediately obvious to us that the midfielder for the Stingers didn't understand the play. He trapped the ball, looking for an immediate pass up the field into our territory. It was a classic mistake we saw often from unsuspecting teams. We had a play designed for just this type of kickoff, a play that rarely failed us. Our forwards raced in a triangulation toward the hapless midfielder with the ball, effectively cutting off any forward passing lanes. At the same time, our midfielders moved down the field, switching with our forwards, blocking any possible crossing passes to their defenders. We were confident that we would shortly have possession. We defenders moved up to cover their other midfielders, leaving all of their forwards racing toward our goal with no ball and no prospects. If, by some slim chance, a pass was able to get through us to them, all three of their forwards would be hopelessly offside.

Their coaches were on the sidelines, screaming at the players to get back and regroup, but it was too late. Our forwards stripped the ball and lofted a pass over to Eric Johnson, who was on the left sideline. He trapped the ball, juked the defender, and crossed the ball about fifteen meters in front of the goal, and it was booted in past the goalkeeper with no problem. This all happened so fast that the Stingers barely had time to react. They were caught with five of their players on our half of the field, while eight of ours were attacking their goal. Less than twenty seconds into the game and we had our first goal.

They were a good team, however, and not prone to panic. Instead, they got mad. They controlled their next kickoff and started an offensive set that was tenacious, if unimaginative. They didn't get a good shot off against us, but on the other hand, they didn't give up the ball very often, either. Every time one of their players got trapped, they managed to pass the ball back, sometimes all the way back to their defenders, only to start another offensive sequence.

Finally, at about the ten-minute mark, the ball came over to the midfielder on my side. We were kind of caught out of position, so my midfielder dropped back to defend while I moved up to meet the ball handler. I dropped down, slide-tackling at the ball, but I missed the ball and ended up cutting the midfielder's legs out from under him. It was an infraction but not a serious foul; I knew it, and my opponent knew it. Even so, he scrambled to his feet and began gesticulating and yelling, trying to draw the attention of the referee. I hopped up, wet and muddy, only to be faced with the referee charging at me, fumbling at his pocket before blowing his whistle and waving a yellow card at me.

"You're kidding," I said. The ref scowled and reached for his pocket, perhaps intending to pull out a red card, which would have forced me to leave the field, and our team would have to play short. I held up my hands to him and backed away, shaking my head. Our coaches, on the far sidelines, were going nuts about the penalty imposed, while in the stands on the near side, the parents and friends of the Stingers were howling for my blood. I backed off the required ten meters, and the referee moved me back even farther before allowing the free kick. The midfielder tried to center the ball to his forwards, but the small delay allowed us to position ourselves to cover everybody, and we took possession of the ball and drove down to the other end of the field.

The seesaw battle continued until about the twenty-five-minute mark. We took the ball and got it out to Eric Johnson on the left side, and he started running down the sidelines with the ball. The ground was a little slippery, so he didn't feel like he could run full out, and the Stingers' defender had the angle on him anyway. The defender caught up to him, lowered his shoulder, and knocked Eric completely out of bounds and on his ass, skidding and rolling on the wet grass of the sidelines. The defender took the ball and moved it back up the field, all the while knowing that the whistle that we fully expected for the foul would never come. Again, our coaches and players on the sidelines started yelling and complaining to the referee until he called a time-out, on our possession, and trotted over to our bench. He stopped in front of our head coach and pulled out his yellow card and waved it in his face, calling him for a violation. We were dumbfounded, and Mr. Reyes looked like he was going to have a stroke. But he kept his mouth shut. The referee restarted the game, awarding possession to the Stingers on the infraction, and the game continued, getting rougher and muddier and less organized as time ticked on.

By the end of the first half, it was obvious that the Stingers were focusing on Eric, apparently with the intent of getting him out of the game. They roughed him up at every opportunity, and by the halftime whistle, he was bruised, muddy, and gasping. One of our assistant coaches jogged over to the referee as he was standing on the sideline talking to one of his line judges, intending to lodge a complaint about the rough and uncalled-for treatment that Eric had put up with, but to no avail. He came back over to our bench, shaking his head ruefully, and let us know what was going on.

"It's a hometown ref making hometown calls, boys," he said. "Let's whip them and then beat it out of town. We are not going to get any fair calls in this game, so don't look for help from any of the officials. Just play your game. Got it?"

We all nodded.

"Eric," Mr. Reyes said, "do you want to sit out the second half? I know you have school practice this afternoon. Maybe you'd better just rest."

"No, sir," said Eric defiantly. "I'm playing. This is the last game, and I am not going to let them drive me off this fucking field. Sir."

"Watch your language, Eric. And get in there and play tough, if that's where you want to be. I'll sub you out for a rest at about the fifteen-minute mark."

I looked over at Eric. He stared back at me, a look of determination in his eyes. I nodded at him, and he nodded back. After a last pull from my water bottle, I stood up, held out my hand to Eric to lift him up onto his feet, and we all trotted out to the field even before the ref blew his whistle.

The second half of the game started out right where we left off, rough-and-tumble, but we knew more about what to expect. The first time Eric touched the ball, their midfielder came barreling over to knock him down, but he was not expecting Eric to be as quick as he was. He did a neat sidestep, and the midfielder skidded out of bounds, waving his hands to try to keep his balance. Eric slid right past the charging defender and ran full out at an angle toward their goal, heedless of the slippery ground. Their keeper came spidering out to cut off Eric's targets at the goal, arms out and head up, until suddenly he dropped and dived headfirst for Eric's knees, intending to, at the least, knock him out of the play, and maybe do some bodily damage in the process. Eric used the outside of his right foot to pass the ball neatly to our center forward, and then he leaped high in the air, allowing the keeper to slide underneath him. He landed on his feet nimbly, goal-side of the keeper, and watched with pleasure as our forward walked the ball in past the last defender and touched it into the back of the net.

That goal finally took the wind out of their sails. We ended up scoring two more times, and Mr. Reyes, true to his word, subbed for Eric at about the eighteen-minute mark. He let him sit and recuperate for the rest of the game. During the last five minutes, the Stingers managed to score a cheap goal on a corner kick that we deflected right to a startled Stingers forward. It bounced off his shin guard and skittered into the corner as our keeper vainly dived for it. By that time, I was sitting on the bench next to Eric, watching the end of the game from underneath a damp towel draped over my head.

At the end of the game, we lined up to congratulate the other team, and the coaches all shook hands. Mr. Reyes, our head coach, normally a very polite, conscientious, and somewhat formal man, pointedly walked away from the referee without shaking his hand, a gesture I had never before seen from him. It probably didn't bother the ref since he didn't know Mr. Reyes or our team at all, but I knew that Mr. Reyes thought long and hard about the snub before allowing himself to deliver it.

We stopped for lunch on the way home, and that revived everyone. We were soaked and muddy, tired and exhilarated. It was our best moment as a team. It was too bad it was also the last moment of that particular team.

Mr. Reyes dropped Eric and me off at the school for our team practice. We were late, but it was obvious to our coaches why, since we were still in our muddy uniforms. We barely made it through that day's practice, holding each other up as we stumbled through our final lap around the field at the end of the afternoon.

I had time to eat dinner and take a long, hot shower before getting on my bike to ride over to Molly's. The rain had stopped hours ago, and the skies were clearing, promising a spectacular sunset. Heather and Josh were both home, too, so the four of us ended up in the family room, watching a movie on HBO. Heather and Josh were on opposite ends of the couch, and Molly and I were sitting together on the floor, leaning back against the sofa. Somewhere in the middle of *An Officer and a Gentleman*, I fell into an exhausted sleep. My friends let me sleep until the end of the movie and then roused me enough to push me out the door. I biked home and fell into bed, not even bothering to take off my clothes or brush my teeth.

- 16 -

THE HOT, LAZY SATURDAY

School had only been in session for two days, and already I was happy about the weekend so I could relax. Saturday morning dawned hot and sunny. Molly and I met Lori at Kip and Davey's soccer game just before ten o'clock at the park where the boys and I had drilled. We all sat together on the sidelines and watched as the boys tried out some of their newly learned skills. We cheered and whistled every time one of them touched the ball, shouting out encouragement. Kids that age tend to drift back into the habits of the group, and Davey and Kip were no exception. It was swarm-ball at its ugliest, but everybody on both teams was having a ball, so it was all okay.

At halftime, the boys came over carrying offerings of orange slices from the team's halftime treat supply. Davey crawled up onto Molly's lap, and Kip, following his brother's lead, jumped into mine.

"Ow!" I complained good-naturedly. "No bouncing, okay?"

"Okay, Sean," he grinned. He gave me one last, small bounce for good measure anyway.

"Do you guys know what you're supposed to be doing out there?" I asked.

"Playing soccer?" replied Kip.

"Sure, playing soccer and having a good time. But how are you supposed to be playing soccer?"

"Oh, yeah," said Davey. "Move to where nobody else is, call for the ball, one-potato look and two-potato pass."

"There you go," said Molly. "Just remember what Sean has been teaching you, and you'll have even more fun out there."

At that point, the boys' coach called his team over to give them second-half instructions. He read off his starting lineup to the players, and as their names were called, they left the sidelines and took their positions on the field. Davey was playing center midfielder, and Kip was right forward.

Just that little reminder at halftime was enough for them to recall their lessons. They mostly stayed at their positions for the rest of their playing time that day, instead of rushing to the ball wherever it might be on the field. It paid off for them toward the end of the third quarter, when the ball squirted out of the pile of players into Davey's area. He scooped up the ball, dribbled down the field for about three steps, and then passed it up to Kip. Kip tried to take the ball in to the net, but was caught up in traffic when he fumbled a little on his trap, and he lost it in the scramble around him. Even so, I was happy to see them work on their positioning and their passes during a game. I hoped that they would be able to see the worth of their drills, even at their young age.

After the game ended, the boys each grabbed a hand and dragged me over to meet their coach, a man they only knew as Coach Bill.

"I'm glad to meet you, Sean," said Coach Bill. "Davey and Kip have been bragging about you almost nonstop."

"Well," I said, somewhat embarrassed, "I've been trying to help..."

"No, no, don't get me wrong," Coach Bill interrupted. "I really am glad to meet you. You couldn't see it very well today in the game because none of the other boys have caught up to them yet, but both Davey and Kip are light years better than they were in the spring. Some of that improvement can be attributed to being a little older and a little bigger, but it's obvious that the time you've spent with them this summer has been beneficial to them. I especially liked that play down by the goal, when Davey passed the ball over to Kip. Very neat."

"Yeah, I saw that, too. Too bad it didn't work out to be a score," I said.

"Well, yes and no," he replied. "At this age, the score of the game doesn't really matter to these kids. The parents care more about wins and losses than the kids do, I'm afraid. All the boys know is they're out there on the field, running and having a good time. A goal is just that: a goal to aim for. Scoring gives them a good feeling right then at the time, but by the time they restart the game afterwards, they've practically forgotten about it. In a couple of years, it might start to matter to them, but for right now, it's just one more thing for them to worry about. And I'm all for giving them less to worry about. I'm happier when they execute a good pass or can clear the ball out of the pack or make a good interception. That's enough for them to think about at this point in their soccer lives."

"That's true, coach," I said. "I've officiated games at this level, and a lot of the time the kids are more interested in what the halftime treat is going to be than in what is happening on the field."

Coach Bill laughed. "Yes, and this team is no exception. I just wish the parents could have the same attitude. Some of them get so competitive through their kids!"

"It only gets worse as the kids get older," I said. "I've got friends on my rec team who are already getting pressure from their parents about playing well so they have a chance for scholarship money for college, and these kids are only thirteen or fourteen years old."

"Well, Sean," he replied, "play the game for fun. If you're good, the rest will find its way to you." He shook my hand and then walked over to talk to some of the parents.

✮ ✮ ✮

Heather dropped Molly and me at Skip's house that afternoon. We could hear sounds of the party wafting over the neighborhood as we got out of the car and found our way to the back yard. There was a large wooden deck attached to the house, off the kitchen, and Skip was there, his girlfriend Maggie Wiggins by his side, holding court among some of the members of the team and their girlfriends. I knew all the guys, and most of the girls I knew at least by sight. I stopped to say hello and introduced Molly to the group.

"I know you," said Skip. "You're Heather's sister, aren't you?"

"Yes, I am, but I prefer to think of her as the sister, not the other way around," shot back Molly with a smile.

"Watch out, Sean," Skip said as he turned to me. "You've got a firecracker here."

"Don't I know it," I said. I dropped our pack of sodas in a corner.

Most athletes tend to date athletic types, and soccer players are no exception. Most of the girls at the party played on one team or another at school or were members of the coveted groups such as cheerleaders, student council, or poms. The surprising exception to this was the girl hanging onto the arm of Theo Jameson, a senior forward on the team and one of Skip's best friends. Her name was Allison Moseley, and her main claim to fame was her voluptuous figure, along with the way she flaunted it. Even here, at a pool party with lots of skin showing on lots of fit bodies, Allison managed to draw attention to herself.

She wore a startlingly bright orange bikini, maybe two sizes too small, so that her fleshy breasts practically spilled out over the top. To accentuate the effect, she had grabbed on to Theo's arm and was squeezing her boobs against him, creating an impressive amount of cleavage and reveling in the stares from many of the boys on the deck.

Molly yanked on my arm and guided me toward the stairs leading down from the deck.

"You're going to start drooling in a minute," she said quietly. We headed for the coolest spot in the yard, the swimming pool. We jumped into the shallow end and waded over to where Jorge Mendoza was lounging. Surprisingly, he had brought his sister, Kristina, along to the party. Kristina was wearing a black one-piece suit that really showed off her trim form and made her darkly tanned skin shine. Beads of water seemed to glisten off the shoulders and arms of both Jorge and Kristina. We said our hellos, casually splashing water on our shoulders to cool off. I looked up at the crowd on the deck just in time to see Eric come out from the kitchen with Keisha Prescott. Eric's eyes practically popped out of his head when he almost bumped into Allison, who giggled and squeezed even harder against poor Theo. Keisha grabbed Eric's arm and pulled him away. He stumbled a little and then spotted us watching him from the pool and stopped to say something to Keisha. She glanced over, and they both stepped off the deck and jumped into the pool by us.

"So, Eric, did you get an eyeful?" I asked.

"Oh, he got an eyeful, all right. And pretty soon he's gonna get an earful," said Keisha.

We all laughed. Molly stood in front of me, about six inches away, and said, "I noticed that you paid particular attention to her chest, too, Mr. Porter. What do you have to say for yourself?"

There was a glint in her eye that warned me to be cautious or I could be expecting some pain. I craned my neck around her to glance up at the deck and then deliberately looked down at her lightly freckled chest. "You know, Molly, you are much more tanned than Allison. In my eyes, that means that she pales in comparison to you."

Molly smiled, a look of delight on her face, as she gave me a light tap on the chest with her forearm.

"Nice save," murmured Jorge, next to me.

There were a few kids trying to get up a volleyball game out in the yard, but it was just too hot, and the pool was too refreshing. Eventually, we worked up enough enthusiasm to set up the net across the pool so we could play water volleyball. Even that collapsed into a free-for-all after a couple of games.

Molly and I tired of the roughhousing very quickly. We tried moving to the side, out of the way, but we still were splashed.

"Come on," I said as I waded along the side. "Let's just go down by the shallow end and sit on the edge for a while."

Eric, Keisha, Jorge, and Kristina all joined us, and for the rest of the afternoon and into the evening, the six of us lounged near the shallow end of the pool.

Skip and Theo fired up the grill and threw hot dogs, bratwursts, and burgers on to cook. Maggie and Allison shuttled back and forth from the kitchen with bags of chips, plates of sliced tomatoes, onions, mustard and ketchup, and bowls of potato salad. A real production line got going as everyone suddenly realized how hungry they were. Skip and Theo were kept busy for the next hour or so, cooking up grub for the rest of us. Every so often, either Allison or Maggie would hand them cold cans of soda, and one time Maggie stuffed a hot dog in a bun into Theo's mouth as he was flipping burgers with one hand and turning brats with the other. He hardly missed a beat, chewing and flipping hamburgers at the same time.

Just as we were leaning back in satisfaction, having downed an impressive amount of food, the girls came out with a huge pan of homemade brownies and a five-gallon tub of ice cream.

It was an effort, but we managed to clean all that up, too. By the time everyone was done, there were just a few brownie crumbs left, and the bottom of the tub was barely covered with the last melting remnants of ice cream.

It was starting to get dark out by the time we finished eating. Skip lit some torches that were placed around the yard and turned on the lights in the pool while turning off all the other lights in the back of the house. The swimming pool, now empty of activity, was a calm, iridescent rectangle of blue-green liquid floating in the middle of the yard. The flickering light from the few torches, along with the reflected light from the water, cast shadows everywhere, dancing and playing across the furniture and bodies in repose around the property.

Skip and Maggie, their duties as cook and scullery maid done, made their way around the deck and pool, stopping to talk for a few moments with each group of kids. When they got around to the six of us, still grouped around a table by the end of the pool, Skip plopped down in an empty chair in mock exhaustion. Maggie stood behind him, casually rubbing his shoulders.

"So, Porter, did you get enough to eat?" he asked.

Eric snorted in amusement, and Molly and Kristina laughed out loud.

"This boy eats more than I ever thought was possible," Molly said.

"Well, don't eat so much you're going to get fat, Porter. Don't forget you're riding the pines this season, not running your ass off in the games," he said with a grin.

"Don't worry about me," I shot back. "That's only true if you don't get slow and lazy. Don't forget who's gunning for your position."

"Hey, do I look scared? You're good, Porter, I'll give you that. You're just not good enough yet." Skip stood up, stretched, and draped his arm around Maggie's shoulder. "Come on, babe. Let's mosey."

The two of them wandered to the next group, and Eric muttered, "'Let's mosey'? Since when did we land in the Wild freaking West?"

Keisha laughed derisively. "Yeah, what arrogance. And he's gonna be captain of the team, right?"

"Aw, Skip's not so bad," I objected. "He's just had a lot of press lately about how good he's going to be this year. I think he's operating under a lot of pressure, much more than he's showing."

"Yeah, well," said Eric, "it's all right if you want to defend him, since you've got to live with him during practices and all. If it's all the same, I'll just not be his best friend, okay?" With that, he reached behind him and pulled another soda out of the cooler.

After the brutal heat of the day, the air felt very cool after the sun went down. We all slipped on T-shirts and shorts and started gathering our stuff together. Mr. Mendoza had already picked up Jorge and Kristina, and Eric and Keisha were leaving very soon. Molly went into the house to use the phone to call Heather to pick us up and then came back and started helping Maggie clean off the remains of the food from the table. I struggled up and started picking up empty plates and soda cans and carrying them over to the trash cans. Keisha came over to say good-bye, giving Molly a brief hug, while Eric genuflected to Skip. They headed around the outside of the house toward the front, giving us a wave as they disappeared around the corner.

A few minutes later, we heard a car honking its horn. Evan and Heather were there to pick us up, so we thanked Skip and Maggie and said good-bye to the stragglers still lounging around the yard. We made our way around to the front, where Heather and her boyfriend were waiting impatiently.

As we threw our gear into the trunk and climbed into the back seat, Molly said, "Don't give me that look, Heather. It's not like you didn't volunteer to give us a ride."

"I know I volunteered," Heather said. "I thought you'd be ready to come home a lot earlier. We're going to miss the first part of the movie."

"So what?" Molly spat back. "You probably weren't going to see the last part, anyway, were you? I've heard about the back rows at the movies, you know."

"Very funny, little sister. Very funny."

The rest of the ride took place in uncomfortable silence. When we got to Molly's house, we clambered out of the car, popped open the trunk, and grabbed our stuff. Evan and Heather took off without a word as soon as they heard the trunk slam closed, and we were left there in a blue-white cloud of exhaust. I looked at Molly. She just shrugged, as if to say, *I don't know what's wrong with her,* and we headed for the rear of the house.

We put our backpacks and the cooler down by the back door. Molly slipped into the garage to grab a handful of blankets, just like before. We walked toward the woods, hand in hand, not saying a word. I could feel that her hand was a little sweaty. It was good to know she was nervous, too, since I had butterflies doing bodily damage to themselves inside my stomach.

We got to the opening in the woods and spread out the blankets. I lay down on my back, and Molly snuggled up in the crook of my arm, her arm draped across my chest and her head nestled against my neck. I languidly ran my hand up and down her body, from shoulder to waist, as we relaxed together. Her hair smelled slightly of chlorine from the pool.

I kissed the top of her head, and she lifted up to give me a soft kiss on the mouth. Her lips were pliant and warm, slightly parted, as we held the kiss. Without breaking contact, she twisted in my arms, rolling over so she was lying partially on top of me, her leg insinuating itself over my knee, and the kiss got harder and hotter. She reached up with her hand and held the back of my neck, pulling me closer to her as her lips moved and her tongue flicked out to touch the tip of mine. I opened my mouth a little more, and she took advantage of the breach and attacked all out, her tongue exploring the recesses of my mouth, teeth to tongue, gums to palate.

I reached down and ran my hand up under her T-shirt, up her back, and under her bikini strap. Pressing the flat of my hand against the middle of her upper back, I could feel the interplay of her muscles and shoulder blades as she moved her arms and her leg. The hem of her shirt was rucking up under her, so she broke our kiss momentarily, lifted herself up, and pulled her shirt up and off. She dropped back down onto my mouth right away, unwilling to be denied the heat and moisture she was finding so entrancing there. I closed my eyes, allowing her to take charge of the force of the kiss. My hand found the clip that held together her bathing suit top, and I fumblingly managed to slip the cloth from its clasp. The strap separated, and Molly twisted her upper body around as my hand glided around her, giving me unobstructed access.

We heated each other up, just like before, until the fires within us could only be quenched in one way.

At the end, Molly lifted her head tiredly, looked me in the eye, and gave me a soft kiss, all buttery and warm, both a thank you and a promise of times to come. She moved to my side as we both worked to catch our breath.

I reached down and pulled off the full rubber and flung it into the woods. I chuckled at the thought of Jake out there, dodging another missile.

"What's so funny, Sean?" Molly asked languidly. She was lying back on the blanket, one knee bent, her arms resting behind her head.

"Nothing," I said. I flopped down on my stomach next to her. "I was just remembering something somebody said once about finding stuff in these woods."

"I'm glad our grove was empty tonight," she said. "I'm kind of surprised that Josh hasn't thought of it yet."

"Maybe he and Shayna have their own little spot already picked out."

She sat up. "I don't think so," she said. "There's still the same number of condoms in his room."

I frowned. "You go checking out his room? How smart is that, Mol? If he finds out, he may just start checking out your room."

She laughed softly. "Oh, he's already tried that and gotten caught. When we were thirteen and Heather was fifteen, Josh got curious about girls, I think. Anyway, Heather found him in her room, pawing through her underwear drawer. Mom and Dad never found out about it, but Heather never let him forget it, either. He still breaks out in a cold sweat if he even has to walk by her closed door."

Ah, I thought to myself. *More ammunition, just in case I need it.* But I didn't say a word about that to Molly.

- 17 -

THE BULLS

Our first varsity soccer game was at home on Friday against one of the smallest schools in our conference. According to our scouts, they didn't have a very talented team, so I was hoping for a little playing time in the second half.

The stands were not even half full. Not many kids at school cared much about soccer yet, but we hoped that would all change as we tore through our schedule. Even before our first game, we were whispering about going on to sectionals and maybe even the state playoffs. We were cocksure, confident we could beat any other school head-to-head. Only a fluke could keep us from our destiny: the playoffs.

And that fluke nearly happened during our first game. The team from Rockland High School won the toss and elected to take the ball. They tapped the ball forward and passed it back to their midfielder, who passed it over to their right midfielder. He immediately launched a booming pass all the way across the field toward the far sidelines. Our right midfielder, Kevin Soranno, went up for the ball, intending to head it up the field. At the same time, Rockland's left forward also elevated. Everybody on the field heard the loud crack when their heads hit, and Kevin went down like a sack of potatoes. The ball went soaring back toward the middle of the field, where it was picked off by a Rockland player. He trapped it, dropped the ball down to his right foot, and launched a rocket at the far right post of the net. Our keeper was one step too slow in following the play, but the ball hit the post and bounced back out to our striker, who promptly cleared the ball out of bounds. By that time, Kevin was on his knees and holding his head with both hands, and the Rockland player he collided with was about five feet away from him, standing with his hands on his knees. I knew he was trying to clear the cobwebs out, having just gotten his bell rung, but at least he was on his feet.

The referee stopped the game and trotted over to check on the fallen players. Both of them shook their heads when asked if they wanted to come out. Kevin climbed to his feet and jogged a few steps, making sure all the parts were in working order, and then walked over to shake hands with the Rockland player.

Rockland took the throw-in, and the game continued. Neither team wanted to test the right side of the field yet, so the ball pretty much stayed away from Kevin and Skip for the rest of the half. Even so, by the time the half ended, we were up 2–0. Rockland never got close to our goal after that first unlucky shot.

We started the second half by playing a little more defensively. Our offense was powerful, but we didn't need to score on the hapless Rockland team any more. They were done for, and they knew it just as well as we did. Skip showed a little razzle-dazzle the few times he managed to touch the ball, but mostly we were just playing keep-away with them. Finally, with about four minutes left to play, the score was 3–0. Our coach made some wholesale substitutions, so the benchwarmers got to play the last few minutes of the game while Skip, Theo, Kevin, and many of the other starters came out. I felt good about being able to go in to substitute for Skip already, during our first game of the season. Skip gave me a high-five as we swapped places, making me feel even better.

THE BULLS

At the final whistle, we subs had hardly broken a sweat. The team went into the locker room to shower and change. We were in a great mood, that first win under our belts, glad to finally get the season underway.

Our head coach, Mr. Neville, was a history teacher, so many of his locker room speeches contained obscure references to battles and soldiers from the past. Half the time, I didn't understand what he was talking about, but that night we interrupted his speech several times with good-natured cheering.

✿ ✿ ✿

The next week, school was back to being a full-time grind. Some of my friends were really smart at school, breezing through on a combination of charm and native smarts, but I had to work hard just to maintain a B average. Molly and Tessa both seemed to get their homework done fast, while it seemed like I struggled just to stay in the same place.

Finally, on Tuesday, the last bell of the day rang. The halls were crowded with kids jostling each other, everybody anxious to get outside while the weather still held. It was a beautiful late summer day, and it seemed like everybody, students and teachers alike, was chafing at having to spend such a great day inside. The physical education teachers were the lucky ones on days like that. They could take their classes out to the track or to the football field, enjoying the good weather, while their co-workers were stuck in their classrooms.

I met up with Jake and Josh on the way to the gym. We were taking the scenic route, leaving school by the front door and walking around the building to enter the locker rooms from the outside. We rounded a corner of the school and saw a small gathering of some of the rougher kids from our school, a group of about seven or eight guys with their hair slicked back and greased up, leather jackets with the collars pulled up, chrome chains and rings hanging from jackets and jeans. They were a group of troublemakers who called themselves the Bulls, I suppose in homage to their leader, a tall, gangly kid with a bad complexion named Richie Del Toro. Richie and his gang were standing in a loose semicircle around the wall. Their body language spoke of somebody inside their circle who was regretting being there.

The three of us stopped as we took in the scene. We glanced at each other and silently agreed that we should take a closer look. Without a word, we started walking toward the group. When we were about fifteen feet away, I could see two smaller bodies trapped inside the semicircle, their backs against the wall. Between the gaps in the crowd, I was surprised to see Jorge and Kristina Mendoza were the ones surrounded.

Richie was the only member of the Bulls standing inside the group. He had a cowlick sticking straight up on top of his greasy head, an errant lock of hair that refused to be controlled by anything Richie put on it. He was derisively known as Alfalfa behind his back, and occasionally to his face.

"I'll betcha you're a hot little tamale, aren't you? Are you a hot one, *Conchita? Como esta* blowjobs?" Richie was saying. He teasingly reached out toward Kristina, who flinched away.

"Leave her alone, you piece of dog shit," yelled Jorge.

"Close it, Jorge. Whore-Hay. What the fuck kind of name is that, anyway?" The group around them tittered as if they were witnessing a star performance on *The Tonight Show*. I noticed Richie loved playing to the crowd.

"It's a better name than Alfalfa, Alfalfa," retorted Jorge.

Richie lunged at him, perhaps intending to slap the smaller freshman around, but Jorge was too slippery. He ducked under Richie's arm and moved behind him. *Big mistake*, I thought. Almost immediately, two of Richie's pals grabbed him by the arms and held tight. Kristina was pressed against the wall, her hand covering her mouth, eyes wide and scared.

This was just too much for me. The three of us pushed our way into the circle, and I grabbed Richie by the shoulder. He was about six inches taller than me, so I had to reach up to grab him, but at that point the size difference between us didn't matter much to me. I was mad.

Richie whirled around as soon as he felt my hand on his shoulder, intending to teach whoever was touching him a lesson in manners, Del Toro style.

"Well, if it isn't the Three Musket-Queers." There was that idiotic twittering again, coming from his pack of hyenas. "What the fuck are you doing here, Porter?" he spat. "Or do you want a little of what we're gonna give to this puny ninth grade spic greaseball?"

"What have you got against ninth graders, Richie?" said Jake. "You seemed to like freshman year so much you went through it twice, if I remember right."

The Bulls all got very quiet. Apparently, Richie didn't like being reminded of how he was held back.

"What did you say?" he asked dangerously, staring daggers at Jake.

"What's the matter with your hearing, Del Toro? I heard him just fine all the way back here," said a voice from beyond the fringe of the Bulls. Richie whirled around to confront this new intrusion, and the crowd parted as Skip, Theo, Eric, and Kevin all walked up.

"He asked what you had against ninth graders, since you seemed to love it so much before," said Skip. "Or are the crops you must be growing in that dirt in your ears making you deaf?"

Richie's face turned an angry red, and he took a step toward Skip. Eric, Theo, and Kevin on one side, Josh and Jake and I on the other, all moved in closer to Richie and his gang.

Suddenly, the odds didn't look quite so good to Richie and his cohorts. They began backpedaling away from all of us, muttering amongst themselves the whole time. They let Jorge go and pretty much forgot about Kristina. I walked over and put my arm around her shoulders protectively. She flinched slightly at the touch but then sighed audibly and hung onto me, grateful for the support.

When they were a safe distance away, Richie turned back to us.

"Don't worry, *Conchita*. I'll be back for that *el blowjob* sometime soon, okay?" The group of them guffawed at Richie's sparkling wit.

Kristina burst into tears and buried her head against me. Jorge came over and hugged her from the other side. I could feel him shaking from the adrenaline rush that must have coursed through him during the altercation.

"Thanks, guys. You got here just in time, man. I thought we were goners." Jorge looked around at all of us, the appreciation shining through his dark eyes.

"We're a team, man. We've gotta stick together," said Skip. "I'm just glad we spotted you when we were over by the corner."

"You've really gotta watch out for them guys," said Eric. "They'll always look for an opportunity, but they won't do anything if they don't have numbers. You know?"

Jorge nodded his head. "I'll remember that. Thanks. I'll also remember that I owe that greasy slimeball a big one."

"You can owe it to him, but don't go trying to pay it off by yourself, Jorge," warned Josh.

"I won't. I know better than that," said Jorge. "Kristina, can you stay on the sidelines while I'm at practice? I don' want you walking home by yourself."

"Good idea," I said. "The group of us can all go that way together."

"Okay," she said. "If you don't mind my watching you guys." She looked around at all the guys around her and blushed a little.

"No, of course not," said Skip. We all started walking to the back of the school. It was time for us to be getting to our respective practices.

The coaches were on the sidelines, going over their notes, so Kristina walked over to one of the benches by them as we all filed into the locker room to change. She stayed there, studying most of the time but occasionally setting her book down to watch us scrimmage. Her eyes followed each of us in turn, the five of us from the soccer team, plus her brother, who willingly stood up to her tormentors.

✡ ✡ ✡

A couple of days later, I was walking down the hall to my third period class with Jake and Eric. I saw Jorge and Kristina just ahead of me, walking slowly in the same direction. I didn't think a thing of it, until I happened to see Richie Del Toro walking with a couple of the Bulls toward us. He was engrossed in his conversation, oblivious to everyone around him. Unlike almost all the other kids in the hallway, Richie carried no books or papers, but instead strutted down the hall with his hands in his jeans pockets. It was to be his undoing.

I saw Jorge move to Kristina's right side so he would be between her and Richie when they passed. Richie was paying absolutely no attention to anything going on around him, confident that people would move out of his way. As the two parties met, Jorge stopped for just a moment and waited until Richie was two steps behind him. He whirled around, dropped to the floor, and swept Richie's legs out from under him in a classic soccer slide tackle. Richie's feet flew up into the air, and he landed square on his backside, his hands still in his pockets. There was a loud thump as he hit, and an echoing thump when his head met the tiles. He started yelling in pain. His friends just stood there and goggled at him, too shocked to take any action. Jorge hopped up and then knelt down on Richie's chest while he was still flat on his back. He grabbed Richie by his greasy hair.

"Do you know why your eyes are so brown, Alfalfa? It's because you are so full of bullshit. Do you hear me?" Jorge was so angry, I thought sparks would fly out of his eyes as he talked softly to Richie. "We have a new word now in Spanish for bullshit, Alfalfa. We call it Del Toro Poo-Poo."

With that, he hopped up, looked quickly around, and grabbed Kristina by the arm and walked swiftly away, never once looking back.

Jake, Eric, and I all burst out laughing. Soon, the whole hallway was clapping and cheering just as a couple of teachers came out to see what the commotion was all about. Richie was still on his back, groaning in pain, and everybody just walked around him without offering to help him in any way. His two cohorts were nowhere to be seen, having abandoned Richie to his own fate. The three of us ambled on, our day suddenly much more pleasant.

At practice that afternoon, the entire soccer team, varsity and JV alike, gathered around Jorge and heard the story all over again. When he got to the part about Del Toro Poo-Poo, everybody whooped and laughed. Jorge was a little embarrassed being the center of attention, but everybody enjoyed hearing about the fall of Alfalfa, now better known as Poo-Poo.

"So, what was Richie's reaction later in the day?" asked one of the younger players. "Anybody got him in a class in the afternoon?"

"I do," said another of the junior varsity players. "But he wasn't there. I don't think he went to any of his classes afterwards."

"That's odd," said Theo. "I wonder why?"

"Maybe he was just too embarrassed to show his face," said Kevin.

"Yeah, maybe," I said. "And maybe not. Watch yourself, Jorge."

"I will, *amigo*. Don' worry. I'm a Latin lover, not a fighter," he said.

We all laughed. Just then, the coaches called us back out to continue with practice, and we all just kind of forgot about poor Poo-Poo for the rest of the day.

The next day at school, I saw Richie first thing in the morning. He was moving slowly and carefully, like an old man. He was a little hunched over, and he was taking small, shuffling steps. People were not quite as careful about staying out of his way as they had been just the day before, but he was concentrating so hard on his walking that he barely noticed. There were beads of sweat on his forehead, and his errant cowlick was waving all over the place.

Between first and second period, Josh came walking up to me.

"Can you believe it?" he said excitedly. "Del Toro's got a broken tailbone. He can't hardly walk, he can't stand up straight, he can't even sit down without hurting, and he's in pain, man. It's just too funny!"

"A broken tailbone? No shit. Well, I guess he won't be bothering Jorge and Kristina anytime soon, will he?" I said.

And so Richie became known as Del Toro Poo-Poo, or Poo-Poo for short. And nobody was afraid to call him that to his face. The Bulls were such a rag-tag bunch, barely able to hold a coherent collective thought together, much less plan out anything more complicated. With their leader down and out, I thought that our troubles with them were pretty much over.

I was wrong.

- 18 -

THE GAME OF LIFE

The next few weeks went by in kind of a blur. There were tests and quizzes to study for, and there was soccer practice every day after school. Our games were every Friday after school, and my weekends were taken up with watching Davey and Kip play soccer on Saturday mornings, doing my chores around the house in the afternoon, then meeting up with some of my friends Saturday night. Sometimes Molly and I would meet up with Tessa, Kristina, Jen, and Sam, and we would go to a movie, or sometimes we would hang around and watch television with some of our friends. Other times, I would get together with Jake or Josh, and we would go to the mall to play video games. It turned out that Josh never did get to use his condoms with Shayna. She broke up with him right after he got them, and now she wouldn't even speak to him. It hurt him, but he wouldn't talk about it at all, and no other girl we knew attracted him that much at the moment. *Let it run its course,* I thought to myself. *It will all work itself out.*

Jake, on the other hand, pretty much walked around with a smile on his face all the time. He wouldn't talk about why, either, but I was willing to wager hard-earned cash that he and Jaimie were finding a way to use up the condoms he got from me.

Our soccer team remained undefeated, winning our games by an average of four goals. Scouts from Division One schools were showing up at our games to watch Skip play, and as a nice side benefit, Theo started getting some good mentions in the local press, too. He was also drawing some scouts to our games.

Coach Neville, always mindful of the future, played his subs as much as he could toward the end of the games, when the outcome was certain. As a result, all of us got a little playing time each game, including our tested-tough freshman backup keeper, Jorge Mendoza.

By the time Sunday rolled around, I was usually pretty exhausted. I was able to sleep in, sometimes not rousing until noon or after. My dad, my brothers, and I would sit around and watch football on TV, and Sunday evenings would be catch-up-on-homework time, from immediately after dinner until bedtime.

Things changed beginning on the last Saturday of September.

✿ ✿ ✿

Molly, Tessa, and I went to Davey and Kip's soccer game in the morning. Each time I watched them play, I could see the results of our lessons taking hold. More and more of their teammates were starting to play positions on the field, and the swarm-ball mentality lessened. The most obvious result of this change was that they were winning a lot of their games now that they were able to control the ball more. Possession is a great offensive tool, Mr. Reyes used to say, and he was right. If your team held the ball for most of the game, the other team couldn't score. It was simple strategy, easy to teach but very tough to learn.

Lori sat next to us on the sidelines. She was looking a little tired herself. Molly was supposed to baby-sit for her later that night, and I had been invited over to watch a movie with Molly and the boys.

Coach Bill came over after the game to chat with us.

"How's your team doing, Sean?" he asked.

"Undefeated. I just wish I could get a little more playing time."

"You'll get your chance. And I know you'll make the most of it when you do," he said. "I've got a favor to ask. I'm going to be out of town next Saturday. Could you stand in as coach for me for their game?"

"Sure, I'll be glad to," I told him. I was surprised he didn't ask one of the parents to do it, but it made me proud that he trusted me with the team.

"We're practicing tomorrow afternoon right here. Can you make it? I'll introduce you to the rest of the team then and explain to them what to expect next game day."

"Sure, that's fine. Is it okay if Molly and Tessa come along, too?"

"Of course. As a matter of fact, I was going to ask Tessa if she could work with my keepers a little bit, anyway, so that works out great." He paused. "If that's all right with you, Tessa. I didn't mean to be presumptuous."

"That's fine, Coach," said Tessa. "I'll be happy to help."

☆ ☆ ☆

It was turning into a beautiful fall evening. I rode my bike over to the Wilkinson house just after dark. The leaves on the trees were turning into their amazing annual display of colors, and some were just starting to fall. I could hear the crunch of dried leaves underneath my tires as I rolled along the street.

I dropped my bike on the front lawn and climbed the steps to the front door. I opened the screen to knock on the door, but it opened before I had a chance.

"Hi, Sean!"

"Hi, Sean!"

The two boys were nearly identical echoes of each other as they jostled to be the first to grab my hand and pull me into the house. The aroma of freshly popped popcorn came from the direction of the kitchen, and I could hear the rattle of ice in glasses from there.

"Come in, Sean. We're going to play Life!" cried Kip.

"What's Life?" I asked with a smile. It was a line in an old song I heard my mom singing occasionally.

"It's a game!" shouted Davey. "Don't you know about Life?"

"I guess not," I answered. "What's it all about?"

"Come on; we'll show you." And off they dragged me, into the family room where the board game was set up on the coffee table.

The three of us sat on the floor around the table. Davey and Kip had already chosen the pieces they would be playing with, and they started running the little cars around the board, following the painted road around and over the bridge and back to the starting point again.

Molly came in with drinks and popcorn. She favored me with a very warm smile as she set out the glasses and cans of soda. She put the big bowl of popcorn on the end of the table nearest the boys and sat down on the floor to my right. She was wearing black jeans and a baggy black sweatshirt that set off the golden red highlights in her hair.

The next couple of hours were spent in the pursuit of careers, families, education, and retirement funds as we played game after game of Life. We laughed and yelled and threw tiny little blue and pink pegs at each other and generally had a great time.

Finally, it was bedtime for Davey and Kip. Molly hustled them up the stairs to get ready for bed. While she was supervising brushing teeth and washing faces and hanging up clothes and putting on pajamas, I cleaned up the family room. I carried the dirty glasses and empty pop cans into the kitchen, threw out the remains of the popcorn, and put the game back into its box. I straightened up the pillows on the couch and crawled around the room, picking up bits of popcorn from the floor. By the time I was finished, Molly was turning out the lights and closing the doors of the boys' rooms, whispering a wish for a good night to each of them in turn. She came down the stairs slowly, walked over to the end table to turn off the lamp, and collapsed onto one end of the couch. As she slouched there, she beckoned to me with one lazy arm, a come-hither wave to her fingers. I knelt on the couch next to her and leaned toward her. Her arm, still hanging out there, snaked around my neck as I bent down to kiss her softly.

"Mmmmm…" she said, her eyes closing. I could see the cares of the world washing out of her face as she relaxed and let the pleasures of the evening begin to work on her.

"Come here," she whispered, pulling me down for another kiss. As our lips met, I felt her open her mouth slightly and her tongue dart out to tease my mouth. I let my tongue peek out to touch tips, poking and teasing and tasting for a few moments.

I was still kneeling over her, so I shifted one knee between her slightly spread legs. I was leaning on my left elbow with my hand resting on the top of her head, and my other hand was at her soft throat, tangled in her hair.

It was late, though, and we didn't want the boys to come down and find us in a compromising position. We contented ourselves with wrapping each other up in our arms on the couch, kissing occasionally as we gazed at the television.

Just before Lori was due home, we disentangled ourselves. I straightened the cushions on the couch while Molly ran upstairs to check on the boys.

"Everything's quiet," she reported when she came back downstairs. We found an old Laurel and Hardy comedy on one of the cable channels and settled back down once again as we waited for Lori to get home.

Right on time, we heard Lori's car in the driveway, followed by her key rattling in the lock at the back door. We stood and came out to the kitchen to greet her as she came in. She looked very tired, but she was smiling easily, something that was missing too often in her life lately. She paid Molly for baby-sitting and bid us both a good night as we headed out the door.

Molly and I talked of nothing on the walk back to her house, and I left her at her front door after giving her one last kiss and an embrace. She turned and went in to the house and turned off the porch light as I got on my bike and rode home.

I was tired but very happy as I got home, thinking of Molly and our evening together with the boys. I dropped my bike by the garage and tried to be quiet as I opened the back door. I stepped into the kitchen. All the lights were on in the house, something that had never occurred before at this time of night.

"Sean? Is that you?" I heard my mother call out from the other room—not a good sign. Suddenly concerned and too conscious of the fragrance of Molly's perfume surrounding me, I walked into the family room to find my mother, my father, and my brother Michael sitting there, staring at me.

"What's the matter?" I asked nervously. I was not sure I really wanted to know.

"Son, there's a phone number here for you to call. They said to call as soon as you got home, no matter what time it was." My dad handed me a piece of paper with a telephone number written on it. I looked up at each of them, but it was obvious that they had told me all they knew. It was apparent they were concerned, too, since they had waited up for me to make sure I got the message. But the message, such as it was, was worrisome, to be certain. I didn't recognize the number.

I walked over to the telephone on the end table by the couch. I dialed the number on the piece of paper, unaware that, a moment later, everything would change.

- 19 -

SKIP AND THEO

I picked up the phone and dialed the number on the slip of paper. An unfamiliar female voice at the other end answered after three rings.

"Hello? This is Sean Porter. I got a message to call this number when I got home."

"Just a minute, Sean," the voice said. There was a thump as the phone was set down on the other end.

"Hello, Sean?"

"This is Sean. Who is this?"

"Oh, I'm sorry. It's Coach Neville, Sean. I've been on the phone with so many people tonight, I forget who I've talked to and who I haven't."

"That's okay, Coach." I was puzzled. *Why is Coach Neville trying to contact me this late on a Saturday night?* "What's up?"

"Sean, this is very hard." He paused for a moment. His voice sounded gravelly. "There's been a terrible car accident. Skip and Theo..." He paused again, perhaps to collect himself. My own heart was beating like a trip-hammer, and my palms were suddenly sweaty. "Skip and Theo were on their way to pick up their dates earlier tonight, when they got into an accident. Another car was involved; Theo's car got pushed off the road and into a tree." His voice was rising in pitch, his emotions raw. He stopped to take a deep breath. "Sean, Skip was killed instantly, and Theo is in very serious condition at the hospital."

"What?" My knees gave out, and I hit the floor with a thump. "What did you say, Coach?"

"Skip is dead, son, and Theo is very badly hurt. I'm trying to contact everybody on the team to let them know. I've talked to almost everyone by now. I've been over to the hospital to meet with Theo's family, and Skip's parents were there, also. It's all so unreal. I don't think anyone realizes quite yet what's happened. Anyway, I've already talked to the principal at school, and he is arranging to have counselors available to everybody on Monday morning. I would like you to get to school early on Monday if you can, and we'll meet as a team, varsity and junior varsity, in the locker room for a few minutes before school starts."

"Okay, Coach. Is there anything else I can do?"

"Not right now, Sean. Just pray. Pray for Skip's family; pray for Theo and his family. I'll be at the hospital as much as I can tomorrow."

"I'll be there, too, as early as I can."

"Thanks, Sean. It's going to be a very sad week next week, I'm afraid." With that, he hung up the phone. I sat on the floor, the dead receiver forgotten in my hand, until the dial tone brought me back to the here and now. I struggled to my feet, hanging up the telephone, and turned to see my mother and father and my brother Mike, all looking at me, concern on their faces.

"We heard sirens earlier tonight. Is this something connected to them?" My mom stood up and came over to wrap me in her arms.

I nodded, not sure if I could speak quite yet. My eyes were burning, and my vision was blurred.

I sniffled a couple of times and got myself under control. I let them know what had happened and about Coach's plan to meet early on Monday morning. We sat up together, the four of us, for about an hour, talking about the accident and how much our town was going to be affected by the tragic news.

Finally, exhaustion set in, and I slowly found my way to my room and shut the door. I needed a shower. I was hoping the hot water would wash away the last hour, clean it up and present it again with better news. I spent about twenty minutes standing there, just letting the scalding water rush over me. The water started cooling as the water heater ran out, so I finally turned the water off and stepped out. I toweled myself dry and slipped on clean underwear. I flopped into bed with no lights on, but it was a very long time before I finally drifted off into a troubled sleep.

I was feeling pretty awful when I got up in the morning. My sleep had been fitful and restless. I couldn't remember any of my dreams, but they left a bad aftertaste, a lingering sour discomfort. I wanted more than anything to cancel soccer practice with Coach Bill's team, but since I didn't have any of their phone numbers, I steeled myself to go and do the best I could. I called Molly as early as I dared, but their house was already up and aware of the bad news. Heather and Evan had heard about it almost immediately. The two seniors ended up at the hospital, where they stayed until the nursing staff finally kicked them, and most of the rest of the senior class, out. She had come home shortly after I had dropped Molly off and awakened the family to give them the news.

Molly said she would call Tessa and the two of them would meet me at the park. My brother Mike dropped me off at the park with my gear about fifteen minutes early, saying he would pick me up after practice.

The girls got there a few minutes later. While we were waiting for the team to show up, Coach Bill explained to us the drills he wanted to work on today. It was hard to pay attention to him, as distracted as the three of us were on that Sunday morning.

The boys on the team started straggling in to the park. Some of them walked; parents dropped others off. Lori came with Davey and Kip and immediately walked over to me and wrapped me up in a warm hug.

"I heard about the accident," she said. "I'm so sorry, Sean."

"Thanks," I said, "but I'm not sure I should be the one to be accepting condolences."

She kept on holding me tightly, as if the sheer strength of her arms could hold off the relentless stroke of the clock.

"I'm sure," she said. "Just because you aren't a blood relation to those boys doesn't mean you aren't hurting right now. They were friends and teammates, and anybody that close is suffering."

"Maybe you're right," I said, and I hugged her back. I did appreciate her concern.

It was a difficult practice session for us. I had trouble concentrating, my thoughts going back again and again to the accident. I knew there was nothing I could have done to prevent it, but that didn't stop me from dwelling on it. I could tell Tessa and Molly were also wrapped up in their own thoughts, no doubt troubled by this sudden introduction of mortality in our midst. It made things a little more difficult for Coach Bill, having three assistants who were not assisting much at all, but he seemed to understand. He carried on with the boys and asked little of us that day.

Michael picked us up after practice, and we dropped Tessa and Molly off at their houses before going home. I wanted to take a shower and get something to eat before I went to the hospital to see Theo.

That afternoon, my dad willingly gave up his NFL jones to drive Molly and me to visit Theo. He stayed in the lobby the whole afternoon while we waited our turn to go in and see Theo. The waiting area was milling with teammates and school friends of Skip and Theo, the boys standing around trying to be stoic and strong, and the girls weeping and hanging onto each other for support. It was no surprise to me that Maggie, Skip's girlfriend, was not there, but I did notice that Allison, the girl hanging on Theo's arm at the pool party, also did not make an appearance.

When it was finally our turn to go into Theo's room, we found that it was nearly as crowded as the waiting room. His parents, brother, two sisters, grandparents, and Coach Neville were all there, surrounding the bed. Theo was in a drug-induced coma, tubes running everywhere, scary machines crowding the walls. He was in traction and had multiple internal injuries. Coach whispered to me that the long-term prognosis was favorable, but they didn't know if he would ever run again until they could bring him out of the coma and get going on his physical therapy. Theo looked so small and frail there, and Coach was sunken in on himself, keeping going by sheer willpower. I felt nearly as badly for him as I did for Theo's family.

Later that evening, we finally left the hospital. Dad drove us slowly past the spot where the accident occurred. There were long skid marks on the road, and the tree they had hit was badly scarred. There were dozens of flowers and candles, tributes to Skip and prayers for Theo, scattered around the tree. It gave the area a look of peace and tranquility, a far cry from its reputation from that day forward.

By the time I got home, I was completely wiped out. I barely had the energy to undress before I crawled between my sheets and fell almost immediately into a dreamless slumber. The start of one of the toughest weeks of my life was just ahead.

- 20 -

THE LONGEST DAY OF SCHOOL EVER

On Monday morning, the teams assembled in the gymnasium before school. Coach Neville stood in front of us, looking tired and worn.

"You know, of course, what has happened," he began. "I do have more information now, and the news is not good. As many of you know, the accident was a hit-and-run. The police have now found the car that pushed Theo's car off the road and into the tree. Unfortunately, it belongs to another student here at the high school, Richard Del Toro."

That set up quite a buzzing in the room.

"Apparently, he and three of his friends were out joyriding, and for some reason they ran Theo and Skip off the road. Richard has been arrested and his car impounded, and they're still looking for Harold Barnes and Vincent Arilio, two of the boys who were in the car with him. The fourth young man, Joey Amonte, is also being held in jail on pending charges."

Harold, Joey, and Vinnie were all members of Del Toro's Bulls. I turned to Jorge, sitting next to me, and whispered that they had all been part of the group that had been hassling his sister and him that day. He just nodded.

"Quiet, now," said Mr. Neville. "Dr. Osgood, our principal, will make an announcement during first period about the

145

accident. He will also announce that school will be closed tomorrow in deference to Skip and his family, so that his friends and teammates can attend his funeral. I will expect to see all of you there. In the meantime, I've got these to hand out."

He reached down and pulled out a box from underneath the table and opened it up. He pulled out black armbands and started handing them out.

"As a show of team solidarity, I would like you all to wear these today. This is a very difficult time for all of us, gentlemen. In light of the events of the weekend, I think we should consider dedicating the balance of this season to Skip and Theo."

There was a murmur of assent from all of us. Nobody on the team even considered disagreeing with the sentiment. Coach Neville asked for a show of hands, and it was a unanimous decision that we would play the rest of our games for our two fallen players.

"Thank you, gentlemen," said Coach. "I'll see you after school for a short practice session."

We all slipped the armbands over our sleeves, and the team quietly shuffled out of the gym to their first period classes.

"Mr. Porter, Mr. Johnson, could I see you two for a moment?" Coach tapped me on the shoulder and caught Eric by the sleeve as we were about to leave.

"Sure, Coach. What's up?" Eric asked after everybody else had left.

Mr. Neville took off his glasses and started absentmindedly wiping the lenses on his tie.

"Despite the circumstances," he began, "I've still got to think about the team and how to salvage this season. I've lost my top two players, and I have to make some fast changes." He paused to collect his thoughts and put his glasses back on. He looked hard at Eric and me.

"You two have been in my thoughts lately. Eric, your speed on the field is exceptional, and we're going to need speed. But your ball handling could use some help. I would like you to work before school with a friend of mine, if you're willing. He might be able to jump-start your skills in a short amount of time."

Eric didn't look too happy about the prospect of getting to school early just to learn how to juggle a soccer ball better, but he wisely kept his mouth shut for the moment.

"In return," continued Coach, "I will be willing to offer you a starting position in the offense, to replace Theo. But," he added, before Eric could answer, "the one depends on the other. If you aren't willing to improve your soccer skills, you won't get the starting nod. Think about it for a moment," he said, and turned to me.

"Sean, Skip and I had been grooming you to take his position after this season. Unfortunately, circumstances have forced me to throw you into the fire. I need you before we were planning. Can you play the right defensive spot, knowing you're going to be trying to fill some big shoes?"

I didn't have to think twice about it. "Yes, sir. I'll do my best."

"I know you will, Sean. I just wish you weren't playing under these conditions." He nodded as if making up his mind about something.

He walked us both to the door of the gym just as the first bell of the day started ringing.

"I'll see you both after school," he said. "We will be talking with the grief counselors today instead of running. This team, this school, has suffered a devastating loss. We can't just pretend the hurt will go away; we need to talk to each other. Everybody needs to talk to a friend, and we are all friends on this team." He put an arm around each of our shoulders as if he was trying to protect us from the ravages of the real world. In retrospect, I guess that's exactly what he was trying to do, in his way.

"Eric, let me know what you want to do by the start of practice on Wednesday, please. Your decision affects what I will have to do on the whole left side of our team," he said as he opened the door for us.

"I don't need to wait, Coach. Let me know when you want us to start, and I'll be here to work on my game. You can count on me." Eric had that same determined look on his face I had seen during our last club game. It now felt like a lifetime ago.

"Okay, good. Then I will let the rest of the team know about our realignment. Thanks, boys. I knew I could rely on both of you. Just remember this: play the game according to the rules, but play your own game. Both things are possible."

He patted us each on the shoulder and then gently pushed us out into the hall and on our way to our first classes of the day.

As I walked down the crowded halls toward my first period class, it was eerily quiet. Everyone was closed in on his or her own thoughts, and those few clusters of kids who were gathered together were talking in hushed tones, as if any undue noise would awaken the sleeping monsters. I got to my classroom just as the final bell rang and sat down at my desk next to Jake, who just nodded to me in greeting, sympathetic to the mood of everyone around him.

The intercom speaker in the corner of the room crackled as the last dying reverberations of the bell were fading, and Dr. Osgood's voice came over the intercom.

"May I have your attention please." He paused as usual, probably to wait for the hubbub in the classrooms to die down. Today that wasn't necessary. "As you are no doubt aware, a tragedy has visited us this weekend. Senior class members Charles 'Skip' Horvath and Theodore Jameson were involved in a traffic accident on Saturday evening. Theo Jameson is in the hospital in serious condition, but is improving. Sadly, Skip Horvath was pronounced dead on arrival. I have spoken to both families and have extended the school's sympathies and best wishes.

"I have arranged to have grief counselors available all day in the nurse's office. Any student who feels the need to talk to a counselor may do so at any time. Teachers have been instructed to write hall passes to any student who wishes to speak to a counselor during their classes.

"Our school will be closed all day tomorrow so that students and faculty can attend Skip Horvath's funeral. Information concerning visitation hours and time and location of the services for Skip will be available by the fifth period and may be picked up in any classroom. School will resume as scheduled on Wednesday morning.

"I am truly sorry I had to interrupt your classes this morning with such terrible news. Thank you for your attention."

For the first time I could recall, there was complete silence both during and after Dr. Osgood's announcement. Usually, announcements concerned only a small group of students or teachers, and everybody else took the opportunity to visit with friends sitting nearby, but today's broadcast was different. The silence was so different than usual, a few kids were looking around bewilderedly, as if they were trying to figure out what was wrong.

All day long, each class was the same. Teachers set aside their lesson plans for the day and tried to get their classes to talk about the accident. Richie Del Toro's involvement was well-known by lunchtime, and none of his Bulls were in attendance that day, probably a good idea from a self-preservation standpoint.

By the end of the school day, everybody I saw looked the same way I felt—ground down until there was nothing left was how Josh put it. Even Toby Mueller, the school's practical joker, was subdued and distracted.

As promised, Coach had a couple of counselors with him when we filed in to the locker room. It was uncharacteristically quiet in there, a not-very-comfortable silence as we walked through the locker room and into one of the classrooms. Everybody seemed to choose their closest friends on the team to sit beside, so it was natural for Eric and me to flop down in chairs together in the same row. He glanced over at me, and I nodded in silent acknowledgement of our connection.

We talked, encouraged by the counselors. We expressed a lot of anger, of course, but I was surprised at the turn the collective conversation took. Before long, the underclassmen were listening as the seniors, and occasionally the juniors on the team, began telling stories about Skip, Theo, and the team. Before long, the stories focused on fun, with plenty of humor, lots of chuckles, and a few tears that caught us unawares at times. I have since learned to call such experiences cathartic, but at the time I was a little surprised at the progression. In retrospect, even at fifteen, I saw the value in turning the tragic experience into something else—something to be learned from, something to be held onto. We all might have treated it differently, but in the end we all felt better for it.

Before he dismissed us for the afternoon, Coach Neville asked us to meet as a team at the church before the service, so we could all sit together.

By the time I got home and sat down to dinner, I didn't want to eat. I was exhausted, the emotions of the day draining me physically, and I felt like I had just lived through the longest day of school ever.

- 21 -

AFFIRMATION OF LIFE

Skip's funeral was scheduled for eleven o'clock on Tuesday morning. My brother Mike, who was living at home while he was attending our local junior college as a freshman, took the day off from his classes to attend the services since he knew a lot of the seniors. He drove me to the church, and we got there a few minutes early so I could meet up with the team.

Coach Neville was gathering everybody just outside, and I walked over to join my teammates. I saw Molly, Heather, and Evan go into the church with a large group of seniors, and I gave Molly a quick, small wave.

"Is everybody here?" asked Coach. "Okay, good. Kevin and John, I have a request."

He looked for them among the teammates. Kevin Soranno was the senior midfielder who played directly in front of Skip on the field, and John Pennington was our starting keeper, also a senior.

"The Horvath family has requested that you two teammates serve as pallbearers today. Unless you have a strenuous objection, I have already accepted on your behalf." Coach looked first at John and then at Kevin, receiving each assent in turn. "All right, good. Someone will signal you when it is time for you to perform your duties. Shall we go in, gentlemen?"

With that, he led us all in to the sanctuary for the beginning of the service.

The next couple of hours were some of the saddest I have ever experienced. Skip's family was nearly inconsolable, and Maggie Wiggins, Skip's girlfriend, was a wreck. Most of the girls, and many of the boys, were sniffling and blowing their noses all during the service. Suddenly, we were not nearly so invulnerable as we were just a few days ago.

Toward the end of the church service, a representative from the funeral home quietly motioned the pallbearers forward, and my two teammates, along with Dr. Osgood, Skip's uncle, and two of his cousins, took their positions by the closed casket. At a signal from the funeral director, they grasped the shiny brass handles and wheeled Skip slowly down the center aisle of the church. When they reached the front steps, they lifted the casket up and carried it down the steps to the hearse.

John later told me he had never lifted anything quite so heavy as that casket and its contents. He also said that later, at the cemetery, when they lifted the casket back out of the hearse and onto a wheeled cart, it was not nearly so hard to do. With a catch in his throat and his eyes glistening, he related to me this first experience with such a burden. I have since found out first-hand that it is, indeed, as he described it: very surprising and startlingly difficult.

After the brief graveside service, the funeral director announced that the family had reserved a banquet hall in town for the afternoon and invited everyone to join them in a celebration of Skip's life. Lots of kids from school and many of the faculty I saw there were opting not to attend the luncheon, but the entire soccer team was planning on going. Michael agreed to drop me off at the banquet hall, and I said I would call him if I needed a ride home.

The mood at the banquet hall was noticeably lighter. It was crowded with Skip's extended family, with family friends and co-workers of his parents, and with the kids and teachers from school who were closest to Skip. There was a large buffet set up against one wall, and there were lots of tables to seat from four to twelve people. Coach Neville commandeered a couple of large tables for the team, and there was plenty of room for everybody.

We all got in line for the buffet. Skip's family had set up bulletin boards on tripods by the first table of salads and had pinned pictures of Skip, baby pictures and more recent ones all jumbled up, for people to look at while they were in line. We recognized a lot of us in the pictures and spent a good deal of time chatting with friends, pointing out pictures and remembering good times that had been recorded by somebody's camera. Molly came over to be with me in the line, and we grabbed plates as we got up to the first table. We made our way through the salad and bread table, to the entrees and vegetables, filling our plates. We carried our plates over to one of the team tables and sat down next to Eric and Keisha, Jorge and Kristina, and some of the other players.

The banquet hall had been reserved for the afternoon and evening, and since there was no real hurry to leave, we didn't. After everyone had eaten their fill, Coach Neville called an impromptu team meeting, inviting anybody in the room to sit in if they wished. Skip's parents were in a corner with consoling relatives, but his sister Ashley, a freshman at school and a good soccer player in her own right, sat in with us, looking for a comfortable place to feel like she belonged. Kevin and John scooted over and made room for her between them, and she pulled her chair in close to listen in on the meeting.

"Can I have everybody's attention, please?" called Coach Neville. He waited a moment for the kids at the tables around him to quiet down. "Thank you. Okay, as you know, we have dedicated the rest of this season to Skip and to Theo. We still have some unfinished business, however. We have some adjustments we need to consider."

He glanced at Ashley. "Are you sure you'll be all right listening in?" he asked her gently. It was obvious she had shed many tears, and there were many more to come, but she nodded without hesitation.

"This team is important..." She wiped her eyes with a tissue as the tears threatened to overtake her, and then she sat up straighter. "Was important to my brother," she continued. "I want to be here, for him."

Coach Neville smiled at her, silently acknowledging her strength. "All right, let's talk for a moment about our lineup. Trent," he said, turning to Trent Abbott, a junior who started as our left midfielder, "I would like you to start in Theo's forward spot." Trent nodded, pleased to be moving into more of a scorer's position. "I would also like to insert Mr. Eric Johnson into Trent's former midfield slot."

The team's collective eyes turned to our table and to Eric, who seemed to be blushing under his dark skin. Keisha was smiling broadly, patting him on the back. There was a smattering of congratulations from all around toward him, and then everybody quieted down. There was still one position, Skip's, to be covered.

"Starting at the right defensive position," said Coach quietly, "will be Sean Porter."

There was another smattering of agreement, mostly led by Eric and Molly, and I felt a lot of hands patting me on the back and shoulder. The announcement was not a real big surprise to anybody on the team, but it really cemented the fact that we didn't have Skip to rely on in the backfield anymore.

"Ladies and gentlemen, please," called out Coach one more time. The shuffling of chairs and the clatter of glasses and cups stopped once again. "I would like to remind you all that we still have half our regular season to go. And, if we are very fortunate, we will advance into the sectionals and the playoffs. We have a lot of hard work ahead of us, and there will be a lot of adjustments in our game that we will need to work hard on, but I know that you all will pull together to make this team work." He lifted his glass of water and held it out in front of him. "To Skip, and to Theo."

We all raised our water glasses.

"To Skip. To Theo." We all took a sip and sealed our bargain.

Coach Neville closed our team meeting, put on his coat, and stopped by to pay his respects to the Horvath family before leaving. A few others left, but a lot of Skip's friends decided to stay, taking advantage of a homework-free, practice-free day.

A little later, small triangles of sandwiches, snacks, and cookies were brought out and set up on the buffet tables for those of us who had stayed. There was a small garden area out the back of the banquet hall, with a gazebo tucked in a corner, half hidden from the sliding doors of the patio area. Molly and I grabbed a plateful of food and slipped through the door to watch the sun go down from the patio. We brought out our jackets, since it had cooled off quite a bit as soon as the sun started getting low in the afternoon sky.

As we were sitting at one of the garden tables on the patio, I thought I heard voices coming from the area of the gazebo, though in the gloom I couldn't see anyone back there. I got up and tiptoed down toward the back, trying to be quiet and careful in the dark.

As I got closer, the sounds separated into two voices. Eric and Keisha were sitting on a bench inside the gazebo, away from the glare of the lights from the patio door. They had their arms wrapped around each other as they talked softly, their hands busily moving under their unbuttoned coats. I ducked back behind a tree and made my way back to the patio, where Molly was waiting. I put my finger to my lips and motioned for her to follow me.

"What?" she said a little impatiently.

"Shhhh!" I whispered. I motioned for her to follow me down toward the gazebo. She sighed dramatically but came down behind me, back to the cover of the tree. As we got closer, we could hear the tiny movements betraying the couple. I exaggeratedly tiptoed forward so Molly would get the idea to be very quiet, and pointed toward the dark area where Eric and Keisha could just be seen. Molly placed her hands on my shoulder and peered around me as I crouched down.

There was no talking going on now. Eric had Keisha wrapped up and pulled to him, his arms inside her coat. They were engaged in a hard, open-mouthed kiss. From the movement of their mouths and cheeks, it was plain that their tongues were fully engaged with each other.

They stayed together for several minutes, enjoying their time in the gazebo, thinking they were alone. Eric whispered something, and I heard a low, throaty giggle come from Keisha.

Molly and I backed out of view silently, back to behind the tree. We stayed off to the side of the garden area, out of sight of the gazebo. Molly held my arm close to her as we huddled together in the cold.

"Wow," she whispered. "That was really something."

"Yeah," I answered quietly.

"That's kind of taking a chance on getting caught, though," she said.

"Maybe it adds to the thrill," I suggested.

She looked at me for a moment. In the dim light, I couldn't read the expression on her face.

Just then, we heard Eric and Keisha walking back toward the banquet hall, arm in arm, talking quietly to each other. Just before they slid the door back and stepped through, I heard Keisha's tinkling laughter as Eric teased her about something.

A moment later, Molly was dragging me by the arm toward the gazebo.

"Come on," she whispered. "It's our turn."

AFFIRMATION OF LIFE

Those words were enough to get my blood racing, and I stumbled after her, suddenly aware of a tightness in my dress pants. She dragged me by the hand up the three steps into the gazebo and into the corner so recently occupied by our friends. She pushed me down onto the bench and sat on my lap, grabbing the sides of my head and pulling herself down to kiss me. Her mouth immediately opened, her tongue darting out to challenge and joust, and she wrapped her arms around my neck.

We mimicked the actions of our friends, holding each other in the chilly night air. But it was cold out. We settled back down on the bench, arms around each other, silent in the dark together for a few moments, content to put up with the temperature for a chance to gaze at the evening sky together. Her head was resting on my shoulder, comfortable and comforting. I was as happy as the day would allow me to be.

At the time, I thought it was kind of weird that we were so intent on being out there with each other on such an occasion and in such a place. However, the advantage of time has since given me a more proper sense of the motivations behind not only our actions, but the course we observed Eric and Keisha traveling.

It was, of course, the affirmation of life, even in the shadow of the certainty of death in which we had so recently walked.

- 22 -

BUSTED

The next day, our teachers really made up for two lost days of lessons by piling on the homework. It was close to dinnertime in the Porter household. I was upstairs in my room, trying to comprehend my algebra, without much success. My mom was in the kitchen getting dinner ready, when I heard her calling up the stairs to me.

"Sean!"

I opened the door to my room to answer her.

"Yeah?"

"Sean, I've got to run to the grocery store for a moment. Your dad should be home in just a few minutes, so we'll plan on eating in about a half an hour. Okay?"

"Okay, Mom. I'll just be up here studying until then." I closed the door and sat back down on the floor. *I'm never going to understand these formulas!*

A few minutes later, I heard footsteps on the stairs but didn't think anything of it until the door to my room opened. I was surprised when I looked up to see Molly standing there. She was still wearing her sweats from cheerleading practice, her hair tied back in a loose ponytail.

"Hey, Mol. What are you doing here?"

She closed the door and sat down beside me.

"I just saw your mom leaving in the car. Isn't anybody else home?" she asked.

"Nope, just me. And now you."

"Good," she growled as she jumped up and wrestled me to the floor.

"What are you doing?" I asked, taken by surprise. I was pretty much caught. She had my wrists trapped beside my head, and her weight was pressed onto her hands as they held my arms down. I probably could have bucked her off, but I had the feeling that would have spoiled the fun for her.

"Oh, I just thought I'd come over and jump on you this afternoon," she said. "I missed you today. I was thinking about you last night and all day today in class. I got all itchy and stuff, so I decided to come over to see if you knew how to scratch my itch."

"Mol, it's really not a good time..." She got a dangerous gleam in her eye when I said that, so I decided not to continue with that line of reasoning.

"I'm going to let go of your left arm," she said. "Don't try anything funny. Just reach into my jacket pocket and get your present out."

"A present? What for?" *Uh-oh, did I miss a special day or something?* Now I was worried.

"For just because. Go ahead, Sean." She let go of my left arm. I slowly reached up and wiggled my hand into the pocket of her jacket. There was a paper bag with something in it in there. I pulled it out.

"Here," she said, reaching for the bag. "I'll hold the sack; you reach in and get your present."

I reached in and pulled out a familiar box.

"Condoms!" I exclaimed. "Molly, you are full of surprises sometimes. Where did you get these?"

She let go of me altogether and grabbed the box.

"I stopped at the drugstore on my way here. I knew you had to be just about out of them, and I need to replace the ones I stole from Josh. So I bought them. No big deal. Besides, I want you to always have one with you. We can't afford to be caught without one when we might need one, you know?" She ripped open the box and pulled out a handful of packets and stuffed them into the paper bag. She wadded up the top of the bag and shoved it into her jacket pocket. "You take the rest of these and keep them safe."

She stood up to let me get up and stash my supply. When she saw where I was keeping them, she laughed.

"Your sock drawer? You, too? Not very original, Porter."

"Hey, when I see a good idea, I'm not afraid to rip it off," I retorted.

"Hmmmm...speaking of ripping it off," she said quietly as she moved up behind me and put her arms around my waist. She hooked her thumbs in my belt and drummed her fingers lightly, setting up a sudden throbbing in my head.

My mom's voice came floating up the stairs. Molly had me so distracted, I hadn't even heard her come home.

"Sean! Dinnertime!"

"Sean! Dinnertime!" Molly echoed softly in my ear, her fingers keeping up their insistent drumming.

"Okay, Mom; be right down!" I shouted out. I turned around, still encased in her arms. "I've got to get downstairs, Molly. What are you going to do?"

"Oh," she said nonchalantly, "they don't know I'm here, so I guess I'll just stay up here in your room until you're done eating."

"Okay," I said, a little flustered. "I'll try to hurry."

"You do that, Sean Porter," she said. She grabbed my hand and guided it up under her sweatshirt to her bare breast. "You hurry back," she said.

Now I was a complete wreck. I stumbled to the door, dimly aware that I was walking a little funny, thanks to Molly. *What the hell is going on here?*

Molly sat on the edge of my bed. "Go on; dinner's waiting," she said with a smile. She made a little shooing motion with one hand.

I went out into the hall and closed the door. I was tempted to turn back and make sure she was really there and not just a product of my fevered imagination, but I didn't. I started down the stairs to the kitchen.

Everyone was sitting down at the table when I walked in. Mom had all the food out, Dad was just reaching for the platter of vegetables, and my two brothers were already digging in. I sat down in a kind of a daze.

"Hiya, Sean. Studying hard?" Stephen said innocently. I looked over at him, but he already had his head back down, shoveling in food as fast as he could. He was twelve years old and starting to really grow fast.

I grabbed a piece of fried chicken and started eating it distractedly.

"Uh…will you excuse me for just a moment?" I didn't wait for an answer but instead got up from the table and ran upstairs to my room and opened the door.

No Molly. Maybe I did imagine it.

Just as I was turning to go back downstairs, I heard a slight noise from my closet. I walked over and peered in. Molly was there. She had removed her sweatshirt and taken one of my dress shirts off a hanger and put it on. She had the tails tied around her bare waist, and the shirt was unbuttoned, showing a healthy gap of bare skin from her throat almost to her belly button. She just looked at me quizzically, one eyebrow raised, not saying a word.

I just shook my head, turned around, and went back downstairs. I wasn't imagining it.

"Is everything all right, Sean?" My mother sounded concerned.

"Everything's fine," I said. "I...I just wanted to make sure I turned off my tape player."

I made it through dinner in nearly record time and excused myself from the table.

"The teachers really loaded it on me today, I'm afraid. I'll be up doing homework the rest of the night," I told my dad.

I walked upstairs and knocked softly on my door before opening it. Molly was back in the closet and peeked out when she heard the door close. She still had on my shirt but had taken off her shoes and socks and her sweatpants, leaving only her panties on. When she saw I was alone, she jumped up into my arms. I automatically caught her, and she put her arms around my neck and kissed me as I held her. I backed up until my knees hit the bed, and I sat down, with Molly still in my lap. She reached down and undid the knot holding the shirt together, and the two halves parted, revealing her body to me, in all its glory.

Again, she took one of my hands and placed it on her breast, pressing it there before dropping her hands down to my lap to work at my belt. I felt her nipple expand as I held her. Almost without volition, I squeezed and kneaded the pliant flesh.

It took a few minutes for my brain to kick in.

"We need to get off the bed so it doesn't make noise," I suggested. I slid down and off the edge, down to the floor, and Molly followed me.

She was energetic, and it was all I could do to keep her quiet so my family would not know what was going on right over their heads. It was an exhausting exercise. Afterwards, we were lying together on the floor, waiting for our heart rates to stabilize. My brain, disconnected from rational thought long ago, tried to get back on track.

"How did you manage to get here?" I asked. There was a vague thought that she had accomplished some sort of deviltry to show up at my house tonight.

"I told my mom I would be studying and eating dinner at Tessa's tonight. Tessa said she'd cover for me."

"Oh." That was about the limit of information I was able to handle for the moment.

Something else occurred to me. "How are we going to get you out of here?" I asked, more talking to myself than to Molly.

She sighed contentedly. "I didn't think that far ahead. It's so comfortable here, maybe I'll just stay." She snuggled closer to me.

I sat up, suddenly aware of where we were and the precarious position we were in.

"Get up, Mol. We've got to get you out of here."

She gave me a sour look but got up and stumbled to the closet to gather up her clothes. I threw my shirt and jeans on and slowly cracked open the door to see what was going on in the world. I could hear the television on downstairs in the family room, my mother and father laughing at some antic being pulled on a comedy they were watching. There was no sign of either of my brothers.

"Come on," I whispered, motioning to her to follow me.

We snuck down the stairs and into the kitchen without being seen. I opened the back door and let her out, thinking that we had escaped. As I was closing the door, though, I heard the front doorbell ring. I walked to the sink and got a glass of water, wondering how I was ever going to get my homework done, when I heard some familiar voices from the living room. I headed toward the front of the house.

Mr. and Mrs. Lehigh were there, talking to my parents. Standing between them was Jake, who looked like he wanted to be anywhere but there. I had a sinking feeling in my stomach when

I saw them. Jake looked up, saw me, and turned away sheepishly. *A bad sign,* I said to myself. *A very bad sign.*

"Sean?" my dad called over to me. "Perhaps you should come over here and hear what Jake's parents have to say, son."

Well, the short form was that Jake and Jaimie got caught with their pants down, literally. In a panic, Jake blurted out to his parents that he had gotten condoms from me, which triggered a memory in Mr. Lehigh's brain, namely seeing me and Josh in his store, picking out rubbers with his help.

"Is this true, Sean?" my mother asked.

"Well...um...yeah, I guess it is," I admitted. "I did go there with Josh, but I was just trying to provide a little moral support for him. It's not like I need them for myself," I bluffed.

"Is that so?" asked my dad. "Maybe we should be calling the O'Tooles and asking them, too." I had a bad feeling that my bluff was about to be called. "I assume you still have that box somewhere in your room, Sean. Bring it down and let's see it."

I was about to protest, about to pull out all the stops about trust and constitutional rights, and why do you think I'm lying to you? But I saw by the look on his face that I wasn't going to win any of those arguments. Muttering under my breath a blue streak along the lines of what I was going to do to Jake once we both got out of our respective jails, I trudged upstairs to try to salvage the situation.

As I opened my door, I remembered. *Molly!* She had left me with nearly a full box of condoms, just that evening. I yanked open my socks drawer and pulled apart my special pair of soccer socks. A dozen foil packets spilled to the floor. *I'm saved!*

I scooped them up and ran downstairs. I held out my cupped hands in triumph, showing the dozen condoms to the Lehighs and my parents. *Accuse me, will you?* I thought to myself.

Mr. Lehigh bent down to look at what I held out. "Interesting. But these are two different types," he said, picking out two similar but definitely different condoms and holding them up for everyone to see.

I looked at Jake. *We're both busted*, he seemed to say to me. Unfortunately, I could only silently agree with him.

Half an hour later, the Lehighs were finally walking down the sidewalk to their car, and I was facing the music in front of my parents.

"I'm very disappointed in you, Sean," said my mother. "I thought we had raised you better than this."

I kept my mouth shut, hoping that my silence would be taken as contrition.

My father was also unhappy with me. "I have to admit I'm a little torn here, Sean. On the one hand, I'm glad to see you are doing your part in taking responsibility for preventing unwanted pregnancies. On the other hand, fifteen is too young to be engaging in sexual practices, no matter how mature you think you are." He sighed. "You've given us no choice, son," said my dad. "I think you've set a new record in this household tonight. None of your brothers has ever gotten anywhere near being grounded for life before. But you've managed it. From now on, until further notice, you are to come straight home from soccer practice. You will not leave the house except in the company of one of us, and you will not have any friends over without getting our permission first. And, especially, you will not be here with any girls, including Molly O'Toole. Am I clear?"

"Yes, sir." I tried to sound as sincere as I could. At that point, I fervently hoped Molly didn't try sneaking into our house again.

My precious stash of condoms was confiscated, and I was sent to my room under threat of doom if I so much as sneezed wrong for the foreseeable future. I was under house arrest, and I had no idea how long my sentence was going to be.

- 23 -

CONTAINED GRIEF AND ANGER

The arrangement my parents worked out was that my dad was going to drop me off at school in the mornings and my mom would be waiting for me at the end of soccer practice in the afternoons. I climbed out of my father's car the next morning and walked dejectedly into school, about five minutes before my first class was to start.

I sat down next to Jake and growled at him.

"Thanks a lot, pal. 'I won't get caught. You can count on me,'" I mimicked him derisively. "I guess I know now what your word is worth," I added disgustedly.

"Look, Sean, I'm really sorry. But we really got caught red-handed. When Jaimie's dad found out about it, he was really pissed, you know? Going on and on about how I stole his daughter's innocence, I could go to jail for rape, all sorts of shit like that. I panicked, okay?"

"That's great to know, Jake. That makes me feel a whole lot better."

"Yeah, well, you at least didn't have to face Mr. Jacks. He was so mad, I didn't think I was going to leave the room alive." He seemed to shiver at the memory. "You know, Jaimie's sister, Tara, has been spying on us, I think. She may have been the one who ratted on us."

"Why would she do that, Jake?"

"Ah, hell, I don't know. She's really been acting weird lately. Remember the picnic? She hasn't gotten any easier to be around."

"That's just too freaky. Okay, Jake, maybe I can understand why it happened. But that doesn't make my situation any better."

"Yeah, I know. All I can say is that I'm sorry, Sean. I really am."

✿ ✿ ✿

I quietly told Molly what happened when I saw her at lunch. She was very upset that she was only seconds away from being caught in my room, but that feeling passed quickly. She got a bright look in her eyes.

"You want to live dangerously, Sean Porter?" she whispered. "I might have another plan to come visit you one of these nights."

I nearly choked on my soda. "Christ, no, Molly! Are you nuts?"

She chuckled. "Maybe I am," she murmured. "Maybe I just am."

✿ ✿ ✿

True to her word, my mom was there to pick me up after soccer practice. It was a cold, silent ride home, and a cold and silent evening spent in my room, catching up on schoolwork. No radio, no stereo, no noise was allowed during my incarceration. I went to bed early, a little scared that I would hear the door creak open and see Molly standing there. But fortunately, nothing of the kind happened.

CONTAINED GRIEF AND ANGER

The rest of the week was more of the same. I talked to my friends at school but had no contact with anyone after I got home. It helped that I was trying to work myself into exhaustion during soccer practice. Coach Neville had knowingly put a lot of pressure on me as Skip's replacement, and I wanted to do the best I could. I was messing up a lot during practice, and it was making some of my teammates nervous and a little mad. My attitude was that I could mess up during practice as long as I played well in the game.

The only truly bright spot to the week was on Thursday afternoon, when Coach Neville announced to the team that Theo had been brought successfully out of his coma and was awake and alert. That news cheered everybody up considerably.

Finally it was Friday, game day. This was to be our first game without Skip and Theo, and it was a home game. There was a general announcement at school in the morning, asking the student body to support the team. We were expecting standing room only at the game.

I was sitting in the locker room with my teammates, half listening while Coach was giving us some last-minute instructions. I was nervous as hell.

"Now, remember, people, this team will probably test our right side early on." Coach Neville looked over in my direction. "So, Sean and Kevin, be ready for anything. Sean, you're an unknown quantity to our opponents, so don't be afraid to show them what you're made of. Kevin should be able to head off some of their attacks, and our sweeper and keeper will be watching out, so just go out and play your game."

I nodded and looked over at Kevin. He was sitting with his head down, lost in his own thoughts. *Thinking about Skip and Theo, no doubt.*

Finally, it was time to take the field. We trotted out and began our warm-ups. When the starting lineups were announced and my name was called, it startled me. I was still half expecting Skip to show up and take his accustomed spot on the field.

We took our positions, and the partisan crowd in the stands gave us a standing ovation as the referee blew his whistle to start the game. It was a great show of support for the team, and we appreciated it.

Just as Coach Neville had predicted, the Hamersville Lions did try our right side at the first opportunity. Now that the game was underway, my nervousness was gone and I could see how their plays were designed. I'd been in baseball games when the ball seemed like it was the size of a grapefruit and I couldn't miss hitting it. For me, this game was just like that. The soccer ball looked to be about the size and weight of a basketball, moving in slow motion across the field. I seemed to have plenty of time to get into position to make a play on it without any interference from the Hamersville midfielders or forwards. I was trapping the ball and moving it up at will, dribbling forward or passing it up to Kevin whenever the Lions worked it over into my area. Three times, then four, they deliberately tested our defense on my side. Each time, they were soundly rebuffed. Finally, they gave up on the maneuver and tried our left side. They were no more successful there, either, and by the halftime whistle, we were up 2–0.

The first forty-five minutes of the game went by incredibly fast. I was still feeling very energetic, almost hyper. I trotted over to the sidelines with the rest of the team, grabbed a paper cup of water, and poured it over my head. I reached for another one to drink. Kevin was there, handing me a cup, a huge smile on his face.

"You're playing great, Sean. I don't think they're going to be trying to get by you anymore this game."

John Pennington chimed in. "That first steal was incredible, Sean. Way to go. I guess I don't have to worry about that side of the field after all, do I?"

"Oh, yes, you do," I said. "It's probably just beginner's luck, so don't go falling asleep on me, okay?"

"All right," said John with a laugh. "You just keep playing the way you're playing, though, and we'll be fine back there with nothing to do."

I was jittery with all the adrenaline pumping through me, anxious to get back on the field. I hopped up and down, pacing the sidelines, wishing the whistle would blow soon so I could start running again. I looked down the bench and saw Coach and Trent leaning over a dismayed Eric, both of them talking intently to him at the same time. Eric looked from one to the other, nodding at each of them in turn, a towel over his head and an untouched cup of water in his hand. I didn't notice anything in the first half that should have caused them to be yammering at him. Then again, I was so intent on protecting my own turf that once the ball left my area, I just tracked it down the field instead of paying attention to who was doing what with it.

The ref blew his whistle to start the second half, and we all trotted out to take our positions.

The full forty-five minutes of the second half seemed to move in some sort of dreamlike state. On the one hand, the time flew by so quickly, it seemed like I was out on the field for about seven or eight minutes. On the other hand, it was like everything was moving in slow motion. I had plenty of time to get to the ball, and each time I would pass long, the ball would arc majestically through the crystal air, taking its sweet time to land just where I wanted it to land. It was a magical, very scary evening, full of contained grief and anger. Grief conflicted with awe at being able to play this game, contradicting the raw fact of our fallen teammates, and sparked a hidden well of anger at Richie Del Toro and his band of cruel idiots. I felt it in me, and I thought I could detect it in my comrades on the pitch. It heightened my senses, until I felt I was balanced on a steady wind, coursing through the air and watching everything unfold from high above. I rode the feeling throughout the second half, letting my emotions manifest themselves in my play. At the end of it all, in a denouement that was only reluctantly admitted, we won the game by a score of 4–1.

After the game, as I was sitting on the bench with the rest of the team, my adrenal glands finally shut down and out of production. I went into a severe case of the shivers, so bad that I could hardly stand. Eric, Jorge, and Kevin helped me back to the locker rooms and sat me down on a bench. Eric ran out to get my father, who came in to find me almost comatose, shivering and exhausted from the emotions of the game. My dad took one arm, and Eric took the other. They guided me out into the parking lot and into the back seat of my dad's car. Once there, I finally just collapsed and pretty much passed out.

I vaguely remember the car doors slamming, the car starting up, and the tires crunching through the gravel of the back parking lot. My mom and my dad were talking about me on the way home, but it all sounded like a huge hive of bees in the car, buzzing and hovering around my ears. I couldn't make out a word they were saying, and I just didn't have the energy to care as I lay there, mostly unconscious and completely wasted.

✿ ✿ ✿

The next week was a very strange combination of sadness, euphoria, and grinding boredom. Our tiny local paper had covered the game, and the *Metro Times* picked up their report on Monday for their High School Sports section. The human-interest side of the story, about our first game after Skip and Theo's accident, was the focus, but they did also have a write-up about the game itself. Eric Johnson was singled out as "the new speedster in the midfield" and praised for scoring a goal on his first start. They also painted an entirely too flattering picture of our defense in general, and Sean Porter specifically, bantering about phrases such as "playing exceptionally well under extraordinary circumstances," and "a surprisingly volatile defensive style," whatever that meant. I thought that if they had seen me in my dad's car after the game, they probably wouldn't have been so complimentary.

Coach Neville announced to the team that Theo was having difficulty coping with the results of the accident. He suggested that we make an effort to stop by the hospital and visit with him sometime that week to try to cheer him up.

Poo-Poo was arraigned on manslaughter charges and was still in the local jail. The others who were with him were released on bond. The rest of the Bulls had changed their ways in light of the troubles facing their leader and friends. They were back in school, but they were making an effort to separate themselves from Poo-Poo. They were sporting a new look, dressing preppy in new clothes, with their hair cut and clean, and, in general, keeping a very low profile. It didn't work very well. They were still hazed and harassed for their association with Del Toro.

Another interesting rumor surfaced during that week. It seemed that Allison Moseley, the buxom ditz who was hanging on Theo at the pool party, was the object of Vinnie Arilio's affections. He was so enraged when he heard about Theo going out with her that he may have convinced Richie to go looking for Theo that Saturday night.

I was still under house arrest myself. Dad dropped me off in the mornings, but by the end of the week, he was getting pretty irritated with the routine. Mom picked me up in the afternoons. I spent the rest of the time at home, either up in my room doing homework or watching TV with the rest of the family. Fortunately, Molly's better instincts kept her from trying to sneak into my house. I missed kissing and holding her, though, and I knew she was missing me, too. On Wednesday at lunch, she told me just how much she missed being with me.

We were sitting together at one of the long tables in the cafeteria with a bunch of other kids. Like cafeterias everywhere, it was noisy and boisterous in the large room. Molly was wearing a plaid wraparound skirt with a big brass safety pin as an accessory holding it together, and a fuzzy sweater that fit her very well. She leaned over to whisper in my ear.

"I really miss you, Sean," she breathily said.

"I miss you, too, Mol," I answered.

"No, Sean," she said. "I really, really miss you." She flicked her tongue against my earlobe.

I flinched back. "What are you doing, Molly?!" *God, not here in the lunchroom,* I thought, panic-stricken.

She grabbed my hand and pressed it to the inside of her thigh, under her skirt. She kept her hand on top of mine to keep me from jerking it away.

"Trying to let you know how much I miss you, silly." She tried to move my hand up farther on her leg, but I was nearly frantic in my efforts to look calm while I tried to yank away from her. As it was, I wasn't going to be able to stand up anytime soon because of her.

She nipped my earlobe between her teeth and bit down lightly, sending shivers through me. "What if I told you I wasn't wearing any panties?" she whispered. That sent even more shivers through me. She grabbed my wrist with both hands and pulled my hand up farther on her leg. I felt the bottom seam of her underwear as my fingers brushed against her. I sighed, but whether in relief or in frustration, I wasn't sure.

She chuckled throatily as she let me go, her skirt falling back in place under the table. "You're just too easy to flip up, Porter," she said. She turned back to her lunch as if nothing had happened.

"Molly, I can't help it if I'm grounded. I wish I wasn't too, you know."

"Well, you'd better figure something out soon. I'm really getting...itchy." She wadded up her wrappers and stood up to leave. She gave me a wink and sauntered away, hips swishing her skirt from side to side, knowing I was watching her.

CONTAINED GRIEF AND ANGER

I groaned in frustration. I was done with lunch but I still couldn't stand up without embarrassing myself. *Damn her,* I thought to myself. She was really going to get me in hot water some day.

☆ ☆ ☆

Our game that Friday was an away game. We took a school bus to Rockton Heights High School while a convoy of kids from school followed us to the game. This game was against our toughest rival in our conference, and we were all worked up about coming away with a victory. There were only three more games in the regular season, and we wanted to be playing at our peak for the playoffs. This game would be a good test for our realigned left offense, as well as our right defense.

Practice this past week had gone well, especially after our win the week before. We worked on plays and made mistakes galore, knowing that it was all a learning process for us as a team. I hoped that the mistakes would be left on the practice field again.

The game was surprisingly emotional. Rockton Heights asked their fans to give a moment of silence in honor of our fallen players. Their entire team came over to our bench and shook our hands before the starting lineups were announced. It brought a lump to my throat, and I didn't think I was the only member of our team who suddenly had blurry vision.

The game was every bit as tough as it was hyped to be. Their defense was strong, and they had one of the best forwards in the conference on their team, playing in the middle. Their left forward, playing on my side of the field, was a cagey senior who was not going to let a sophomore like me get the best of him. He was trash-talking at me through the first half, taunting and daring me to challenge him, both on and off the ball. Just before the end of the half, he took a give-and-go from his midfielder and tried to end-run me, but I slid down and managed to knock the ball out of bounds. On the throw-in, Rockton sent most of their players up, leaving only two defenders and the keeper back, trying to make the most of a scoring opportunity. I saw that they were going to throw across to the middle, so I signaled to Kevin to switch, and I raced over just as the throw was made. I got there in time to step in front of the intended receiver, trapped the ball, and headed upfield as fast as I could go. Their defensive midfielder angled over to cut me off, but I saw Eric streaking down the middle, wide open and calling for the ball. I passed it over to him and took off past the startled defender into the open space on the side. Eric trapped the ball, took two steps with it, and rocketed it back over to me. The last defender was caught between us, undecided about who he should cover. His momentary hesitation cost him. He ran toward me, leaving Eric unguarded, so I crossed the ball. Eric then powered it into the back of the net unobstructed. I ran over to him, yelling and screaming, and he jumped up into me, knocking us both to the ground. We got up just as the rest of the team rushed over to us to congratulate us on the goal. We trotted back over to our side for the kickoff. A moment later, the whistle ending the first half sounded.

The second half didn't go quite so well. Rockton made some adjustments to their game and scored two quick goals in succession before we could figure out their changes. The game seesawed back and forth from then on. First, Rockton took the offensive, and then we tried attacking. No one scored until a hand ball was called inside the box on one of their defensemen. We scored on the penalty kick, and time ran out in regulation with the score tied, 2–2.

We played a ten-minute overtime period scoreless and had one more overtime period to play in sudden death. If nobody scored, we would have to go to a penalty-kick shoot-off to decide the game. This was something neither side wanted.

We were on the bench, trying to catch our breath before the start of the second overtime period. The batteries were just about drained on all of the starters. Coach was considering substituting some of his players in favor of fresh legs. In the end, he opted for experience on the field at that crucial stage.

It was a mistake. Rockton did substitute, and their fresh players were able to control the ball while we were always one step behind because of our weariness. In the sixth minute, they had a corner kick against us, and they made the most of it. The kick came out to about eighteen meters from goal. Kevin made a play on the ball but stumbled as he went for it. The Rockton midfielder passed it back to the kicker on the side, angling out from the corner, who fired it in at the goal. He was mine to cover, and I didn't get to him in time. John tried diving for it but was a fraction too late. The ball hit the back of the net and made it flutter. Rockton had defeated us in the second overtime period, 3–2. We congratulated them and trudged over to the bench to pack up our gear. We wearily stripped off our spikes, sodden socks, and shin guards, and stuffed them into our bags.

We walked dejectedly to the bus and climbed on for the long ride back to our school. On the way back, as we were sucking down water from a big cooler set up in the back, Coach tried to put a positive spin on the game. He congratulated us on our play and admonished us that one loss so far in the season was of little consequence. We were all too tired to do anything but sit there and listen to his words wash over us, each drawn in on our own thoughts about where we might have done better during the game.

By the time we got back to the school, the caravan that had gone to support us at the game had already arrived. Instead of leaving to go home, nearly all the kids and parents had stayed in the school parking lot to wait for our bus. They were applauding and cheering us as we stumbled out and onto the blacktop of the parking lot. To a man, the entire team was surprised and gratified at the show of support. I saw Molly, and Heather and Evan, and Toby and Jen and Sam, and Jake and Kayla, and Josh, and everybody else there, standing around us in a semicircle as we gathered our gear and moved off into the crowd. My parents were there, too, with my brother Stephen. My dad grabbed my bag and carried it to the car as my mom put her arm around my shoulder, heedless of the grime and sweat. She held me close as we walked slowly through the parking lot. I crawled into the back seat and lay back, my head lolling against the rear cushion.

As he started the car, my dad said, "You played a great game tonight, son. We're very proud of you."

I had nothing to say to that. Exhaustion leaked from every pore. Finally, I managed to mumble, "Thank you."

"You know," continued my father, "your mother and I have been talking about you. We think you might have been grounded for long enough. We'll talk about lifting at least part of your sentence in the morning."

"Okay," I mumbled, too tired to say more.

- 24 -

TRICKS AND TREATS

I was indeed paroled. I had a certain amount of my freedom back, but I had to call my parents and let them know where I was and what I was doing at all times. It was a pain, but it was better than it had been.

The next Monday, the *Metro Times* carried an even bigger story about our game, even though we had lost. I was embarrassed to read that I was being touted as "the defensive specialist who is also a scoring threat" after my assist in the first half.

I didn't want all the attention I was starting to get. Hell, I was only fifteen years old. I wanted to just go out and have fun playing the game.

By the end of October, the Rockton game was our only loss. We would be seeded first in the conference playoffs, and Rockton was seeded second. We might have a chance to play them again for the conference finals, with luck.

I still wasn't allowed to go out and hang out with just Molly, and we weren't able to wangle any time alone. Molly was complaining more and more about being unable to scratch her *itch*. I was beginning to think of her as being much more sexually driven than any other kids I knew, which was saying a lot. I was worried that the boyfriend-girlfriend relationship was suffering because of our inability to have any intimate time together.

Besides that, I was getting pretty horny too, and her complaints didn't help much.

Around two weeks before the end of October, Molly and Tessa decided they would have a costume party at Molly's house on the Saturday before Halloween. I asked my parents if I could go. They called up Molly's parents to find out if the O'Tooles or the Navarrones were going to be there to chaperone. Since both sets of parents were planning on being at the house during the party, my parents reluctantly agreed to let me go. Now, I had to come up with a good costume.

In the end, laziness won out over creativity. My dad had a cowboy outfit, complete with holster and cap gun, tucked away in a closet. I pulled it out and tried it on. It fit well enough, and with a cheap felt cowboy hat that I found scrunched up and stuck in a corner of the closet, I was set for the party.

I got over to Molly's early to help the girls get the basement decorated. The Navarrones and the O'Tooles were all there, except for Heather, busy getting sodas packed in ice, black lights hung up, and streamers and fake spider webs strung. Mr. and Mrs. O'Toole were creating a mini haunted house in the laundry room, with a mannequin's head painted to look like it had been decapitated from a body, a bowl of peeled grapes for eyeballs, and rubber bats and spiders hanging all around. Lisbeth, Josh, and Tessa were hanging streamers from walls and ceilings. I helped Mr. Navarrone get the drinks and ice set up, along with paper cups, napkins, and garbage baskets placed in the corners of the large room. Molly was in the kitchen getting snacks ready, putting chips and popcorn and nuts in big bowls. Later on, they would be ordering pizzas to be delivered for everybody.

We were just putting the last of the decorations up when kids started showing up for the party. Mostly ninth and tenth graders were invited, but these things had a way of expanding sometimes. Josh and Molly ran upstairs to their rooms to change into their costumes and came down just as the doorbell started to ring. Josh was a monk of some sort, wearing a hooded robe with a rope for a belt, his bare feet in sandals. Molly was a hippie girl, complete with a huge afro-style wig and rose-colored glasses. They greeted kids at the door as they came up.

The first to arrive were Jen and Sam, dressed like the *American Gothic* farmer and wife. They were both thin and tall, so it was a natural for them. Sam wore bib overalls and carried a pitchfork, and Jen had on a gingham dress that buttoned to her throat, her hair pulled back tight on her head. Toby, nearly the smallest kid in school, came in a Superman costume, complete with cape, which made us all laugh (which was, after all, the point for Toby). Eric was a priest, Keisha a nun. Jorge took the easy way out and came in his soccer uniform, but Kristina went all out, dressing up as Catwoman, just like Eartha Kitt. Jake was a pirate, with a hook for a hand and a stuffed parrot glued to his shoulder. Jake was still barred from seeing Jaimie, so Kayla came with him, looking absolutely stunning as Jeannie the genie, complete with billowy balloon pants with elastic at the waist and ankles, a pink halter top, and a little cap with a wispy veil that fell behind her head.

All in all, there were about thirty kids at the party, more girls than boys. We had the music playing loud, and there was a strobe light pulsing in a corner of the room. Some kids were dancing occasionally, mostly just standing in one place and jerking around. Some kids brought their disco moves with them and were working it out. Most of the lights were out, with just the strobe on one end and the black lights on the other, but either Molly's parents or Tessa's parents were circulating almost constantly, coming down from the kitchen with plates of snacks and chips, refilling the ice chest, checking on drinks, emptying trash containers, and keeping a sharp eye on the proceedings.

Mr. O'Toole stationed himself in the haunted house, where all the lights were off. He took great pleasure in guiding each kid around and through the spider webs, to the bowl of peeled eyes, and then to the severed head, where he switched on a spot-light to illuminate it in all its gruesome glory. Each time he did that, he got a very satisfying scream from every girl, and a few of the guys even jumped back at the sudden sight of it. I could tell he was very pleased with himself. After all the partygoers had gone through the room, he closed the door and went upstairs to join the other adults, leaving just the spotlight on the head as a deterrent to mischief.

After a couple of hours, it was apparent to the adults that we were reasonably well behaved. We had not brought any alcohol or drugs, and we were having a good time despite their presence. Our good behavior lulled them into coming down less and less to check on us. Molly and Tessa were still making occasional trips up to the kitchen for more snacks or sodas, so there was little reason for the parents to come down anymore. Besides, we were making enough noise. How much trouble could we get into?

Somebody suggested a variation on the old spin-the-bottle game. Since it was a big basement, there were two doors lead-ing to the utility area, one by the furnace and one leading to the laundry room. After some negotiation, it was decided that all the boys would sit in a circle by the laundry door. All the girls would be at the other end of the large room, sitting on the floor by the furnace door. There was a soda bottle in the middle of each circle. It was decided that there would be two spins of each bottle. The first spin would determine who would meet at the laundry room end, where the haunted house had been set up. The second spin would determine who would meet at the furnace end, where there was virtually no light at all.

There was a lot of squealing and giggling going on from the girls' end of the room as we guys gathered around in our cir-cle, laughing and joking about who would end up with whom. When Molly gave the go-ahead, I grabbed our bottle and gave it a spin at the same time Tessa twirled the bottle by the girls. We weren't supposed to let the other circle know who was going to each area. Everybody wanted it to be a surprise.

The bottle stopped, pointing at Toby first. He got up and went in the door to await his partner. I spun the bottle a second time, and it ended up pointing at Eric. He went through the door at our end and headed toward the furnace side. We could hear more giggles and low talk coming from the other end of the room. The agreed-upon time was the length of the next full song on the album playing on the record player, which was loud enough to be heard anywhere in the basement (and probably the whole house). The rest of us spent the time refilling glasses and grabbing another piece of pizza while we waited for the song to end.

At the end of their time, Toby and Eric came back out to our group. Eric had a smile on his face, but Toby looked absolutely shell-shocked.

"Who were you back there with?" asked Josh.

"Kendra," said Eric, grinning. Kendra was a sophomore at school, medium height with a plain face and mousy brown hair. She had, in Toby's words, "big bazooms," though, and she was, it was rumored, generous with her favors. She had come to the party in a tavern wench costume, with a fair amount of cleavage showing to spark the interest of us boys. "She told me she liked chocolate," he added with a smile.

We whooped and hollered at that information, glad that the current activity had gotten off to such a good start. We turned to Toby and asked him about who he had ended up with. He hesitated before answering.

"Ummm...it was Jen," he said sheepishly. Everybody else started laughing at the thought of tiny Toby alone with tall Jen Davies. He glanced at me with a sad look in his eyes, though. I was the only one of his friends who really knew how he felt about Jen, and I knew it hurt him to be the butt of this particular joke. I wondered if Jen had said anything bad to him. *Hey, it's nothing,* he seemed to say to me as he shrugged and sat back down again in the circle. He grabbed the bottle and gave it a spin.

This time, Jake was picked to go to the laundry room side, and I was on the furnace side. As I passed by him, I heard the door at the other end open, and Kayla was walking toward me, heading for the laundry room. She stopped and smiled at me, and then, making sure I was blocking Jake's view, she started to lift her pink halter. It was just a tease, though, and she let her top drop back into place. She swished by me with a smile and a murmured, "Excuse me, Sean."

As she brushed by me, I turned to stare after her and almost fell down when I bumped up against a metal post. Embarrassed, I continued down toward the furnace, just as the door opened again, and Tessa walked in.

We sat down and leaned against the plywood wall, my arm comfortably around her shoulder in a friendly manner. We chatted for a couple of minutes about nothing at all, until Tessa turned to me and said softly, "Molly says you're a good kisser."

I was a little surprised, but I wasn't so dense that I couldn't pick up on the hint. I bent over and kissed her softly. Her hand sneaked up and wrapped itself around my neck while we kissed, her fingers tangling in my hair. It was a sweet, noncommittal, friendly and brief contact, and we stood up together and moved apart just as the song was ending. We each headed for our respective doors, and this time when I passed Kayla, she just smiled at me and continued on her way.

"Okay, who were you guys with?" asked Eric.

"My sister," replied Jake disgustedly.

"I was with Tessa," I said. Nobody had much to say about either of those, so we sat back down, and Jake spun the bottle.

We kept on playing for about a half an hour, with some of the guys coming back with tales of kisses and hugs, others with no activity to report. Josh came back out one time looking very sheepish, saying only that he had been back there with the legendary Kendra. At the same time, I thought I heard an increased volume of whispers and giggles from the other side of the room.

Finally, the bottle landed on me again, sending me back to the furnace side. Scott Taylor, costumed as a doctor in scrubs, was chosen for the laundry room side, and we walked through the door together. As I headed down the dark room, Molly was walking toward me. She stopped when she got to me, reached up and put her arms around my neck, and pulled herself up to give me a very wet kiss as she pressed her body against me. My internal connectors burned away as the heat she generated burst forth.

"Just a little reminder of what you've been missing," she whispered as she backed away from me. She smiled and continued on toward the other side of the room.

I saw the far door open once again but couldn't see who came in. I made my way down to the furnace area, until my foot bumped up against the leg of whoever was sitting there, leaning back against the wall.

"Who's there?" I whispered.

There was no answer, but I did feel a small hand grasp mine and pull me down, urging me to sit beside her. I sat, and the person still held my hand but now pressed my palm up against her bare midriff.

"Hi, Sean," Kayla whispered.

I was still in a minor state of arousal from Molly's kiss, and Kayla's voice activated more burners, stoking the fire. I slipped my arm around her shoulder, and she naturally moved in and raised her face for our first kiss in months. I could make out the almost white radiance of her fine hair as she moved closer to me, and I closed my eyes as our lips met. She clutched both her hands to my wrist on her belly, pressing my hand harder into her stomach as we melted into each other. Our first soft kiss was followed by a much hungrier one.

We were pretty much lost together, unaware that our song had ended until a small shaft of light fell across us as the door opened. We stopped kissing and looked up, startled. Molly was staring back at us, frozen in the act of opening the door as she saw Kayla and me holding each other.

Oh, shit on a stick, I thought to myself. *I have just opened a large, economy-sized can of worms.*

The game went on for a few more spins, but my heart wasn't in it anymore. It really didn't matter because the bottle never pointed at me again that night. The room had gotten noticeably quieter, so much so that it was noticed even upstairs. Soon, one or another of the parents started making quick trips down to see what was going on. They were ostensibly walking around checking on snacks and stuff, but they were also quietly counting heads. The game stopped and kids began milling around again, sometimes dancing, sometimes just grouping and yakking.

A slow song began playing, and Molly slipped her arm into mine, guiding me out into the middle of the room so we could dance close.

"What was that with you and Jake's little sister?" she asked quietly. Too quietly.

"It was nothing, Mol. I was just playing the game, you know?" I whispered. I dropped her hand and put both arms around her waist.

"It looked like you were enjoying playing the game a little too much, Sean."

"Hey, come on. Give me a break," I pleaded. "I kissed Tessa, too. I'm sure she told you about it. Besides, don't try to tell me you didn't give Scotty a little peck on the cheek."

"Okay," she admitted. "I did kiss him. But I also heard the song end, which is more than you can say."

"Hey, she's just a kid. It was probably her first time kissing a boy. I just wanted to give her something to remember, that's all."

"I'll bet it wasn't her first time kissing a boy," Molly muttered. But she let it drop, for which I was silently grateful. I had the sinking feeling that this was not the last time this subject would come up between us.

Molly seemed a little distracted the rest of the evening, but I figured it was because we were at her house and she and her brother had a lot of work to do for the party.

Maybe that was it. Then again, maybe it wasn't.

- 25 -

THE PLAYOFFS

We entered the conference playoffs as the team favored to win. Our local paper was helping to fuel the interest by featuring pictures and biographies of each of the starters in the week prior to the first game of the playoffs. I got a lot of razzing at school the day after my picture and bio appeared. I was pretty uncomfortable with all this attention, but I was in the minority among my teammates. Most of the rest of the guys on the team were really enjoying their moment in the spotlight.

We waltzed through our first playoff game against the eighth-seeded team, winning 5–1. John Pennington's defensive adjustments on the field were solid, and Kevin and I stopped just about every ball that came our way.

Our second-round opponent gave us a tougher game, but the result was still a win, this time 3–1. By now, the big-city newspapers were paying attention, too. The *Metro Times* had us rated in the top twenty in the state, a huge boost for us. Their small article about our win in the second round also pointed out what their reporter considered to be a major flaw in our game, however. He wrote that he wasn't sure we had the depth to win against Rockton Heights, the only team to defeat us in the regular season.

Coach Neville made sure he read that article to us during our warm-ups the next afternoon. He posted copies of it on every locker as a reminder of what was expected of us. He wanted us to confound expectations, and he had every confidence that we could.

Since we were seeded first in the tournament, we had the home-field advantage. Rockton came to us to play the championship game, and we made sure the stands were packed with fans. We wanted it loud, and we got it. The cheerleaders, normally only required to perform at football games in the fall, voluntarily showed up to lead the crowd. They cajoled people to slide over closer to each other so that more people could sit down. They worked the crowd until there were no gaps to be seen at all. Heather O'Toole even went so far as to climb up into the stands and act as a traffic cop, moving people around and filling in spaces. She got a lot of laughter and no small amount of applause for her efforts as she picked her way back down to the sidelines, her golden-red ponytail swishing back and forth.

And it was all very much worthwhile. Rockton Heights came into the game a little overconfident. We capitalized on that, scoring our first goal within the first ten minutes. By the final whistle, we had trounced the toughest competition we could find in our conference, beating them 4–1. I even scored a goal, only my second as a varsity player, and it was very satisfying to get that goal in the conference finals. We were conference champs, the first team from our school to win the title in soccer.

Sectional playoffs didn't start until the next weekend, so we had Saturday and Sunday off from practice. This gave our scouting and coaching staff time to prepare for an unfamiliar opponent. We would enter the sectionals seeded fourth out of eight conference champions. The winner of the sectional tournament would go downstate for the state tournament, again a single-elimination tournament for the eight winners of sectionals from around the state.

The Monday *Metro Times* ran a big story about our conference win. The story traced our season from the beginning that had held so much promise, the schools that had been scouting Skip, and our wins up until the accident. Then, the article continued with how our team's makeup had changed so much because of the loss of our top two players, the struggles, and ultimately the triumphs of the team. Surprisingly, they assigned a large amount of our team's success to "the quiet sophomore with the loud game, defensive standout Sean Porter." There were quotes from some of my teammates about me, and Coach Neville was quoted extensively in the article. There was even a picture taken of me during the Rockton Heights game for the conference championship, frozen just at the moment the ball left my foot on a pass upfield. I hadn't even been aware of a reporter talking to anybody, so it all caught me by surprise.

By the time the Friday of the first sectional game dawned, the *Times* had come out with their picks for All-Conference honors for all the metropolitan conferences. I was shocked when I got to school and was informed, via an announcement by Dr. Osgood over the intercom, that I had been selected as one of the All-Conference defensemen for our conference, despite the fact that I had not begun the season as a starter for our team.

A college about an hour's bus ride away was hosting sectionals. We were nervous and tense on the ride down. Again, a caravan of cars containing kids and parents supporting us followed our bus to the host field.

Because of the All-Conference selection and the article in the *Metro Times*, our opponents started focusing on me a little more. They were double-teaming me and making an effort to pass the ball into the middle of the field before I could get to it. That was fine by me. I sure didn't want to trip over my own two feet in an attempt to save the game. If the opposing team was accommodating me by keeping the ball out of my area, so much the better. The end result of that strategy was that when the ball got down into our half of the field, the available playing area, from our adversary's point of view, shrank down in width by a third. It worked just fine to our advantage, especially since we then were presented with an open side when we cleared the ball, the side that Kevin and I patrolled.

On one opportunity, John Pennington picked up a weak rolling shot, ran up a few steps, and rolled the ball over to me on the right side. There was only one guy by me, so I let the ball pass me and took its momentum up the field. I was to the midfield stripe by the time anybody came close enough to challenge me, and by then, our offense had a set play in position. I lofted a pass up to the middle, and the play developed just the way it was designed, with a Trent Abbott goal and our first sectional win the result.

Each successive sectional game was against tougher opponents, but we made it through, winning our three games 1–0, 3–2, and 3–1. We were state tournament bound.

The next weekend, we left by bus on Thursday for our game downstate on Friday. Once again, there were eight teams in the tournament. The first two games would be played Friday and Sunday, and the championship game would be held the next weekend.

In our first game, we played the Planey Warriors, a team that was very experienced, having been here the previous year. They put together some play sets that were completely different from anything we had ever seen before, led by their senior All-American forward, Jesse Wilhoit. They moved the ball in to Jesse every chance they got, and Mike Evanson, our junior sweeper, along with both of us defensive players, were hard put to keep him from scoring at will. As it was, he collected three quick goals within the first twenty minutes of the first half. We were in real trouble of being blown out for the first time all season.

Finally, we dropped our defensive center midfielder back, so in effect we had left and right sweepers, and that seemed to stymie the Warriors. We managed to neutralize Wilhoit with the new arrangement. Any time the ball came down into our end of the field, we were able to clear it back out to midfield.

At halftime, we were down 3–1, but we were feeling much better about how we were playing than we did during the first few minutes of the game. Eric and Trent let us know that the Warriors had a weaker player on defense on their side of the field. If we could clear the ball up to them, they felt they could make a play on goal.

A few minutes into the second half, their confidence was rewarded. The ball cleared to Eric on the left, and he lit his afterburners. He torched the defenders, streaking down the sidelines and angling in toward the middle. Trent dropped over to cover the left side as Eric charged the middle. At the very last possible moment, he passed the ball over to Trent, who stepped toward the ball with his left foot and launched a high bullet at the far post. The ball just slipped under the top rail and clanged against the back post of the goal. It was now 3–2, and the Warriors were on the defensive.

About seven minutes later, a similar play developed, but this time Trent gave Eric a give-and-go past the defender, and it was Eric's goal that tied the game.

At about the eighty-five-minute mark, Kevin and I switched positions on an errant pass by the Warriors. I took the ball up toward midfield. Our opponents were so worried about Eric and Trent on the far side that they made the mistake of letting me advance the ball. Their midfielders were holding their positions, which meant I just had their left defender in front of me. I faked a pass into the middle, giving myself a looping pass around their defender, picking the ball up again behind him. I came in toward the goal just as their sweeper and goalie decided I was a threat, but it was too late. I threaded a pass in to Trent, who tapped it in for the winning goal. We were advancing to the semi-finals, winning the game 4–3.

On Sunday afternoon, we were facing the Rock Falls Lions, another perennial soccer power from downstate. We were pretty tired from the game on Friday, but we figured the Lions would be tired from their win on Friday, too.

We were wrong. This was our first trip downstate, and emotions played a huge part in our win on Friday, leaving us pretty drained for Sunday's game. Not so the Lions. They had been here before and knew what it meant to leave it all on the field in the first game. They didn't make that mistake this year. They razzled us, they dazzled us, they embarrassed us. We went down in flames. We got trounced, completely and thoroughly beaten. We walked off the field after ninety minutes, knowing we still had a lot to learn about tournament play. The final score was 5–1.

Our season was over.

The only true bright moment after that humiliating loss was the following Monday, when the *Metro Times* announced their All-State team. Of course, leading the team was Jesse Wilhoit, the All-American forward from Planey. But, to my surprise and my team's delight, I was chosen as a second-team All-State selection on defense, only the second player in our school's history to make the list. The first to have been so honored was, of course, my mentor, Skip Horvath.

And I truly was honored. All I had wanted to do was go out and play the game, and here I was, being recognized for playing it my way, just as Coach Neville had advised. My hard work, and the hard work of Coach Neville and Coach Reyes and all my other coaches and assistants and teammates, had paid off dividends I had never even dared dream of.

- 26 -

A WALK IN THE SNOW

Ever since the All-State selections had been announced, my parents had fallen back into their old parenting ways, pretty much letting me be a teenaged kid. As long as I didn't get myself into trouble again (or find myself being dragged, kicking and screaming, into trouble, such as what Jake did to me), and as long as I kept my grades up, they were willing to pretty much stay off my back.

All during the postseason, from the conference tournament all the way to the state playoffs, Molly was acting funny around me. It was as if she was distracted or something. And to tell the truth, all during that month, I was plenty busy. The homework load didn't ease up just because we were still playing soccer, and our games were no longer local affairs. We were traveling longer distances to play, and the further we got in the tournaments, the farther we had to travel. As a result, I didn't have any time on the weekends to spend with Molly, and during the week, all I could spare was a quick phone call occasionally.

She was still really friendly during school, but it seemed like she was distant and distracted whenever I called her. Monosyllabic answers to my questions, no prompting from her to help the conversation along, and uncomfortable silences were the norm. It got so that I didn't like to call her at night, content just to see her at school instead.

Finally, though, the soccer season ended. I had a weekend free, so when I saw her at lunch on Wednesday, I asked her if she could do something on Friday night.

"Ummm...I don't know for sure yet," she evaded. "Call me tonight, okay, Sean? Look, I've got to go. I've got a meeting set up with my adviser. I'll talk to you later."

She abruptly got up from the table and threw the rest of her lunch away and left the cafeteria, leaving me feeling awfully alone among a sea of students.

That night, after dinner, I dialed her number. Josh answered the phone.

"Dude, what did you do?" he asked.

I was puzzled. "What are you talking about?" I asked.

"Man, she's really in outer space tonight. She was snapping at all of us at dinner and even yelled at the dog. I laughed at her when she did that and almost got my head handed to me."

"Great. I wonder what the hell is going on."

"Well," he said, "I hope you can figure it out before she gets on the phone. But you did something to piss her off, Sean; bet on it."

There was a loud clunk as he let the handset drop. *Great,* I thought to myself. *I'm in trouble, and I don't know why.*

I heard Josh calling Molly to the phone. A few moments later, she picked up the handset.

"Hello?"

"Hi, Mol. It's me."

"Oh. Hi."

Silence. *Uh-oh.*

"Um, you said I should call," I prompted.

"Oh, yes. That's right, I did." She took a deep breath. "Sean, I need to talk about something, okay?"

"Sure, go ahead," I said. My heart started beating a little faster, and my stomach was doing tricky things. I wished I had gotten myself some water or something to drink before I dialed. Maybe that would have helped calm me down.

"It's about us, Sean. I think we've got problems we're not talking about."

"What problems, Molly? Besides, we're talking now, aren't we?" I knew they were weak arguments, but they were all I had at the moment. I was still trying to wade through the minefield of this conversation.

"We haven't been talking before now, though. I'm just not comfortable right now with where we are, Sean. I know you've felt it, too. Ever since the costume party..."

"Wait a minute. The costume party? You mean the one at your house?"

"Of course the one at my house." She sounded exasperated with me. "What other costume party have you gone to? Never mind; I don't want to know."

"Molly..."

"Shut up for a minute, Sean, and let me work this out. Ever since the costume party, when I saw you kissing Jake's little sister..."

"Molly..."

"I saw you kissing Kayla, Sean. And you both looked like you were enjoying it."

"Molly..."

"And you were both enjoying it. I can't get that image out of my mind, Sean."

"But you kissed Scotty."

"Didn't you hear me? I said you were both enjoying it. That's the part that has been really bothering me, Sean." I could hear the tears just starting on the other end of the phone. My stomach dropped into my toes.

"Look, Molly..."

"Just let me talk for a minute, okay?" She took a deep breath to get herself back under control. I tried it, too, but it didn't work for me. "I'm afraid you're not taking this relationship very seriously, Sean. I thought you loved me. I thought you were committed to me. But ever since that party, I haven't been able to convince myself that you are in this with me one hundred percent." She stopped again. I could just detect a sob trying to work its way out of her and into the open. "I think we're going to have to stop seeing each other for a while," she whispered.

"Molly…" But I had nothing to say. She had said it all. When I didn't respond, the sob that had been waiting for its opportunity finally escaped. Without another word, she set the telephone down and broke the connection. No slamming it down in anger, just a quiet click. The thunderous sound of that click seemed to drop an entire wall of bricks onto me.

Shit.

The whole next day at school, I walked around numb. At lunchtime, Molly found somewhere else to sit. I ate with Jake and Eric and Keisha and Toby, but I just couldn't track any of their conversations. I thought Josh had probably clued in Jake about Molly and me, so he at least was a little sympathetic. Even so, I really didn't want to spill out my personal problems to the table, so I endured some good-natured ribbing about my long face. It was a rough day, but at least I could go home right after school and try to bury myself in homework. It was one of the few times I was grateful to my teachers for piling it on.

Friday was a little better. I had gotten over the shock of Molly calling it off, but it still hurt. I understood more now how Josh must have felt when Shayna broke up with him back in September. I thought I would make it through the day without too much pain.

No such luck.

It all began around lunchtime. I was walking toward the cafeteria with Jake, when Toby came up and grabbed my arm.

"Man, you're not gonna believe what I just heard," he said as he tugged on me. Out of the corner of my eye, I could see Jake frantically waving his hand at Toby, trying to get him to shut up about something. I turned toward him. His hand dropped like it suddenly weighed about fifty pounds, and he got this innocent look on his face that immediately made me suspicious.

"What?" I asked sharply.

"Who, me?" he asked. By the look on my face, he realized how stupid that sounded, so he dropped the act. We made our way to some empty seats at our usual table and sat down.

"Okay, guys, what gives?" I asked.

Toby and Jake glanced at each other.

"Okay," said Jake. "You're probably going to hear about it from somebody else later today anyway, so you might as well hear it from your friends first." He glanced around to make sure someone wasn't listening in, as if it mattered.

Toby leaned in close and spoke quietly. "Molly's going out with someone else on Saturday."

I stared at him and then looked at Jake. He gazed back at me solemnly. "She's got a date?" I asked stupidly.

Jake nodded. "Scotty asked her out. She said yes. They're going to some party that Tessa knows about somewhere. Hey, I'm sorry, Sean."

I nodded mutely. I told myself we had broken up; she was free to go out if she wanted. It didn't help. *It's only been two days!* I was still trying to process our conversation from Wednesday, and she was already going out with someone else? It didn't make any sense to me. And she told me she didn't enjoy her session with Scott in the laundry room.

Or did she really say that?

I started running our conversation back through my mind. *Hold on, there's something wrong here. She was upset that I seemed to be enjoying kissing Kayla, but she never said she didn't enjoy kissing Scott that night.*

Maybe there was more to this breakup than she was telling me.

Not that, ultimately, it was going to make any difference. Whether she and Scott were going out because of the costume party or not didn't really matter. Whether there was an attraction there before our breakup really didn't matter at this point, either. We were done with each other. How we got there was just reopening wounds that should stay closed and healing.

But this news really did hurt.

And Josh and Toby were absolutely right. I heard from five or six other friends that Molly was going out with Scott on Saturday. *Bad news travels fast,* I thought to myself.

Then, just before my last class of the day, Jake found me in the hall.

"Sean. You're not going to like this news at all, but I just heard from somebody who saw them that Molly and Scott went to a movie together last weekend. While you were at the state tournament, she was already going out with somebody else. Man, I'm really sorry to have to bring you this news, Sean."

He looked as sorry as he sounded. I would have felt sorry for him, but I was busy feeling sorry for myself and couldn't spare any for my friend.

Now I really felt like crap.

Friday night, Josh and Jake and I met at the mall, and I lost myself in a maze of pinball and arcade games, dumping quarter after quarter into the machines. Air hockey, I discovered, was a very good outlet for anger and frustration. Even when I was winning, I was slamming the puck as hard as I could, trying to break that little disk into a zillion pieces. I felt oddly better after about a half dozen battles at the table.

On Saturday, I tried to lose myself in chores around the house. The grass wasn't growing, but there were leaves to rake, gutters to clean, and the garage to sweep out. I finished the afternoon by taking my soccer ball back behind the garage and kicking it against the back, chasing down the rebound, dribbling back to an imaginary line, and firing the ball against the wall again. It was getting pretty cold out, but by the time I was done, I was breathing hard and sweating from my exertions. I just wasn't tired enough to stop thinking about Molly going out with Scott that night, though. It was like a splinter in my thumb. I had to worry it and pick at it until it throbbed so I could be unhappy about how much more it hurt now that it was getting infected.

I trudged into the house and stripped off my soaked sweat-shirt and T-shirt. I dumped them in the laundry basket in my room and headed for the shower. The sky had just started spit-ting little wet clumps of snow flurries. *Oh, good,* I thought to myself. *Now the weather is turning bad on me, too. What next?*

I spent the next several hours looking at the television but not really seeing anything. I would switch to one channel, watch for a few minutes, then get up and walk over to the selector on the TV and switch to a different channel. I would sit back down, only to get up a few minutes later and go through the motions again. Nothing grabbed my interest enough to stay with it. I got more and more frustrated as I continually flipped through all the channels, only to start all over again at the beginning.

Finally, I decided that taking a walk in the freezing weather suited my mood. Maybe I could walk far enough to tire myself out so I could just go to sleep. I slipped on my letter jacket, slapped a baseball cap on my head, made sure I had gloves in the pockets, and trudged out the door.

I walked aimlessly around the neighborhood, not paying any attention to where I was or where I'd been. I just walked through the building snow and slush, head down, hands thrust in jeans pockets, staring at where my next step would land.

Eventually, I found myself stopped on the sidewalk by Jake and Kayla's house. No lights were on at the front of the house, but it didn't matter. I didn't want to see anybody anyway. I walked up their driveway and around the garage into the field in back.

My body was on autopilot, my mind switched off. I was letting my feet take me where they wanted to go, or so I thought.

I shuffled through the accumulating snow all the way across the field and into the stand of trees. The snow was reflecting what little light there was outside, and my feet found the worn path through the woods easily. My body stopped, and it was a few minutes before my brain reconnected. I was standing on the path, shoulders hunched against the cold and wet. Ahead of me was the tree Jake and I had climbed so long ago. I mentally shrugged, telling myself it was a lesson in futility to even think of going up there, but my feet began to move again in that direction.

I pulled out my gloves and put them on and reached up to climb the tree. The branches and limbs were slippery and wet as I climbed higher. I got to the branch I had sat on months ago, and glanced at the back of the O'Toole house. No lights were on there, either.

Wait a minute. There was a dim glow coming from one window. I slid over to the branch on the other side of the tree and stood up on it to try to peer into the window. I knew it was Molly's room. *She probably just left a closet light on or something,* I told myself. *She's not there. She's out with Scotty,* I reminded myself. *She's not there.*

My eyes adjusted to the light coming from the window, and standing on the branch allowed me to see most of the room. The faint light was coming from her bedside lamp. It was so dim because she had thrown a T-shirt or something over it to cut down on the glare. Scott and Molly were lying on her bed together, kissing and holding each other. As I watched, my eyes grew more accustomed to the amount of light available. I saw Scott's hand move tentatively up from Molly's waist, brushing along the nap of her sweater to softly grasp her breast. I saw Molly arch her back a little, making her chest rise, pushing harder against his hand. Her mouth opened as she kissed him harder, and she pulled him tighter to her, keeping her upper body turned just slightly so that he didn't lose contact with her.

I saw him drop his hand down and urgently scramble for the hem of her sweater, anxious to slip beneath it. I saw the fabric of the sweater rise into a ridge as his hand and arm slid up, eager to reclaim possession of her breast.

I stayed there in the tree, unaware of the temperature or the snow or anything else surrounding me as I watched Molly push Scott away for a moment so she could sit up and pull the sweater over her head. Her bra was askew on her, one cup pushed up where Scott had wormed his fingers underneath. She reached behind her and unfastened the bra, pulling it off her shoulders and tossing it onto the floor. She lay back down and pulled Scott back to her for a kiss. He took the advantage Molly was giving him and grabbed at her clumsily as he was brought back down to her.

I continued to watch as Molly took charge of an apparently inexperienced Scotty. She rolled him over so she was partially on top of him, slipping her knee between his legs as she rose up slightly, guiding her swollen breast to his lips. He licked and kissed her turgid nipple, but it looked like he wasn't sure what she wanted. He let his hands slide down her bare back as he suckled at her breast. He tried to slip under her jeans and onto her butt, but her pants were too tight. He contented himself with grasping her over her jeans.

I stayed there the whole time. I saw it all. I watched Molly unsnap first her jeans and then Scott's. I watched as he watched her, unable to believe his luck. I felt the knife go into my chest and slice down to my stomach as I saw her move over him, her hands now on his shoulders, her head back in pleasure, her eyes closed in concentration. I saw her open her eyes and say something to him, saw her reach down and take his hand, saw her press it to her breast as she moved up and down on him. I watched it all, hardly able to blink, as she rode herself nearly to completion.

I saw Scotty tense up, saw his hips working up and down frantically. His movements were inhibiting Molly's, keeping her from cresting, and in a perverse way, I was glad to see it.

I couldn't bear any more. I closed my eyes against the vision and then concentrated on getting out of the tree. I did not want to look at the window, so I turned to face back into the woods as I climbed down. I dropped to the ground, slipped in the accumulating snow, and fell on my ass. I leaned back against the tree as I felt the sting of tears in my eyes. I intensely regretted coming to the tree, and I was miserable and cold and wet and suddenly very tired.

I dragged myself up to my feet and shuffled back out to the path. As I was making my way through the woods and toward the field, my subconscious noted, for future consideration, something that I did not register at the time: another set of footprints in the snow, feet quite a bit smaller and narrower than mine, paralleling my path through the woods.

- 27 -

THE FLYING MENDOZAS

Even while it seemed like my personal life was going into the crapper, my soccer-playing alter ego was flourishing. In the two weeks since my selection as an All-State athlete, even snooty upperclassmen were saying hello to me at school. It was an odd juxtaposition. On the one hand, Molly and Tessa were barely speaking to me. On the other hand, I was becoming something of a BMOC, a big man on campus. The other jocks in school, football players and basketball players and track and field guys, finally were accepting the fact that soccer could actually be a real sport. The members of the varsity and junior varsity soccer teams were finally being accepted into the Fraternity of Sweat.

The next weekend, my family and I were invited down to the state capital for a reception for all the All-State honorees. Soccer still wasn't a first-tier sport, so the governor wasn't going to come, opting instead to send the lieutenant governor in his place. We checked into the sponsoring hotel on Friday evening. There was an informal party for the All-Staters in one of the conference rooms that night after dinner. It was a chance for the players from around the state to get together socially, so we could try to get to know each other. Parents and families were there for the weekend but were only invited to the formal dinner and ceremonies on Saturday night. Friday night's party was reserved for the athletes.

I walked into the room a little nervously. I only knew a couple of the guys by sight, having played against them during the tournaments. I hadn't ever met any of them before, since there wasn't anybody else from my school, or for that matter from my home conference, who was selected. I saw Jesse Wilhoit, the All-American forward from Planey, standing with a couple of other guys near the soda bar. He glanced over at me, leaned in to his group to say something, and then started walking toward me.

"Sean Porter?" he asked as he came up to me.

"Yeah," I answered. "You're Jesse Wilhoit, right?"

"Right," he said. "We played against each other a couple of weeks ago. You torched me pretty good that game, Porter."

Suddenly embarrassed, I quickly replied, "No, I didn't. I think you scored three quick ones on us early in the game, didn't you?"

He grinned. "Yep, I did, but then your guys on defense shut me down. That was a cute trick, using a double sweeper. Didn't hurt your offense any to do that, either, did it?"

I smiled. "No, I guess it didn't."

"And, if I remember right, you got the assist on the winning goal that game, didn't you?" he asked.

"Well," I said hesitantly, "yeah, I guess I did."

"See? You did torch me." He laughed. "Set on fire by a sophomore! Boy, that felt good, let me tell you." He started steering me toward the group he had left to come talk to me.

"It felt good?" I asked. It was a puzzling thing to say. I hesitated for a step. I glanced at his face, perhaps expecting to see anger or a hint of sarcasm, but he was smiling. His expression was nothing but open, honest, and friendly.

"You betcha," he said as he stopped with me. He raised his eyebrows and jerked his head in the direction of the others, convincing me to continue strolling over toward the group watching us. "I was way too big for my britches all season long. I was headed for a fall. I'm just glad it happened now, when I was still playing high school soccer. I've got a full ride to the University of Florida next year, and I would have really been in deep shit if I had walked in there thinking I was King Soccer and then have somebody there kick my ass like you did. So, you see, you did me a big favor in that game," he finished as we stepped up to the others.

"Okay, if you say so," I said doubtfully.

Jesse introduced me to Wayne Phillips, a senior keeper, and to Harlan Corwin, a junior forward, both from Rock Falls, the state champions.

"Jesse's been telling us about your game against Planey," said Wayne. "I'm glad you got that out of your system before you played us."

"Well, we were on a high for Friday's match, but by the time we got to you guys, reality had set in," I replied. "Besides, your team was really good. You deserved to win State."

We fell quite naturally into an easy friendship that evening, and I relaxed and enjoyed meeting all the guys. There was just one other sophomore on the All-State team, a midfielder named Spencer Goldman, from South High School in the city. I saw him standing near the door, looking uncomfortable, so I excused myself from the group and went over and introduced myself. I insisted he come over with me, which he reluctantly did. Jesse, Wayne, and Harlan treated him with the same respect they had shown me. It made me realize that these guys were all here for the same reasons: because they loved the game they played, and they were recognized as being good at the game, just like everybody else in the room. It created a real sense of camaraderie among all of us.

The next night at the banquet, Jesse made sure we sat with his family at a large round table. My mom and dad and my brothers, Michael and Stephen, were falling all over themselves over the fact that they were sitting at the table of the state's only soccer All-American. Jesse and I just laughed at the absurdity of it all. Jesse introduced his parents and his younger sister, Anna, a pretty, dark-haired freshman with shiny braces on her teeth. She had to be embarrassed by those braces, because she rarely smiled. When she did smile, though, her whole face lit up, and she turned from merely pretty into something extraordinarily precious, and I couldn't help staring at her in awe.

Later on, after dinner and dessert, and after the lieutenant governor had given his speech and handed out plaques to all the players, a band over in the back corner of the room began to play. Jesse, having noticed the effect Anna was having on me, amused himself by insisting I dance with her. After cajoling me mercilessly, joined by Michael and Stephen, I finally got up and asked her if she would like to dance. Her face turned beet red, but I was rewarded with one of her radiant smiles as she nodded and stood. She was nearly as tall as I was and very self-conscious as we walked to the dance floor and found a space. It was a fast song, so we shook and jumped all over the place together, hidden in the middle of the crowd. Her hair bobbed up and down as she danced, and even though I tried not to stare, I couldn't help but notice how her body moved. Unfortunately, all that did was remind me of how much I had missed warm female companionship now that Molly was getting her itch scratched somewhere else. I certainly wasn't going to try anything with Anna, especially with her big brother around, but it was apparent that I was a horny young man who was temporarily smitten.

To my surprise, I found myself having fun with Anna. We ended up staying out on the dance floor, shaking and shucking to the fast songs, box-stepping to the slow songs, and even standing there, side by side, watching the band play on those occasions when the beat was one of those in-between rhythms that I have always found it hard to dance to. She was comfortable staying by my side, and I fell into an easy association with her. By the last set, we were holding hands in between dances, neither of us willing to go back to our table and possibly break the spell.

Finally, though, the band played their last song. Anna and I were just about the last couple left on the dance floor, and we stayed there, dancing close, until the echoes of the last notes bounced off the walls and faded into quiet. Only then did we reluctantly turn to walk back to our table. Jesse and Michael were still sitting there, paying absolutely no attention to us. Apparently, they were becoming good friends from the look of things. Wayne and Harlan and a couple of other All-Staters were also there, sitting in on their conversation. When Anna and I walked up, she dropped my hand before her brother could see her and say anything. We sat with the others, until a few minutes later it was clear that the party was breaking up. As we all walked toward the banquet hall doors, Anna and I delayed as much as we could, lagging behind the others on the way down the hall toward the elevators. Jesse managed to herd everybody into one elevator, and, with a little smile on his face and a twinkle in his eye, pressed the button to close the door just as Anna and I got to them. He winked at us just before the doors closed, leaving us to get our own elevator. Anna's cheeks turned red, and she shyly reached for my hand once the coast was clear. We stood there, hand in hand, as we waited for the next elevator.

An older couple got on the elevator with us, so we stepped to the back corner, silently holding hands, until we got to the fourth floor, where the Wilhoits were staying. I walked her to her door, which was left open a crack. We stood facing each other silently, each of us nervous about what might be expected of us by the other, until I finally slipped my arms around her and pulled her to me. She put her arms around my neck as I kissed her softly on her lips. I could feel the heat radiating from her cheeks as she flushed, so I let her go and dropped my arms, stepping back.

"Good night, Anna," I said quietly. "I'm glad you were here tonight." I turned to go back to the elevator.

"Sean?"

I turned back to her.

"Thank you for tonight. I'll remember it always," she said. She had one hand on the doorknob, the other at her throat. I tried to memorize how she looked in just that moment, so I could recall the vision she presented as she stood there, shy and smiling her dazzling, beautiful smile, shot through with white and silver.

✫ ✫ ✫

Back at school the next Monday, I very quickly fell back into the routine and only occasionally thought about calling or writing to Anna, until finally, I hardly thought about her at all.

Around Valentine's Day, our school held its annual turnabout dance. Back when my parents were going to school, a turnabout dance was themed around Sadie Hawkins Day, a fictional holiday created by cartoonist Al Capp. They dressed up like hillbillies straight out of *Li'L Abner* and Dogpatch, his comic strip creation. By now, though, our school had dropped the Sadie Hawkins name. The bib overalls and blacked-out teeth and hay stuck in your hair had been abandoned in favor of casual, comfortable clothes, and the event was moved from mid-November to February. It was still a turnabout event, though, with the girls asking the guys out, asking the boys to dance, all that stuff.

A bunch of us decided to go to the dance as a big group instead of putting ourselves through the pressure cooker of finding dates. Josh had been going out with Andrea Coulter since just before Christmas, and they were going to be joining Toby, Jake, Jorge, Kristina, Ashley Horvath, Becky Steinman, and me at the dance and at a local restaurant afterwards for desserts and sodas.

The dance was held in the school gym, and it was decorated Dogpatch style, with hand-painted banners and signs, bales of straw, and crockery jugs marked "XXX" with magic marker, I suppose as a sop to the old traditions.

I met up with the group at the dance, and we wandered slowly around the gym, stopping to catch up with our friends, checking out who was with whom. I stopped and traded back-slaps and high-fives with some of the kids I knew. I happened to glance over toward the double doors of the gym and saw Kevin Soranno and John Pennington come in the door with their dates, and there was a big crowd gathering around them. Jorge, Kristina, Ashley, and I headed their way, intending to say hello, when the people standing around them parted momentarily. I got a glimpse of a wheelchair being pushed through the door by a man who looked like he was somebody's father. As we got up to the edge, John and Kevin spotted us and waved the group back to let us through, just as Mr. Jameson was able to wheel Theo into the room and to the side. Theo saw me and smiled, all the while nodding and waving at all the well-wishers gathering around.

"Porter!" he called in a surprisingly strong voice. "Damn, boy, it's good to see you. I've been reading about you, and these guys here," he said, jerking his thumb at Kevin and John, "can't seem to shut up about you. Congratulations!"

"Thanks, Theo. We all have been thinking about you, too, obviously. How are you feeling?"

"Pretty damn great right about now, but I think that's because I'm living better through chemistry. I've got a whole damn drugstore running through my veins right now."

"Wow, it's really good to see you. This is such a surprise."

"I don't think I'm going to get out on the dance floor tonight, but I'm getting closer," he said with a smile. He looked over my shoulder and saw Ashley Horvath standing behind me, peeking around to see Theo sitting there. His face kind of crumpled.

"Oh, Ash, I'm sorry. I didn't see you there. How are you doing?" Seeing Skip's sister wasn't something he was expecting, and it was affecting him.

Ashley could see it, too, and rushed over and knelt to give Theo a fierce hug. "I'm doing okay, Theo," she quietly whispered to him. "I'm glad to see you're doing better, too."

"Yeah," he whispered back to her, "I'm doing better. It's been really tough. But it's been tough on everybody, especially you. You sure you're doing okay? Say, you didn't bring this sorry excuse for a soccer player, did you?"

She looked up at me, and her face tinged pink. "No," she said, smiling. "I just came with along with Sean's friends, that's all."

"Well, if he tries anything, you come look for me. I'll give him what-for," he said as he let her go. His eyes were shining with unshed tears, for Ashley, for Skip, for himself.

"Thanks, Theo. I will." She turned then and walked away quickly. I thought she needed a moment to compose herself, so I shook Theo's hand, assured him I would talk to him later, and handed him back to John and Kevin before going off to catch up with Ashley.

She was still slowly walking away, staying close to the wall, when I jogged up and put my hand on her shoulder.

"Ash?" I asked gently. "Are you okay?"

She turned, melted into my arms, and sobbed. "I miss him so much, Sean," she cried. Her face was buried in my shoulder, and I could feel the sobs wracking her.

"So do I, Ashley," I whispered. "So do I."

She got herself under control and stood up on her tiptoes to kiss my cheek. "Thanks, Sean," she said. "Thanks for being a friend."

"Aw, cut it out," I said. I wiped the last of her tears off her cheek with my fingertips. "Go fix your makeup, kiddo. I'll be right over there," I continued, pointing to where Jorge and Kristina were standing, waiting for us.

"Okay," she said. She headed toward the girl's restroom. Kristina saw where she was going and met her on the way. She started chattering to Ashley as they pushed open the door. I knew Kristina was trying to distract her, take her mind off her dead brother with idle gossip. She was very perceptive about other people's moods and feelings, a sympathy that came naturally to her. I walked over to Jorge to wait for them to return.

"She's upset about Theo and Skip?" asked Jorge.

"Yeah. She really misses her brother. Hey, Jorge, why don't you work on getting her to dance with you? When they do the men's choice dance, you should ask her," I suggested.

"You t'ink?" he asked. "I dunno, man, I don' wanna get shot down, you know? I t'ink you da man in her eyes right now, Sean."

Well, that surprised me. I hadn't thought of Ashley in that way before. In fact, I really hadn't thought of any girl in that way too much since my split with Molly, except maybe for Anna Wilhoit. Sure, like any red-blooded teenager, I was in lust with nearly every girl I saw, but I was also a bit of a romantic. *Me and Ashley? Nah.*

The girls came out of the washroom together. Ashley was laughing at something Kristina had just said and was turned to her, hand on Kristina's arm, as they sauntered our way. I looked at both of them a little more closely. Ashley had on a skirt and sweater. She was very slim, barely five feet tall. She had light brown hair cut just to her shoulders, and when she smiled, her silver braces flashed. She was extraordinarily cute.

Unfortunately for Ashley, she was walking next to somebody who, I suddenly realized, made her look thin and drab in comparison. Kristina, walking beside her, was devastating. She tended to dress either in black or in white, which set off her coloring very well, and tonight was no exception. She had on a sleek black dress that was very modest at the hem and neck, but snug enough to show off her very fit form. Her hair was jet black and long, almost to the middle of her back, and she had thick bangs that were cut below her dark eyebrows. Her skin glowed, and her eyes flashed with amusement as they glanced our way. I noticed that she seemed to almost glide across the floor, instead of walking with a stride like Ashley.

Damn, I thought to myself. *Have these two always looked this good?*

That was the moment that I realized I might be completely over Miss Molly O'Toole.

The four of us wound our way across the gym to the rest of our group, now congregated against the folded-up bleachers. As soon as we walked up to them, Becky grabbed my hand and dragged me out to the dance floor. Becks also played soccer, but only recreationally. I had acted as referee for one of her games during the summer, but I didn't get to know her until school started. She was almost my height, with dark blonde, almost brown hair that she almost always wore in a short ponytail. Tonight, however, her hair was down, just touching her shoulders. We were dancing fast to an old Chuck Berry song. Her hair was swinging back and forth across her face, first hiding and then revealing her features as she moved. It was almost hypnotic in its metronome sway. By the time the song ended, I was a little lightheaded just from watching her hair fly around. We held hands companionably on our way back to the group.

Just as the next song, a Beach Boys record, started up, Ashley took my hand and led me back out. I was still trying to get used to this sudden popularity, but I was willing to enjoy the ride as long as the wheel went around. Ashley was gyrating around, moving her hips while keeping her feet nearly still, and I smiled to myself as I danced with her. She was such a quiet, shy girl; it was odd to think that she was actually swinging her hips to and fro like this, in public and everything.

By the time we made it off the dance floor and back to the group, I was breathing a little more heavily. Dancing with these girls was hard work. Fortunately, a slow song came on, and I was just breathing a mental sigh of relief when Kristina beat Ashley to me, reaching for my hand and wordlessly leading me back out to the dance floor. She flowed into my arms effortlessly and seemed to mold herself to me, resting her head on my shoulder as we box-stepped around the floor. I was sorry when the song ended and Kristina slipped away from me, leading me back to our group while still holding my sweaty hand.

The next fast set began, and Ashley pulled me back out for another dance. When that one was done, Josh's girlfriend, Andrea, came my way as Becky took Josh out. I pleaded exhaustion, so she took Jorge out to boogie. I watched all the kids grooving and jiving out on the floor. Out in the middle of the crowd, I could see Molly dancing and shimmying with Trent. I looked around and saw Scotty leaning against the wall, looking sourly out toward Molly and Trent. He looked very unhappy. *Welcome to the Molly's Exes Club,* I thought. I raised my paper cup to him in a mock salute, but he wasn't paying any attention to me. *Just as well, probably.*

My eyes kept on dragging back to Ashley and to Kristina. There was quite a contrast between the two, but they were both very attractive girls. Ashley was swaying back and forth with Toby, who had his hands on her hips as they danced together. I thought they looked good together. I glanced over at Kristina, who was gliding around Jake, her lithe body moving with all the grace of a leopard. As I watched, she glanced over at me. Our eyes met, nearly stopping my heart, until she dropped her gaze, moving around Jake in a sinuous move to the music.

Becky grabbed me for another fast song. Strands of her hair were getting matted with sweat as she swung her head back and forth to the beat. I led her more toward the middle of the floor, just to see who was with whom on the dance floor.

The song ended, and almost immediately, another slow song came on. This time, Kristina didn't even wait for us to get off the dance floor. She met Becky and me at the edge, and Becks wordlessly stepped aside in what almost felt like an unspoken agreement, letting Kristina slip her hand in mine and guide me back out. This time I put both arms around her waist and held her to me. As she laid her head on my shoulder, I felt her take a deep breath and pull me even tighter to her. The feel of her body against mine triggered some rather dirty thoughts in me.

By the time the song ended, we were right in the middle of the crowded dance floor. Without letting go of me, Kristina looked up into my eyes wordlessly. I could have sworn she was waiting for me to kiss her, but that couldn't be. *Could it?* A fraction before the hesitation turned into embarrassment, she turned, releasing me from her arms, and slowly made her way back toward our side of the gym. She held her hand behind her and wiggled her fingers at me, confident enough not to turn around to see if I was following her. I took the hint and reached for her. I held her hand as we walked, and she didn't let go until we were back within the circle of our friends.

Jorge looked at me silently. I shrugged at him. He rolled his eyes, as if to tell me that I was the densest fool he knew, and turned away to say something to Jake. Ashley said she wanted to go find Theo and roll him around the dance floor, and took off to look for him. I heard the opening samba beat of Santana's "*Oye Como Va*" start up, and Jorge leaped up, grabbing Kristina by the arm, and the two of them practically ran out to the dance floor to do some cutting to the strong Latin beat.

And dance they did. I didn't know Jorge had those kinds of moves in him, but he was absolutely sensational out there, putting on a real show for everybody. All the boys' eyes, however, were on his sister. She was swaying and pouting, dipping and twirling, stalking and stretching like a cat and practically purring with pleasure all during the dance. It was unlike anything I had ever seen before, and I was enthralled. In fact, most of the other dancers out there stopped to watch in appreciation, marveling at the two Mendozas showing 'em how.

As Kristina and Jorge flowed together across the floor, I had the distinct impression that, even though Kristina was concentrating on dancing with her brother, her focus was toward me. There was nothing she was doing that I could say with any certainty was aimed at me, but I still had the feeling that she knew exactly where I was all the time. Her sudden exhibitionistic fervor was for my benefit. Whether it was a conscious effort on her part or not, it had a definite effect on me. I could not tear my eyes from the dance, nor did I want to stop watching. And when the final notes of the song echoed into the gymnasium, the two of them stood there in a pose, oriented toward each other, arms upraised, still as statues while their schoolmates, having seen a side of them that had been unknown up until just that moment, broke into applause and cheering for the display. The sudden barrage of cheering and clapping seemed to snap them out of their trance, and they looked around them, somewhat embarrassed over the attention they were getting. Panting and sweating from their exertions, they dropped their arms, turned and smiled at each other, and then walked back toward the group of us. We were standing there, mouths agape in awe, having just witnessed a true transformation among kids we all thought we knew pretty well.

Everything after that was denouement since the music stopped a couple of songs later. We all gathered our coats and headed for the door and the restaurant, laughing and teasing each other easily. Ashley rejoined us by the door, having spun Theo around for one song and stood by him while they watched the Flying Mendozas. We all piled into a couple of cars and headed out.

When the evening finally ended after an hour of ice cream and pop and cake and coffee, our rides were showing up to pick us up. Mr. Mendoza drove up to take Jorge and Kristina home, just as my brother Michael rolled up to give Jake and me a ride home. Right before she got into the car, Kristina took my arm and pulled her lips up to my ear.

"Please call me, Sean. Please," she whispered. Without another word, she ducked into the car and pulled the door shut behind her. I knew saying those words cost her a lot. I promised myself that I would do my best to not disappoint her.

And I did remember. It was late the next day, Sunday, when I finally got up the nerve to call her house. Jorge answered the phone.

"It's about damn time, Porter," he admonished me.

"What are you talking about, Jorge?"

"She asked you to call, man. No, she din' tell me, but I know her well enough. She did ask you, right?"

"Yeah, she did, and…"

"And nothin', man. She been on pins an needles all day, waitin'. I knew she was nervous about somethin', and I finally figured it out. If you wasn' gonna call soon, I was gonna come over there an' kick your ass, man."

"What the hell are you talking about?"

"Kristina, man, what choo think? You know how hard it was for her to grovel like that, asking you to call? You better do the right thing wit' her, man." He sounded as serious as he did when he was sitting on top of Del Toro that day in the hallway.

"Just get her, will you? And don't worry, man," I tried to assure him. "Of course I'll do the right thing."

"I know you will, Sean. I just wanted you to know how much this means to her, thass all." He set the telephone down and went to get his sister.

A quiet voice. "Hello?"

"Hi," I said. Then, as an afterthought, I decided I had better introduce myself, since she probably didn't recognize my voice over the telephone. "It's Sean."

She giggled. "Of course it's you," she said. I could hear the smile in her voice, and it made me smile, too.

We talked about nothing for about twenty minutes, until I could hear a heavy voice rumbling in the background.

"I've got to go, Sean," she said softly. "Thank you for calling."

"Uh, wait a minute, Kristina," I said hurriedly. "Do you…I mean, would you…uh…maybe we could…what I mean is…" Boy, was my tongue ever getting tangled now. *Where did I suddenly get this attack of nerves?* I took a deep breath and started all over.

"What I mean is, would you like to do something next weekend with me?" I finally finished.

"Sure," she replied quietly. "What would you like to do?"

"Well, maybe we could go to a movie or something."

"Okay," she said. "I'll ask my parents and let you know tomorrow at school. Is that all right?"

"Uh, sure, that's fine," I said dumbly. "See you tomorrow, then."

"Good night, Sean. Thank you for calling." She hung up the phone, leaving me standing there stupidly, a dead line humming in my ear, resonating in a sonic harmony with the memory of the sweetness of her voice.

- 28 -

RESPECT

On Friday night, Michael drove me over to pick up Kristina. We were meeting Josh and Andrea at the mall, and then we were going to go see a movie.

I knocked on the front door, and Mr. Mendoza opened it. He stepped aside, gesturing me in. He was not very tall but he was substantial. I could see just how Jorge would look in twenty years.

I stepped into the hallway. Mr. Mendoza held out his hand and, in a heavy accent, said, "Welcome, Sean. Kristina will be here in *uno momento.*"

The smaller Mendoza children, four all told, were peeking at me from doorways, whispering to each other and giggling. I felt like I was on display as I shook Mr. Mendoza's hand.

Jorge came out of the kitchen, his mother trailing behind, and came over to me.

"Hey, Sean," he said with a smile.

His father turned to him and said something in Spanish.

Jorge turned back to me, a grimace on his face. "My father has asked me to translate for him. He says that he is very glad to meet you. He also said he wishes to say something to you."

"Okay," I said, suddenly apprehensive. This was a new one on me.

Mr. Mendoza looked at me as he spoke, and I stayed facing him as Jorge translated.

"He says that Kristina is his oldest daughter and so is very special to him, just as his oldest son is special to him." Jorge's voice was expressionless as he spoke. I saw Kristina, dressed in a simple black sweater and cotton pants, just coming in from the hallway. I glanced at her and smiled before turning back to her father. She looked a little embarrassed but said nothing.

Her father glanced back to see her standing in the doorway and then turned and continued.

"We have tried to raise our children to respect all others, even when we ourselves have not been shown that same respect," Jorge continued translating. "It is a sad fact of life that not all people have been taught how to respect others."

Jorge stopped, firing off a burst of Spanish to his father. It sounded like a question, or maybe a complaint. His father answered back implacably, and Jorge, resigned, continued translating.

"He says that he expects you to treat his daughter with the respect she is due. If you do not, he will know, and he will have words with you about it."

He did not look like a man I would want to have "words" with, particularly alone in a small locked room. Still facing him, I composed my reply before opening my mouth.

"I give you my word that I will give Kristina every consideration I can. I think of her as a good friend, and Jorge is a good friend, and I would do nothing to harm either friendship."

Jorge translated for me. Mr. Mendoza nodded, held out his hand, and shook mine to seal the deal. He smiled then, and turned and held out his arm, as if presenting his daughter to a crowd. Kristina came up to him, kissed him on the cheek, and we headed out the door to Michael's car.

It was always awkward when you had to be driven around because you were too young to drive yourself. Picking up a date was even more so. We solved the problem by squeezing into the front seat with Michael. It was crowded, but I certainly didn't mind. As a side benefit, Mike didn't feel so much like a chauffeur, either.

"I'm sorry you had to go through that with my father," Kristina said as we started down the street.

"Hey, it's just fine," I assured her. "I know he worries about you and wants to protect you, and all that."

"Yes, well, he's decided that the best way to get his point across is to speak Spanish and have Jorge translate. In reality, he speaks English nearly as well as we do. He's just trying to make an impression on you," she said with a smile.

"Oh, he made an impression on me, all right," I said. "He scared me a little," I added.

"He'll be glad to know that," she said with a laugh. She shifted a little, and the contact I felt with her, up my side and my arm, from my hip and down my leg, got just a little more substantial. We stayed in unacknowledged close contact with each other, just like that, all the way to the mall.

Once we met up with Josh and Andrea at the mall, thoughts of the punishment Mr. Mendoza might be planning to wreak upon me if I got too improper were banished, and we had a great time together. When we got to the movie theater, we settled in with popcorn and sodas, into one of the side rows of the auditorium. Andrea and Kristina were sitting between Josh and me. By the middle of the first reel of film, our hands had found each other's. We spent the rest of the movie in awareness of each other, maintaining contact with clasped hands and knees just touching.

On the way home, Kristina and I once again squeezed into the front of Michael's car, and Andrea and Josh climbed into the back. We dropped off Andrea first, and Josh walked her to her door, giving her a long kiss good night before trudging back to the car for a ride back to his house.

Kristina's house was our next stop, and I walked her to her door, also. I wondered if Mr. Mendoza was watching through the curtains, making sure I treated his daughter properly. I looked at the windows nervously. Kristina probably guessed my thoughts, because she had a small, secret smile on her face as she stood there, waiting for me to make up my mind about what to do. Finally, she took both my hands in hers and turned me to face her.

"Good night, Sean. Thank you for a very nice evening." She leaned in toward me just a fraction, watching me. I bucked up my courage and bent toward her, and our lips touched softly for just a moment. She turned toward the door and opened it, flooding the landing with light from the hallway.

"Kristina?" She turned around and looked at me quizzically. "Did you really have a good time tonight? What I mean is, would you go out with me again?"

She smiled her secret smile again. "Yes, Sean, I would love to go out with you again."

The pressure I had been feeling, but had tried to ignore, dissipated into vapor, to my immense relief. I headed back to the car, my feet barely making contact with the sidewalk.

The whole next week at school, I didn't have much of a chance to talk with Kristina. I kept on telling myself that it was just one date, not a lifetime commitment, and to chill out about it. It didn't help. I called her on Tuesday evening, but her father said she couldn't come to the phone. I called her on Wednesday, but she wasn't home. I called her on Thursday, very near panic. She had me thinking that I had done something wrong, that she didn't want to see me again, that she was evading me. She answered the phone on the second ring.

"*Sí,* hello?"

"Kristina? Hi, it's me, Sean."

"Oh, Sean, I was hoping you would call," she said. She sounded happy, not upset. *Did I worry all week for nothing?*

"You were?" I asked before I could think about it. "I thought maybe you didn't want to talk to me."

"Why would you think that, silly?" She sounded amused.

"Well...ummm...I called the other night, and then again last night..."

"Oh, that," she dismissed. "My father just told me tonight that you had called. He wouldn't let me call you back. He says it's not ladylike to be calling boys."

"That's okay," I said, relieved. "I just wasn't sure if I was making a pest out of myself or not, that's all."

She giggled, a tinkling sound that sent shivers up and down my spine. "You can be a pest, if you'd like," she said softly. "I won't mind."

"Um, would you like to do something with me this week-end?"

"Of course. What did you want to do?"

"Well, Eric and Keisha were thinking about going out to the bowling alley on Saturday night. It's something about using glow-in-the-dark pins or something. Would you like to try it?"

"Okay. What time?"

"I'll call Eric and find out and call you back," I suggested.

"No, don't call back tonight. Just tell me tomorrow at school or call me tomorrow night. I'll ask my parents if it's okay, but I'm sure they will say it's fine as long as I don't stay out past eleven."

"I'll talk to you tomorrow then. Bye."

"Bye, Sean. Thank you for calling." The telephone clicked in my ear as the connection was broken.

Eric, who had just gotten his driver's license, picked me up Saturday night for our dates. It was so wonderful having a little more freedom instead of relying on older brothers or parents for rides. My birthday was coming up soon and I could hardly wait to take my driver's test and get my license.

We picked up Keisha and then drove over to Kristina's house. I thought I must have passed some sort of test with her parents, because she came bounding out the front door and down the sidewalk, waving back toward the house as she headed for our car. I didn't have to go through a grilling from her father this time. Maybe he figured he had scared me sufficiently that first time, which was true, or maybe he had come to trust me a little bit. I hoped to be trustworthy, not only in his eyes, but in Kristina's, too. She climbed into the back seat with me, and as soon as we were down the street and out of sight of her house, she scooted over to sit next to me. I took her hand and held it in mine, glad of even that little touch.

At the bowling alley, most of the lights were out. There was a disco ball rotating above the alleys, with a spotlight shining on it, scattering shattered rays of light all over the interior. Some of the bowling pins had been painted with fluorescent colors, and there were black lights shining down from the pinsetters, making the pins glow at the far end of the dark alleys, giving the place a surreal feel. There was loud music playing; the pulse of the bass was thumping and reverberating through the floor and into our bodies.

Kristina was a terrible bowler. She had only gone bowling once before in her life and the challenge of trying to knock the pins down in the dark was beyond her. Nearly every time she whipped the ball down the alley, it ended up in the gutter, usually within about ten feet of the foul line. She didn't care though, and neither did the rest of us. We were laughing and joking about how awful we all were at this game. On the rare occasions when Kristina actually managed to knock a few pins over, she would jump up and squeal excitedly, hands in the air in triumph, and then she would run over to me and jump into my arms joyfully. I loved it every time she did that, being able to hold her tightly with a crowd all around us. Those were special moments for me.

On the ride home after we finished bowling, we snuggled up in the cold back seat, her arms threaded through mine as we waited for the heater to kick in. Keisha and Eric were pointedly ignoring us, so I took the opportunity to lift up her chin and lean toward her. Her eyes were wide and solemn, an infinitely deep pool of brown and black, with her lips slightly parted in anticipation of this moment.

I kissed her. Softly, oh so softly and gently, I paid homage to her soft and sensitive lips. Her eyes closed, and she pressed toward me for more. I turned in my seat and slipped my arm around her waist as we continued kissing. I was getting very warm but it had little to do with the car heater. I was hoping she was feeling the same.

She was wearing a long coat that buttoned down the front with four large buttons. I stopped kissing her and gazed into her eyes as my hand found the coat button near her waist and fumbled to open it up. I wanted to be closer to her, but I didn't want her to be cold. I just wanted to slide my arm inside her coat to hold her closely. I finally was able to push the button through the buttonhole, and as I slipped my arm inside her coat, my fingers accidentally brushed against the bump of her breast, barely hard enough to feel. But I saw her eyes widen, and she jerked a little. By then, my hand was on her waist and she understood that it was an accident. However, I was afraid the damage might be done. She relaxed, though, and moved to kiss me again, a soft and tender touching that washed away all worry.

We stayed just that way until we pulled into her driveway. We walked to her front door, but this time the light didn't come on. I pulled her to me.

"Are you okay?" I asked quietly.

I thought she might have blushed just a little. "Of course I am. Why wouldn't I be?"

"Um…well, it's nothing," I stammered.

"Look, Sean, I...there was a boy I liked, when we lived in Texas." She paused. "I was only thirteen, almost fourteen. We... he and I...he is the only other boy I've ever kissed, Sean, besides you."

"It's okay, Kristina."

"No, I just want you to know that I have no...experience... in this."

Tears were just starting to well in those deep, dark eyes.

"So," she continued hesitantly, "I'm a little frightened sometimes, Sean. If you don't want to see me anymore, I understand... but..."

I was devastated by her words. "Don't you want to go out with me, Kristina? I thought you liked me."

She hugged herself to me. I instinctively held her tight, trying to understand what she was saying.

"I do like you, Sean, and I do want to go out with you. It's just...I mean...I can't...you know...I can't be like some of the other girls, and...if you don't want to be with such an...inexperienced...person..."

"Hold on a minute," I said. I held her by her arms and moved her back a little so I could look in her eyes. "You think I won't like you just because you're not like Molly or someone?" She didn't move, but her eyes told me the truth. "That is the most ridiculous thing I have ever heard you say, Kristina. I like you because you are *you,* not because of anything you might or might not have done in the past, or for any, um, favors you might give in the future."

"Really?" The tears started spilling, but I thought it might be from relief instead of sadness.

"Really. Don't get me wrong here, Kristina. I would love to share something beyond a few kisses with you. Hell, I'll come right out and tell you that I lust after you." She finally smiled, a very good sign. "I would jump your bones in a heartbeat if I

228

thought you would be willing. But I know you're not, and it's all okay. I like you for who you are, and your innocence is all a part of you. If you want to wait, I'll wait. Maybe some days I'll be a little impatient, but just tell me to back off and lighten up, Kristina, and I promise I will. And that's no lie."

She sobbed and crushed herself to me, holding me as tightly as she possibly could.

"Hey," I said. She looked up at me, her head still against my chest. "Would you go out with me again?" I asked.

Eyes shining, she lifted up and kissed me, pressing hard against my lips with hers.

"Yes, of course," she said happily. She gave me one last quick kiss before turning to the door. "Thank you, Sean. Thank you for understanding. Call me?"

"Maybe even tonight, when I get home," I threatened, even though we both knew I wouldn't. Her parents would never let her talk on the telephone this late.

My feet never touched the sidewalk as I strolled back to Eric's car.

Over the course of the next week, I called her so we could chat in the evening a couple of times, and she even managed to call me once, a very short, whispered conversation. I was impressed, since she apparently managed to sneak that call in to me, a huge accomplishment considering there were seven other family members in her house at the time.

In the back seat of Eric's car the next weekend, we were snuggling and sharing small kisses again. This time, when I brushed against her as I put my arm around her waist, she didn't flinch or look upset at all. In fact, she kissed me hard and opened her mouth just a little, allowing her tongue to slip out and brush lightly against my lips. Encouraged, I let the tip of my tongue touch hers, and the contact was electric. Her mouth opened a little more, her tongue got a little more daring, and she was making small noises deep within her as she felt her passions begin to escalate. As we kissed, her body turned slightly away from me. My hand at her waist was moved from her side to her tummy, over her sweater.

I was so involved in enjoying the development of our new way of kissing that the change in her body language didn't register with me at first. Finally, one of those odd contact switches in my brain clicked and it occurred to me that this was her silent signal to me that it was probably okay to take our physical relationship up another step. I slowly, cautiously, allowed my hand to move up the outside of her sweater, ready to call an instant retreat at the first sign of discomfort. I felt the nubby cotton of the knit of her sweater, and then I could feel the harder edge of the bottom of her bra beneath. Still no sign of hesitation came from her; in fact, her kissing got hotter and wetter as my hand moved farther up, finally cupping her small breast through the layers of clothing. I caressed and lightly squeezed her.

Unfortunately, it was a short ride to her house, and we arrived way too soon for my liking. But arrive we did, so we scooted out of the back seat and I walked her, as usual, to her door.

This time, her good night kiss held quite a bit of heat, no doubt left over from our activities of a few moments before.

"You are a surprising young lady," I said as I held her there.

Again, I thought I could detect a blush. "I don't want you to think I'm cold," she whispered.

"Hey, I've seen you dance. You are anything but cold, sweetie." I kissed her again.

"You ain't seen nothin' yet," she said. "My momma taught me a dance..." She stopped talking abruptly, and this time I knew she was blushing fiercely. It made my blood race a little faster through me.

"Will you dance it for me?" I asked teasingly.

"Oh, maybe some day," she replied coquettishly. "If you're a very good boy." She pecked me on the lips and turned to the door. "Good night, *mas querido*. Sleep well."

Sleep well, she said. It would be a very long time before I could get the image of Kristina Mendoza, her cinnamon skin glowing as she danced alone just for me, out of my mind long enough to be able to fall asleep.

- 29 -

TRUST BETRAYED

Tryouts for the girl's varsity and junior varsity soccer teams were held at the beginning of March. Jen, Ashley, and Molly won positions on the JV team, while Kristina and Tessa both made the varsity team. Practice was every day after school, starting about the second week of March. The girls were doing a lot of running laps, out on the track when the weather cooperated and in the gymnasium when it didn't. There was a lot of good-natured complaining about it among the team members, but they knew the benefits of all that boring lap running would pay off once the season began.

Because of her practice schedule, I couldn't see or call Kristina much during the week. Her parents were very strict anyway, and with so much of her free time taken up with soccer, she only had time for homework after dinner. No time for poor Sean.

I had a plan, though. My sixteenth birthday was the first week of April, and Toby's was the same week. We came up with the idea that we should have a combined birthday party to celebrate. My parents offered to host the party, so all our friends were invited over to my house on the first Saturday of April. Toby and I asked Ashley and Kristina if they could come over early in the afternoon to hang out with us while we got the basement ready for the party, which they did. Toby and Ashley had become something of an item ever since the turnabout dance in February. They discovered a remarkable compatibility together that began on the dance floor and expanded from there. I was really happy about it for Toby's sake, because it meant that he was finally getting over his serious crush on Jen Davies, who still was madly in love with Sam. Ashley was a better fit for him, anyway, since she didn't tower over him by a foot like Jen did. The four of us had a great afternoon getting set for the party, watching TV, and gossiping about our friends.

Most of our friends were at the party. The music was loud, but there were some quieter, darker corners for the couples (though my parents made sure they patrolled those areas frequently). Drinks were spilled, chips and dips were consumed in huge quantities, and everybody seemed to be having a very good time.

At one point during the height of the party, Eric came over to me.

"How's it going, Sean? Another year older, huh?" he said.

"Yeah, the time's really flying now," I replied. "One day, you're a fifteen-year-old punk. The next thing you know, you've got your driver's license and you've got a bunch more new friends needing rides."

"Don't I know it. I got my license and all of a sudden, I had to start driving my younger brother and sister around all the time. Got old pretty quick," he complained. I could sympathize. My brother Michael was more than happy to see me get my license, since that meant that I could drive our younger brother Stephen around now instead of him having to cart the both of us. "Hey, have you heard the rumors going around about your old girlfriend?" he asked.

I shook my head. *This oughta be good,* I thought to myself.

"You know she broke up with Scotty, right?" he asked. I hadn't known, but then I wasn't paying a lot of attention to what Molly was up to lately, either. "Well, Scott's been spreading some dirt about her. About how she was putting out for him so easy at first but then shut him out after a while. Calling her an ice bitch, things like that."

"You're kidding."

"Nope. Ask Keisha. She's really been getting the down-and-dirty from the rumor mills in the girls' johns at school. Anyway, the story that Keisha picked up is that Molly was two-timing Scotty with Trent and then dropped them both and jumped on Mikey Evanson."

"You have got to be shitting me, Eric. Molly is doing this? What the hell is wrong with her?"

Jake walked up just in time to hear my question. "You guys talking about Molly 'I'll Do Anything for a Long Hard One' O'Toole? Yeah, I heard, too," he said.

"I don't believe it," I said, shaking my head at the news. "What the hell is she trying to prove?"

"I don't know, but her brother better not find out about it," said Jake, glancing over in Josh's direction.

"On a happier note, man, it looks like you and Kristina have got things going," said Eric. "You're a lucky dude. She's one of a kind."

"Yeah, well, my track record for keeping women happy is a pretty dismal 0–1 so far," I said. "I'm trying, but who knows how successful I'll be."

"You know the secret to keeping a woman happy, don't you?" asked Eric. Jake and I looked at each other questioningly and then both said no.

"Just repeat after me: 'Yes, dear, of course it was my fault. Anything you want, my little love-muffin,' and everything will be hunky-dory," he said.

We all laughed.

"Lessons in life we could all learn from," said Jake.

As a birthday party treat, my parents agreed to let me drive Josh and Andrea and Kristina home after the party. I was using my mom's car, a '75 Buick Century with a split bench seat in the front. Josh and Andrea got into the back, and Kristina slid over next to me as I started up the old beast. We were barely out of the driveway when I heard giggling and kissing noises coming from the back. Kristina looked at me and smiled, taking my arm and holding it as I tooled down the street.

In almost no time at all, I was pulling into Andrea's driveway. I stopped the car, throwing it into park while we waited for them to disentangle from each other and walk up to her front door. While Josh was kissing her and saying good night, I slipped my arm around Kristina's shoulder. She tilted her head up, and I bent down and kissed her tenderly and softly, just the way I knew she liked to be kissed.

The back door opened, and Josh climbed back in.

"All right, you guys, that's enough," he complained good-naturedly. "Can't you see I'm lonely back here? It's bad enough I don't have my girlfriend here. I have to watch you two and your disgusting public display of affection?"

I took my arm back from around Kristina's shoulder and put the car in reverse. As I was looking through the back window, backing out of the driveway, I glanced at Josh.

"It's not exactly a public place, I don't think. But we'll stop anyway, because we are sensitive to your loneliness," I said.

"Thank you very much," he shot back. "Thank you from the bottom of my bottom."

"Josh! That's gross!" Kristina complained, but I could see she was smiling as she said it.

I drove through the side streets to Josh's house and dropped him off. I was reluctant to drive straight to Kristina's house, wanting to spend as many minutes with her as I could, so I turned in the opposite direction, intending to just drive around for a few minutes with her by my side.

"Good, I don't want to go home just yet," she whispered when she saw that I had turned in a different direction.

We drove slowly down the street.

"Stop over there," she said, pointing to a dark area in the middle of the next block. I pulled over to the curb, in front of a new house under construction. There were no lights around us as we came to a stop under a tree, the streetlights on the corner too far away to afford much light here in the middle of the block.

It was chilly out, so I left the car running with the lights off. I turned to her and put my arm around her once more. She turned into me, slipping her arm around my back as she tilted her face up, inviting me to kiss her. I bent down and pressed my lips to hers in a soft, warm, and tender kiss. I planted lots of little kisses on her lips, the corners of her mouth, her cheeks, and her chin, receiving lots in return. I didn't want to rush her in any way, so I contented myself to nibbling and kissing her softly. Finally, her lips found their way to mine, and I could feel her trembling as her mouth opened just slightly and the tip of her tongue just touched my mouth. My lips parted, and my tongue slipped out to meet hers, tip to tip, before retreating and breaking the kiss. I nuzzled her throat, feeling the heat radiating from her skin just below her ear, and returned for another kiss. Her lips and tongue were bolder now, being guided in their explorations by her rising temperature, until, after several brief darting jabs at each other, our mouths finally opened and our lips sealed onto each other as our tongues intertwined in our first truly hot, wet, demanding kiss.

She moaned into my mouth and twisted her body so she could hold me tighter against her. My hand snaked around her waist to hold her tightly to me. My knee was pressed against hers, our torsos twisted around as I struggled to get even closer to her around the steering column of the car. She reached up and threw her arm around my neck as we kissed, and I could feel her sweater inch up from her jeans so that two of my fingers were resting against the hot skin of her lower back.

Just that small touch of her soft skin lit the afterburners in my body, and my blood raced through me, making me feel flushed and swollen. My fingers slipped under her sweater, still at her waist, and rested there, reveling in the feel of her incredibly smooth skin. My hand warmed from the touch, my fingers tingling, as I pressed my palm hard against her back.

We stayed like that for a time, kissing each other, until the headlights of a car turning down the street from the corner interrupted our reverie. We both glanced at the clock on the dashboard.

"I've got to get home," she said regretfully. "Jorge is probably already there, and my parents will be worried that I didn't come home with him."

I reluctantly let go of her, wishing fervently we could have continued, but I had made a promise to myself that she would guide me. I would only go as far as she was unhesitatingly willing to go and would not push her to go beyond. I could see now, though, that it would not be an easy promise to keep.

Two minutes later, I was walking her to her door. The porch light went on as soon as we stepped to the door. She reached up and kissed me lightly on my cheek just before the front door opened, and she stepped inside.

"Thank you, Sean," she said. "Good night."

It was a long time before I finally fell asleep, thoughts of my raven-haired beauty keeping me occupied.

☆ ☆ ☆

Just as soccer practice had started for the school teams, the recreational teams for all ages were starting to gear up. I got a call from Davey and Kip's coach, Bill Pinella, asking if I would be his assistant coach for the spring session. To help seal the deal,

238

he had asked Lori Wilkinson to call me, too. She told me that the boys were clamoring to see me again.

"It seems to them like it's been years since they saw you," she said.

"Well, it's been since the fall sometime," I recalled.

"So, will you do it? Will you help out Bill with his team?"

"Sure, Lori; I'll be glad to," I said.

Bill and I met a couple of times at his house to go over some drills he had in mind for the team. He was going to be out of town for a couple of games and he insisted on letting me make my own lineups for those games.

The first couple of practices we held were just information-gathering exercises for us, watching the boys kick the ball around, timing them as they ran up and down the field, and asking each one which position he liked to play best and why. They still had plenty of soccer left to play before they got locked into a specific position or even labeled defense or offense, so we didn't take anything they said too seriously, knowing full well how changeable kids that age could be.

After the second practice, I recruited Jorge to come along to some of our practices. We had a core of three boys who were most interested in playing keeper, so Jorge took those three aside for about twenty minutes each time and worked with them on punting, blocking, and moving their defensive players around the field. The three keepers got more and more enthusiastic about trying out their new knowledge in a game, so we dedicated the last half of each practice to scrimmaging, dividing the team in half and playing either a half-field game or a full-field scrimmage. Sometimes we drew lanes on the field with cornstarch and flour, making them stay within their lanes. Some days, the lanes had about ten feet of space between them, sometimes we drew them so they overlapped, but the rule always was don't step out of the lane. We knew that when it came to game time, they would follow the ball anyway, but we were trying to convince them that if they played positions, they would be able to move the ball better. Some days it worked; some days it didn't.

Lori came down whenever she could to watch at least the last half of practice. She asked if I could work with the boys again on the side. I was gratified, as I had been looking forward to helping them out again. She also mentioned that Molly was still baby-sitting for her occasionally, but she had noticed that she was pretty unhappy lately and asked if I knew anything about it.

"Nope, I don't," I said. "Molly and I haven't really spoken much since around November."

"I'm sorry to hear that, Sean," she said. "I thought you two made a really cute couple."

"Well, at the time I thought so too, but what can you do?" I replied.

She could tell I really didn't care to talk about it, so she dropped the subject.

☆ ☆ ☆

A couple of weeks after my birthday, I borrowed my mom's car and picked up Kristina for our Saturday date. It had been a warm and sunny day, the first real promise of the summer to come. We decided to forego the movie we were going to see and instead drove to Silver Lake, a town close to us that had built up around its namesake body of water. There was a public prom-enade all around the lake, with park benches and gazebos and a band shell. We parked the car at dusk and just started meander-ing around the lake, pausing and sitting when we felt like it, walking and holding hands when we got tired of sitting.

It took us a couple of hours to make our way completely around the lake, and we were chilled by the time we got back to the car. Ours was the only car left in the lot as I started it up and threw the fan and heater on high.

"Ohhh, I'm so cold," she complained as she scooted over to nestle up against me. I put my arm around her and pulled her tighter to me.

"Snuggle up here; I'll warm you up," I said as I wrapped my arms around her. She twisted around to press more of herself up against me, trying to take advantage of my body heat. I unzipped my light jacket and pulled it around her as she shivered against me, her face tucked under my arm and her arms drawn in to her.

I felt the beginnings of heat coming from the floorboards. "It's warming up now," I said. She just shook her head and burrowed deeper into me, now snaking her arms around me, inside my jacket, to hold me around my waist.

"You could probably safely come out now," I said as I felt my feet begin to warm. She shook her head again, staying right where she was. "Come on, you can do it," I said encouragingly. Again, she shook her head and pulled even tighter on me. I grasped her shoulders and gently pulled her out from her warm cocoon. She lifted her head and smiled at me and then moved up closer to me. I bent down and kissed her softly. She practically purred as I kissed her, her pleasure and contentment obvious, even to me.

I felt her lips open slightly, her signal that she wanted more. I let the tip of my tongue peek out and touch her warm lips, and they parted a little more as her own tongue came out to meet mine, tips touching and caressing, exchanging information on a cellular level.

My own internal temperature climbed, and I stopped kissing her long enough to reach for the zipper of her coat. She watched me solemnly as I slowly lowered the tab and opened her coat so I could slip my arms around her. When I did, my hands encircling her waist, she closed her eyes and lifted her face up to kiss me again, opening her lips a little more and becoming more daring with her tongue in my mouth.

My hand found its way to the hem of her sweatshirt, and my fingers wormed their way underneath, encountering the soft skin of her tummy. I could feel the depression of her belly button, but that particular area was not my goal at the moment, as my hand slipped up her sternum to find her small breasts. I grasped one and squeezed, slid my hand over to fondle the other, then moved back to the first, almost as if comparing the roundness and firmness of her feminine charms. I managed to fumble with the front clasp of her bra, until the encasing material magically parted to allow me access to her hot, desirable flesh.

The heater of my car kept on pumping out hot air, and our own interior thermostats were turned up to maximum. After paying homage to her upper body, Kristina apparently comfortable with this intimacy, I moved my hand down to the snap of her jeans, but that tripped a circuit breaker in her. She froze and grabbed my hand, stopping me from continuing.

"No, Sean, please. I can't." She was breathing very hard, and I knew that what she did was nearly as difficult on her as it was on me, but I couldn't deny her. I looked into those huge brown eyes, looking so longingly at me, and took my hand completely away from her pants and pulled her by the waist to me. I lowered my face to her and kissed her soft lips, bending to her will without reservation. We kissed and cuddled for a time, lost in our own thoughts of wishes and acceptance, unspoken longings and unfulfilled desires balanced by the unreserved respect of our individual silent vows. Our kisses became more and more chaste, until finally they were as we had started, soft and tender and loving.

✰ ✰ ✰

Two weeks later, I had a very busy weekend planned. The girls had their first game on Friday night, and I was going to watch the varsity team play. There was a pizza party planned for after the game, and Kristina and I were going to go. On Saturday morning, she was coming over to my house to work on a project we were doing together for our English class. We had the same teacher, but were in different classes, so the assignments were the same for both classes. Then, later in the afternoon, Davey and Kip had their first game of the season. I was hoping that the lane drills we had been using would pay off during a game situation and was anxious to see how it worked.

The weekend started out great. The girls played hard on Friday, winning their game 3–0. Tessa tallied her first shutout as a varsity keeper, and Kristina scored the final goal, powering a shot in from just inside the box after taking a crossing pass.

After the game, we all went to a local hangout and ordered pizzas and sodas, talking about the game and laughing over some of the little errors that didn't affect the outcome at all. Most of the team was there, along with a bunch of friends of the team, including Jorge, Molly, Toby, and Ashley. Tessa had decided, sometime over the course of the spring, that maybe I wasn't the devil incarnate and was back to being relatively friendly to me again. Molly still didn't talk to me much, but we weren't enemies either, so everybody at the pizza place was comfortable and happy that they got their first win under their belts. I ended up driving Jorge and Kristina back to their house afterwards. Jorge, in his usual considerate way, quickly slipped out of the car as soon as it was stopped, giving Kristina and me a moment together so we could share one quick kiss. It wasn't nearly enough, but it had to do.

On Saturday, Kristina's mother dropped her off at my house so we could work on the project. Mrs. Mendoza came in for a moment and chatted with my mom in the kitchen. I'm sure she wanted to make sure Kristina and I hadn't just cooked up a plan to be alone, but we really did have homework to do. My brother Michael was home, too, coming in and out of the house for drinks and snacks as he washed and waxed his recent purchase, a 1977 Honda Accord.

After about an hour, my mom called us in to the kitchen for lunch. As we were eating, she said, "I hope you guys don't mind cleaning up after lunch. I have to go to my bridge club this afternoon."

"No, Mom, that's all right," I said.

"If you need anything, Michael is working on his car in the driveway," she added.

"Okay, no problem. We'll just be working here." We were set up in the family room and had the stereo going. Kristina went back in to continue working while I cleaned up the kitchen after lunch.

When I got done in the kitchen, I walked into the family room to get back to work. Kristina was lying on the floor on her stomach, one leg bent up into the air, writing in the journal we were creating. It was a warm spring Saturday, and she was wearing a short T-shirt that had ridden up just a little to leave a thin strip of skin showing above her shorts. She looked absolutely delicious, so scrumptious that I just couldn't resist. I knelt down next to her and kissed the gap between her T-shirt and her shorts. She squirmed a little.

"Stop it, Sean," she said, but she really didn't sound like she meant it, so I did it again.

"Sean!" she complained, but there was a laugh in her voice. She pretended to keep on writing as I scooted down and kissed the back of her bent knee. She squirmed again, but it wasn't to get away from me. This squirm had a definite hint of excitement in it, especially when she straightened out her leg for me. It seemed like an open invitation to me, so I did it again, this time eliciting a humming "Mmmmmmm" from her.

I kissed my way up the back of her thigh, all the way up to the hem of her shorts, and worked my way back down again to the back of her knee. Her leg was silky smooth on my lips, and

I could feel the fires begin to stoke within me as I continued. I worked my way slowly back up her thigh, nibbling and kissing along one leg and running just my fingertips, so lightly I was barely touching her, up her other thigh. Her legs parted slightly, an involuntary reaction that I didn't think she even realized was happening. She laid still, the journal forgotten as she concentrated on the signals being transmitted through her nervous system.

I began to caress just a little more with my fingertips, still reveling in the silken feel of her skin on my lips and tongue and fingers. I kissed and caressed up and down her legs, each time a memorable journey of discovery. Finally, as I approached the hem of her shorts, I grasped the material in my teeth for a moment and then stuck my tongue up the leg of her baggy shorts as far as I could. I pushed up the material with my face as I traced along her skin, until I got to the edge of her panties, tasting the salt on her skin from her thigh to the crease along the bottom of her butt.

I teased her, and worked myself up, by kissing and nibbling the skin of her legs. As I played with her, I could feel her trembling slightly. *Is it excitement? Nervousness? Desire? Fear?*

I was about to suggest we go up to my room, away from the possibility of discovery by my brother, when the telephone rang.

"Shit," I muttered. I scrambled up from the floor and reached for the phone.

"Is Kristina there, please?" It was her mother's voice. *Oh, great,* I thought. *A hell of a time for her to be calling.* I didn't say anything, just handed the phone over to Kristina. She was flushed and nervous as she reached for the handset.

"Hello?" She paused, listening. *"Si, Mama. Si. Adios."*

She turned to me after hanging up the phone. "My mom is coming to pick me up. I'm sorry, Sean." She looked crestfallen, but I thought she might have been a little relieved that we didn't have more time to go even further than we did. I, on the other hand, was not relieved at all. In fact, I was in some discomfort, having been left in the lurch, in a manner of speaking. I wondered if there was any factual basis behind the theory of taking a cold shower.

Looking at the clock, though, I realized I might not have time for that cold shower. Davey and Kip's soccer game was starting shortly. As soon as Kristina's mother picked her up, I would have to borrow Michael's car and get to the game. Frustration mounted on frustration. It wasn't Kristina's fault that her mother called, and I had to be going anyway, but I still felt like I had been put through the wringer by circumstances beyond my control.

We picked up our study materials in silence. Kristina's shoulders were a little hunched, and she kept on glancing at me with a worried expression. I knew she had detected my mood, and it was upsetting her, but I couldn't find the right words to say to her to ease her mind. I just wasn't in a conciliatory mood, so I let her suffer a little.

A car honked from the driveway. Kristina headed for the front door, books and papers in her arms. I opened the door for her. I still couldn't think of anything meaningful to say to her.

"I'll see you later," I said lamely.

"Okay, Sean." There was a hint of tears in her eyes that I tried to ignore. "Good luck at the game this afternoon. Will you call me later?"

"Sure, I'll call you tonight after I get back home," I said. Maybe by then I could come up with the proper words to tell her how much I cared for her, words that just escaped me now.

I closed the door and sighed, disgusted with myself, and trudged upstairs to change my clothes for the game. I did have just enough time to test out that cold shower theory.

It didn't work.

☆ ☆ ☆

Michael was going out with some buddies that night, so he let me borrow his nice, clean car so I could get to the soccer game. I got there with just minutes to spare, so I ran out onto the field to give Coach Bill a hand with warm-ups. The referee came over to inspect the team and patiently explained to the young boys about how the game was to come to a stop whenever he blew his whistle. He also talked for just a moment about throw-ins, hand balls, and other fairly common things that were bound to come up in the course of a game, explaining how he would be calling the infractions he saw. The information was nothing new to Bill or me, but it was good to have the boys reminded of the rules of the game by someone in a uniform.

We took the boys over to the sidelines and talked to them briefly before giving them their positions for the start of the game.

"How shall we play the game today, boys?" asked Coach Bill.

"Zones and lanes!" they shouted.

"Right! Okay, remember that your lanes overlap. That means that you, Justin," he said, pointing to the boy who would be playing center forward, "can move a little bit into Joey's lane on the left or into Davey's lane on the right."

"Oh...*kay!*" shouted Justin.

"Now, Joey," he said, turning to his left forward, "can you go into Justin's lane?"

"Yup," said Joey.

"Right. And can you go into Davey's lane?" asked Bill.

"No way, Jose!" Joey yelled. All the kids started laughing.

"That's right," called out Coach Bill. The boys quieted down a little. "Play your lanes and pass the ball."

Davey called out our passing chant, "One-potato look, two-potato pass!"

"Exactly right!" exclaimed Bill. "Are you ready? Okay, team, go out there and show them how this game is played!"

They all jumped up and down, shouting and hooting as Bill called out their names and sent them out to the field to take their positions. Davey was playing forward on the right; Kip was our center midfielder. We had three boys in reserve to substitute where we needed them. We were playing twelve-minute quarters, and I knew by the end of the game, some of our kids would be dog-tired. We would be able to substitute nine of the twelve players during the game, which meant that three boys would have to play the whole game. We mapped out a plan so that those three would rotate into the goalkeeper's jersey for one quarter each, so at least they wouldn't be out running the entire time.

We were playing a newly formed team, and their coach was one of the dads who had been "volunteered" for the job. He was willing, but he really didn't know the game very well. Our team, on the other hand, was almost entirely intact from the fall session, so they were more experienced. Coach Bill had let me introduce some new drills to our practices, many of them techniques I had found to be particularly useful when I was learning the basics of positions and ball handling. We felt we had a pretty talented team on our hands by this point. Bill and I stayed on the sidelines, shouting out encouragement and moving our players up or back on the field as we saw how the game was developing. We made sure we were on the opposite side of the field from where the parents were sitting, reasoning that our instructions could be separated by the players from the general noise and hubbub coming from the spectators' side.

It all worked beautifully. Our boys pretty much played their lanes, with just a few excursions back into swarm-ball soccer, while the opposing team's players all followed the path of the ball in a mob. The end result, forty-eight minutes of game time later, was our first win of the season, 7–1. Davey had scored three of the goals, Justin scored two, and Joey and Kip each had one goal. After we were up 4–0, around the middle of the second quarter, we even pulled one player off the field, willing to play short for the sake of fair play. We stayed that way through the entire second half, and still, even playing down one player, we outscored them 3–1 during that time.

All of the moms and dads of the boys on our team were going nuts on the other side of the field, getting louder and crazier with each goal. When the referee blew his whistle to end the game, they all came rushing out onto the field as if we had won a major championship or something. Bill and I just watched from the sidelines as our boys were overrun by the mob of parents washing onto the field to congratulate them.

Somebody suggested that everybody could meet at a local pizza parlor for a victory celebration. Since it was late in the afternoon and everybody was hungry, it was agreed that we would have a team dinner.

As Bill and I were packing up our equipment, Lori Wilkinson came over to us, Davey and Kip at her side looking upset.

"Bill, I hate to ask you this, but I can't go to the pizza party tonight. I'm meeting some friends for dinner, and I have to get home and get ready. I've got a baby-sitter scheduled to be there in just a few minutes, but the boys really want to go with the rest of the team." She looked at the two of us and smiled. "Do you think I could impose on you to drop them off at our house after the party?"

Davey and Kip's eyes lit up at hearing that. How could we refuse?

"Of course, Lori. I'll be glad to," he said.

"I have my brother's car here, too," I added. "If it's okay with you that they ride with me, I'll take them over to the party so you don't have to drop them off."

"Oh, Sean, that would be lovely." She turned to the boys. "Okay, you guys, listen up. Sean and Coach Bill are in charge. What they say goes. Do you understand?"

"Yes, Mom!"

"Yes, Mom!"

"And wear your seat belts. No excuses!" she added.

"We will, Mom."

"We always do, Mom."

"All right," she said, giving each of them a hug and a kiss before walking off toward the parking lot. She turned and waved at us as she crossed the field.

By the time we got all the pizzas, it was later than we had anticipated. Most of the boys were starting to fade, and Bill kept looking at his watch worriedly.

"What's the matter?" I asked.

"My kids are home alone. My wife is working tonight, and I've got to get home and take care of them," he said.

"So go," I told him. "I know where the Wilkinson house is. I'll drop off Davey and Kip for you."

"Are you sure, Sean? I mean, Lori asked me to take them, but…"

"I'm sure. Everything will be fine. Lori's a friend; I know she'll understand. Go, take care of your own kids."

Bill thanked me and took off for home. I waited until the boys were stuffed full of pizza and sodas and herded them out to the parking lot. They scrambled into the back seat of the Accord and fastened their seat belts. By the time I carefully pulled out into the street, they were nodding off.

They were fast asleep by the time I got to their house. I pulled into the driveway and got out of the car. I reached into the back seat and unfastened Davey's seat belt first. I picked up the dead weight of the sleeping boy, hitched him up so he was kind of draped on my shoulder, and trudged up to the front door. I was holding him up with both hands, so I kicked at the door, hoping that the baby-sitter, if she was still there, would hear me and open the door for me.

I wasn't too surprised when Molly O'Toole opened the door. I remembered hearing about some sort of cheerleading competition that was going on that weekend, and Molly standing there in her cheerleading skirt and letter sweater reminded me of it. She must have come here directly from the competition instead of going home to change first. When she saw me, her eyes widened, until it registered that Davey was asleep in my arms. She held the door open for me so I could carry him into the house. I climbed the stairs and set him down on his bed and then went back down and out to the car to get Kip. Molly had followed me upstairs, and she was able to wake Davey enough to help him get into his pajamas and climb under the covers of his bed. As soon as his head touched the pillow, he was back asleep.

I waited downstairs, pacing back and forth in the family room, as Molly got Kip into bed. I was uncomfortable being there, but I didn't want to be so rude as to just simply leave without a word. There was an artist's pad and colored pencils on the couch and a bowl of wax fruit on the coffee table. It looked like Molly was making good use of her time waiting for the boys to show up by working on some art homework. I picked up the pad and looked at it. It wasn't bad, even for a half-finished drawing, but the perspective of the curve of the bowl looked wrong to me. *Not that I could do any better,* I reminded myself. In fact, I had trouble drawing a stick figure, so I really had no right to criticize Molly's work.

I put the pad down as I heard her come down the stairs.

"Not bad," I said, indicating her drawing.

She just shrugged. "I'm not real happy with it," she said, sitting down on the couch and picking up the paper. "See? I just can't get this bowl right." She flipped over the pad to show me some previous attempts at the still life. She was right. She was struggling with it, but each subsequent drawing was better than the previous one.

"Don't worry about it. You'll get it," I said. I flopped down in the easy chair. I suddenly realized I was nearly as tired as the boys. It had been a long day.

Molly picked up a bunch of wax grapes, their finish red and dusky, and let them roll from one hand to the other absentmindedly.

"I could get how the grapes are round," she said, "but that bowl is really tough." She held up the bunch, looking at them critically. "Most of these fruit have a curve to them. Why is the bowl so difficult?"

She tossed the grapes back into the bowl and picked up an artificial banana.

"Even this," she said, looking at the yellow fruit, "has a shape I can handle."

She glanced at me then and held the end of the banana lightly against her closed lips. My tired mind registered how her pupils dilated slightly, but the recognition didn't bubble up to the conscious areas of my brain until, still holding the tip to her lips, she said, "I like bananas." Her lips parted slightly, her eyelids drooped just a little, and the banana seemed to slide into her mouth a fraction.

My brain may have been befuddled, but my body certainly recognized the signals. I felt a little light-headed as contacts closed, synapses fired, and blood flow was suddenly redirected.

"Do you like tasty fruit, Sean?" she whispered. "I know you do." Her fingers were sliding slowly up and down the wax banana as she held it close to her mouth and played with it. I was frozen there, my hands nailed to the arms of the chair, my legs out in front of me, as I stared at her uncomprehendingly. I was just peripherally aware that I was feeling a considerable pressure within my sweatpants, and Molly's eyes were naturally drawn to my crotch.

"Oh, yes, I see that you do," she whispered as she stared, eyes shining, at my obvious excitement. Her legs parted slightly as she sat up, leaning in toward me just a little. She dropped her hands down to her lap as I watched, riveted there. I watched and did nothing as she slowly lifted up her skirt, sliding the hem up her thighs until her pale blue underwear was showing. She still held the banana with her other hand, and once her legs were fully exposed to me, she slowly rubbed the banana across her panties, between her legs. When the tip of the wax fruit touched her center, she sighed, leaned back, and slitted her eyes, watching me the entire time she was turning us both on.

"I've missed you, Sean," she whispered hypnotically. "Have you missed me?" I just stared at her, not really able to comprehend what she was saying. My brain was seriously disconnected from all that was happening.

"I've missed you a lot," she whispered. She leaned forward, dropped to her knees on the floor, and crawled over to me. She put a hand on each of my knees and pushed them up along the tops of my thighs, letting them pause at my hips. She was looking into my face, her eyes now bright and shining and confident, as she reached for the elastic waistband of my sweat pants. She grabbed the sweats and the elastic of my underwear at the same time, and pulled them both down.

I sank even farther into the chair and groaned, closing my eyes as the sensations raced through me like a tidal wave. *It's not going to take long to get me off, considering my frustrations of earlier in the afternoon,* I thought disjointedly. My crotch humped up into her hand, desperately seeking the completion that I could not bring to myself, already dangerously near to that climax. I felt something warm and moist and looked down to see Molly with a different sort of banana, a fleshy appendage instead of a wax substitute, in her mouth. She was still looking up at me, and now her eyes looked amused. When she saw me watching her, she opened her mouth just a little while she used her tongue on me, just so I could watch her, kicking up my temperature even more.

When she was satisfied she had my attention, she stood up and grabbed my arm, pulling me up and out of the chair.

I stood on wobbly legs as she shucked my sweats off. I lifted one leg at a time and allowed her to pull them down and off my feet, pulling my shoes off with them. When I was naked from the waist down, she coaxed me down onto the floor. I lay down on my back, arms at my sides. When she had me positioned just right, she finally let go of me so she could stand and reach under her skirt to take off her panties and toss them aside. She joined me on the floor, straddling me. She lifted up her hips and, with her hands, positioned me against herself and sat down on me. The entire time, my subliminal brain was screaming, *NoNoNoNo,* but my traitorous body was crying out for more.

She was as tight, hot, and wet as I remembered her. I let my hands rest on her hips as she rode me up and down, taking her pleasure, her skirt hiding our coupling from view.

I was still pretty much out of it. I didn't even think about what we were doing, in a full state of denial, right up until the end, when my completion triggered her own. It wasn't until she finally collapsed down on top of me that it occurred to me, much too late, that we were unprotected.

That thought, more than anything, snapped me out of my funk. I pushed her off me and rolled away from her. I stood up and looked down at her in disgust. She didn't shy away from me but looked boldly back at me, lying there on the floor, a small smile on her face as if to say, *I've won you back after all.*

I turned away from her, nauseated by the smell of our mating, sick to my stomach at what we had done, furious at myself and at her. I found my clothes and put them on as quickly as I could. I shoved my feet into my shoes without tying them. I had to get out of there.

Without a word, I ran out the door and jumped into my car. I started it up and backed out into the street without looking, jammed the car into gear, and took off for home. My house was dark when I got there, but I didn't want any lights on. I ran upstairs to my room, tears burning in my eyes. I stripped off all my clothes and scrubbed at my crotch with my sweat pants to try to remove the feel of Molly, to no avail. I stumbled down the hall naked, to the bathroom. I turned on the shower and crawled in. The water was scalding as I sat huddled in the corner of the shower stall, shivering and miserable. Tears were coursing down my cheeks as I recoiled at what I had done. To myself, to Molly, to Kristina. I hated myself at that moment. I stayed there, miserable and wet, as the water pounded down on me, slowly getting cooler and cooler, until it was icy cold. Only then did I manage to reach up and shut it off, but I could not move from the cold floor of the shower. I stayed there for a long, long time, convinced that I was the most amoral, evil, worthless person I knew, utterly without virtue or value.

And I was absolutely devastated at what I had done to Kristina and her trust. I could never face her again. I never wanted to face anybody ever again.

I think I passed out there, amid floating images of a cinnamon-skinned innocent, a cunning strawberry blonde vixen, a lovely dark-haired angel with braces, and a temptress with white-blonde hair dressed in a genie's costume circling and harrowing my tortured mind until blessed unconsciousness claimed me.

If you enjoyed Sean's tale so far, here is a preview of the continuation. The second book is titled *The Balance Point: Playing the Game II,* available soon.

- 1 -

SEAN PORTER'S DILEMMA

You wonder, sometimes, how you get into these situations. Looking back, I have to believe that, somewhere along the timeline of my life, I was led to this point, that I would be here no matter how I led my life. But I digress…

In the spring of 1981, I was experiencing a crisis. I was a six-teen-year-old soccer jock with girl trouble brewing, ready to spill out and burn me good. On this particular weekend, I had spent Saturday afternoon doing homework and fooling around with Kristina Mendoza, the girl I had been dating for a few weeks, only to end up frustrated when her mother called. Our fun was interrupted, and she had to go home. Later that same afternoon, I helped coach a team of younger kids, a boy's under-eight soccer team, to their first win of the season, and we all celebrated by going out for pizza and sodas afterwards. Davey and Kip, two kids I had been working with who were on the team, fell asleep in my car as I was driving them home. I carried them into their house, where my old girlfriend, Molly O'Toole, was baby-sitting. One thing led to another, and before I could stop it, Molly and I were going at it on the family room floor.

Now, here it was, Sunday afternoon, and I still couldn't work up the courage to call Kristina, even though I knew she was waiting to hear from me. Not only did I screw Molly, but I had the feeling I had royally screwed myself. I had no idea what I should do.

So I did nothing, which was even worse. I hid at home most of the day, even though it was a gorgeous spring Sunday. I didn't want to see anybody; I didn't want to talk to anybody. I couldn't even stand being in my own skin. I tried to tell myself to give Kristina a call, pretend that everything was all right, but I knew things weren't all right, and I knew my voice would betray me. I thought about calling her brother, Jorge, one of my best friends, but I wouldn't know how to explain it to him, either. My best buddy Jake would be sympathetic, but he had his own troubles ever since he was caught with his pants down, literally, with his next-door neighbor, Jaimie.

It was just too much of a dilemma for a sixteen-year-old kid.

So I stayed locked away from the world at large, hiding in my room (it almost sounds like a Brian Wilson song; in fact, it felt like a Brian Wilson song). I dreaded going to school on Monday, but I knew I wouldn't be able to effectively fake an illness. Mom and Dad had seen it all with my older brother Mike, and he pretty much ruined it for me, as well as my younger brother Stephen, when it came to trying to scam the parents.

Monday morning dawned cold and rainy, perfect for my mood. In the hallway before first class, I imagined that everybody around me was whispering and pointing at me accusingly, knowing practically firsthand what had happened over the weekend. I kept my head buried in my locker, trying to will myself into some sort of invisibility.

By lunchtime, I was a wreck. I wanted to move away, start life over under a new identity. Everything, including what little future I had, looked bleak. And then things got really bad.

I was standing under the canopy of one of the rear doors of the school during lunch. It was one of the spots where the smokers tended to congregate, but I was hoping that the weather would discourage a lot of them. Of course, today I couldn't be that lucky. I was enveloped in a blue-white cloud of cigarette smoke as I tried to choke down my sandwich. Finally, I had had enough. I disgustedly tossed the rest of my lunch away and yanked open the door. I thought maybe the library would be a safe place to hang out for the rest of my lunch period. It was, after all, foreign territory to most of my acquaintances. I headed in that direction, only to bump into Jorge Mendoza.

Jorge was a couple of inches shorter than me, but what he lacked in height, he more than made up for in ferocity. He grabbed the front of my shirt and pushed me back against the wall.

"What the hell is going on, Sean?" he growled.

I put my hands up in resignation and tried bluffing. "What do you mean? Get off of me, Jorge."

"You know what I mean," he said. "Rumor has it you're back together with Molly. So tell me, Porter. What the hell is going on?"

"No, I'm definitely not back together with Molly. Where did you hear that?"

"The usual sources," he admitted. He let me go but still stood close to me, not about to give me a chance to slip away. "So how would a rumor like that get started?"

"Uh," I said cleverly. My mind was scrambling for something plausible to say and was coming up blank, as usual.

"You din' call Kristina all weekend, either. And she's pretty upset about it. It's pretty suspicious, Sean," he continued.

I desperately needed a friend in my corner if I had any hope of redeeming myself in Kristina's eyes. I had to hope that Jorge was that friend.

"Look, Jorge, I need your help. You've got to talk to Kristina for me."

"Why, *amigo?* Why don' you talk to her yourself?"

"Because I am drowning in a lake of shit, and when she hears about this, she's probably going to throw an anchor at me instead of tossing a safety rope." I put my arm around his shoulder and turned with him to walk down the hallway. I felt his shoulder muscles bunch up as if he wanted to shrug off my arm, but I was determined to enlist his help. I hung on to him until I finally felt him relax a little. Not much, but enough. "I'll tell you all I have to tell, Jorge, but you've got to help me convince your sister that I'm not the bad guy here," I pleaded.

He looked at me out of the corner of his eye, but at least he didn't shove me away and bury me. I steered him toward the library, where we might be able to find a corner where we could whisper. A place where I could confess my sins.

The library was nearly empty. I guided him to a table away from the windows and the doors, and we sat down across from each other. We both put our arms on the table and leaned in toward each other so we could quietly converse. Jorge's eyes were hard and dark as he sat across from me, implacable and cold.

I laid myself bare and told him nearly everything. I told him about studying with Kristina in the morning and about teasing with her after lunch. I told him about the soccer game and how well the boys had played, and especially how the keepers had seemed to grasp what Jorge had tried to teach them. I told him about going out for a pizza celebration afterward, about how the boys had fallen asleep, and about how Molly had answered the door at the Wilkinson house. I told him about putting them to bed and about how I was looking at Molly's art project. I confessed about being lulled by her, and I told him about her little play with the wax banana and how she used it to her advantage. I told him about ending up on the floor with Molly, sparing no detail, offering no excuses, letting him see the Sean Porter I had come to loathe. The only thing I didn't tell him was how his sister looked on my family room floor, how she squirmed as I played my tune on the backs of her legs. I needed an ally, after all, not another enemy.

"Sean, you really screwed up," whispered Jorge as he shook his head.

"I know I did. I've been beating myself up about it since it happened. But what do I do about it?" I asked in desperation.

"I dunno. Lemme work on it a little." Jorge stood up from the table and walked away, still shaking his head.

Maybe I had found an ally. I hoped I had. Then again, maybe I had given him all the ammunition he needed to bury me.

CPSIA information can be obtained at www.ICGtesting.com
Printed in the USA
BVOW012322280313

316768BV00020B/615/P